MISGUIDED TRUTH

A DR. SAMANTHA JENKINS MYSTERY

STEPHANIE KREML

This book is a work of fiction. Names, characters, places, and incidents are the product of the author's imagination or are used fictitiously. Any resemblance to actual events, locales, or persons, living or dead, is coincidental.

ISBN: 978-1-955921-06-0 (ebook); 978-1-955921-13-8 (paperback); 978-1-955921-14-5 (hardcover)

www.stephaniekreml.com

 Created with Vellum

1

As Dr. Samantha Jenkins uncovered a troubling detail in the medical records, she missed a seemingly innocent compliment that came from her patient across the exam room. Sam was hunched over a bulky computer, navigating through a sea of medical data, her focus zeroing in on Cindy Bergstrom's most recent lab results. The creatinine level at 1.4 wasn't alarmingly high but was certainly above the normal range for a woman of her age. What concerned Sam more was the gradual increase in this metabolite over the past few years, mirroring Mrs. Bergstrom's blood pressure, which had only recently been addressed.

"I just wanted to say you've been the nicest so far," Mrs. Bergstrom repeated, after receiving no response.

Sam raised her eyes from the screen and straightened her back, blinking in surprise at the comment. She turned to look over her shoulder at the woman seated on the exam table behind her. "I'm sorry, Mrs. Bergstrom? Could you repeat that, please?"

Her patient sighed. "Please, Doctor, call me Cindy.

After all, you've been calling me by my first name every night at the diner."

Sam forced a small smile at Cindy's request for informality—along with the irony. After all, Cindy was the one who'd insisted on calling Sam "Doctor" at the diner the first time they'd met. She'd had Sam pegged from the get-go when she'd walked up to Sam's table to get her order. "We don't get many unfamiliar faces around here—are you the new doc who's fillin' in this week?"

But Cindy's labs had created a shadow in Sam's mind during the otherwise mundane follow-up appointment. Given her history of borderline-high blood pressure, Sam found herself wondering if Cindy's kidneys were starting to feel the strain. She didn't want to second-guess Dr. Carlisle's judgment, but she wondered why he hadn't started her on medication sooner.

Then again, as Sam had crisscrossed the state, subbing in at small clinics in tiny towns, she'd noticed that many of the older docs weren't quite as aggressive treating some chronic conditions, like high blood pressure. In fact, it seemed a few of these docs continued to practice according to the guidelines that were current when they'd been in training, which, in some cases, may have been several decades in the past.

"I was just sayin' that you're the nicest doctor that's filled in so far," Cindy elaborated, locking her bright blue eyes with Sam's.

Sam broadened her smile. "Thank you." Her gaze moved back to the dinosaur of a computer. While she appreciated the compliment, she was more worried about the implications of the lab results.

Cindy was in for a follow-up visit after she'd started an ACE inhibitor a couple of weeks before. Sam's thoughts lingered on the identity of the prescribing doctor—probably another *locum* like her, a transient shadow in the wake of Dr. Carlisle's untimely departure. Was he one of the physicians Cindy had alluded to in her comment?

Sam asked, "Are you having any problems with the lisinopril that Dr. Najeeb prescribed?"

"Like, what kind of problems?"

"Well, some people have issues with a cough, headache, sometimes dizziness—"

"Now that you mention it, I did feel a little dizzy after I started taking it, but that's gone away. I have been coughing a lot more, though." To demonstrate, Cindy coughed a couple of times, shifting herself on the exam table, the white sanitation paper crackling beneath her.

"I think it might be better if we switch you to a different medication," Sam said, "one that will help with your blood pressure and provide some protection for your heart."

"My heart?" Cindy's eyes widened.

"Even though most people with high blood pressure may feel fine, the elevated pressure can lead to kidney problems, heart failure, stroke—"

"My pa died from heart failure. And he had high blood pressure, too. He was on so many pills." Cindy shook her head slowly, her gaze becoming distant. "Thank goodness he had benefits through the VA. I don't know what we would've done otherwise. They even covered most of his stay at his nursing home. And right before . . . the end, they had to hook him up to that kidney machine. Every chance I got, I dragged Sarah with me to the VA hospital in Timmons so she could see her grandpa." A wistful smile crossed Cindy's face. "She loved her grandpa so much when she was little. They had this special bond. But now he's gone, and she's a moody teen . . ." She looked up at

Sam, sudden awareness on her face. "So his blood pressure caused all that?"

"Possibly." Sam didn't want to speculate too much without knowing more about Cindy's father, but it was a common clinical picture. "It sounds like it was very difficult for all of you. I'm sorry he went through that."

"It's okay, Doctor. He's been gone five years now, and he lived a good life." Cindy took a deep breath and looked at Sam earnestly. "But if I can keep from having that stuff happen to me, I'm all for it. What do I need to do?"

Sam was a little reluctant to change medications for someone she was seeing for the first time, especially since she knew she wouldn't be able to see Cindy for another follow-up visit—Sam's *locum* assignment at this clinic was only for two weeks. But since Cindy had only recently started taking lisinopril at a very low dose, and since Sam could informally follow up with her at the diner, she ventured forward.

"Is that cough bothering you?"

"Yeah, actually, it is." Cindy covered her mouth and coughed again. "I thought maybe I had a cold or something, but I never did have a runny nose or anything like that." She made a face. "And you know, it's not great when you start coughing right as you're serving your customers."

Sam didn't fault the previous doctor for initiating Cindy's treatment with lisinopril; it was a commonly prescribed first-line option, and he was the one who'd ordered the labs Sam was now reviewing, with the previous set of labs from a couple of years prior. Back then, Cindy's creatinine had been 1.0, right at the high-end of normal.

However, since Cindy was experiencing a well-known side effect, and with her family history of heart failure, Sam believed it would be in Cindy's best interest to switch her to another medication. Besides helping with blood pressure, as Sam had relayed to Cindy, it could provide some extra protection for the heart—at least according to the latest studies. "Would it be okay if I changed your medication?"

"I'll do whatever you want me to do, Doctor. Like I said, you're the nicest one who's filled in since Dr. Carlisle died."

"Okay, I'm going to switch you to losartan," Sam said. "It acts in a very similar way to the other medication, just in a different part of the pathway that regulates blood pressure. It shouldn't cause a cough like lisinopril, but—" She glanced at Cindy's labs on the computer monitor again, double-checking her electrolytes. "You'll want to avoid things that are high in potassium."

Sam then elaborated a little further on the precautions Cindy needed to take with her new medication, offering additional advice. Despite Cindy's nods and attentive gaze, Sam sensed the information was too much for her to take in all at once, and that she might be overwhelmed.

"Hang on a sec." Sam pulled up a web browser on the computer, clicked and scrolled and clicked a few times, sending several jobs to the printer in the hallway. Just some patient education handouts on treating high blood pressure—including the types of medications, along with lifestyle changes, diet recommendations, etc. Pretty dry stuff, but she knew she'd dumped a lot of information on Cindy, and she hoped these would help answer some of the questions Cindy would inevitably have in the following days.

She went out into the hallway to retrieve the printouts and ran into Bonnie, the nurse practitioner who also worked at the clinic. Bonnie always seemed to have a comforting presence, despite her careworn features, her hair pulled back in a practical bun. Sam had assumed Dr. Carlisle had been Bonnie's supervising physician, since

NPs couldn't practice in Texas without one, but she wondered who was supervising Bonnie now.

"It's so wonderful that you do this," Bonnie said when she saw the papers Sam had gathered from the printer. "Not everyone takes the time to make sure our patients understand our treatment plans."

"Really, it doesn't take much to print these out," Sam said, "and, in the long run, I think it actually saves time."

"I agree." Bonnie hesitated briefly before offering, "Would you like to come over for dinner tomorrow? I figured you're probably getting tired of eating diner food every night."

"Oh, thank you," Sam said. "But I wouldn't want to impose."

Bonnie waved her hand with a smile. "You wouldn't be imposing. I'm having Olivia over with another friend. We get together every once in a while, and I thought it would be nice to have you join us."

"Then I would love to," Sam said. Despite enjoying the southern cooking at the only diner in Dry Wells, she was beginning to crave something different. "Thanks for inviting me."

As Bonnie got called away to see another patient, Sam returned to Cindy's room. She rolled her stool closer to the exam table and went over the handouts with Cindy, pointing out which salt substitutes to avoid with her new medications. When Sam handed over the stack of papers, Cindy clutched them as if they were her lifeline.

"I'll send the new prescription to the pharmacy," Sam said as she scooted her stool over to the computer. "And we'll see you again in a couple of weeks to make sure you're doing okay."

"So, does that mean you're staying?" A hopeful look came across Cindy's face. "Like I said, you're the nicest one who's been here since Dr. Carlisle died. You actually take the time to explain what's going on with me."

Sam spun around to face Cindy. "I don't understand what—"

"You said, '*we'll* see you . . .'"

Sam paused as she processed her misstep. "I meant that we—as in this office—will see you for the follow-up appointment." She shrugged. "I guess I said 'we' out of habit."

"But this town needs you." Cindy leaned forward, placing her hands on the table's edge on either side of her knees, her legs swinging with a youthful energy that belied her age. She mustered a timid smile as she looked directly at Sam. "Plus, everyone likes you."

Sam flushed. "Thanks." It was great to be wanted, but she had another assignment on the other side of the state the following month, and she wasn't certain she wanted to live in this small town permanently. "I'm only scheduled to be here through the end of next week, and I'm sure the next doctor will take excellent care of you."

Cindy looked crestfallen. "It's because of what happened to Dr. Carlisle, isn't it?" Her voice was laden with resignation.

"No, I need to—" Sam cut herself off. She didn't want to get into her personal issues with Cindy; she was supposed to focus on her patients' needs. But then she thought about what Cindy had just said.

Sam had presumed that Dr. Carlisle, who used to own the practice, had died of an illness several months before. From what she knew, he'd been practicing there for over twenty years, and she'd assumed that Olivia, the office manager and the late doctor's widow, was having difficulty finding a new doctor to take over the practice in this small Texas town. She'd figured that's why Olivia had been using a *locum tenens* agency to send a series of doctors—like Sam—for short-term assignments to fill in until she found a permanent replacement.

But Cindy's comment had stirred Sam's curiosity.

"What happened to Dr. Carlisle?"

Cindy bowed her head, her lips pursed in self-reproach as she blinked rapidly. "I shouldn't have said anything, because now you definitely won't want to stay here."

Sam edged her stool closer, bridging the gap between them. She looked up into Cindy's eyes, visible through a cascade of dark hair flecked with silver gray. Placing her hand gently over Cindy's, which was tightly gripping the table's edge, Sam offered a comforting touch.

"It's okay." Sam squeezed Cindy's hand and cautiously probed again. "What happened to Dr. Carlisle?"

"I thought you already knew," Cindy said, darting her eyes briefly at the closed door. "There aren't too many secrets in our town. But maybe they kept it from you, so you wouldn't be scared off."

Sam raised her eyebrows. "Scared off from what?"

"You'll find out eventually, anyway," Cindy mumbled, avoiding Sam's eyes, focusing on the floor. "I'm sure as soon as I leave, you'll Google it."

"I'd rather hear it from you," Sam said. "What happened to Dr. Carlisle?"

Cindy turned her attention back to Sam, taking a deep breath to muster courage for her forthcoming revelation.

"Dr. Carlisle was murdered."

2

"What? He was murdered?" Sam was hit by an unexpected surge of surprise, a frosty shiver traversing her frame as her heart leapt, merging shock with morbid intrigue, reminiscent of puzzles past.

Cindy shifted on the exam table again, the crackling of the paper under her filling the silence, like the patter of rain droplets hinting at a coming storm. She shook her head. "I shouldn't have said nothing, because now you're going to leave too."

"No, no," Sam said instinctively, though she regretted her denial as soon as the words came out of her mouth. She certainly couldn't stay, but she wanted to ask more questions. Instead, she waited patiently. Her main goal now was to calm Cindy down.

After a moment, Cindy lowered her voice and said, "He was found in his front hallway, beaten to death. There's not a lot of bad stuff that happens here, so the sheriff called in the Texas Rangers to help with the investigation. So far, all they've said is they think it was someone passing through town, that it was a home invasion. They think Dr. Carlisle just got unlucky, and someone on their way down to Houston was lookin' for drug money or something." Her gaze met Sam's, holding it steadily. "But like I said, usually there's nothin' bad going on around here. Well, except that case over in Timmons. But that's a weird thing, and I should just stop talkin'."

"What case in Timmons?" Sam asked, her curiosity further engaged.

"A doctor's on trial for some deaths at the VA hospital over there—same place my dad was." Cindy shivered. "But like I said, I should just shut up. I'm making you think this place is full of sinister folk."

She closed her eyes for a moment as she straightened up on the table, composing herself and tucking her hair behind her ears.

"Anyways, Doctor. I hope you stay, since you really seem to care about us."

"Oh, thank you, Mrs. B—Cindy."

"When did you want me to come back again?"

"Right," Sam said as she wheeled her stool back over to the computer. "Let's have you come back in two weeks to see how you're tolerating your new medication. We'll also check your blood pressure again to see if there's any improvement or if we need to increase the dose."

"Then I'll see you at that visit?" Cindy asked hopefully.

Sam smiled, chastising herself inwardly for using the word "we" again. In two weeks she'd be gone.

So instead of deflating Cindy's hopes, she gave a noncommittal answer. "We'll see."

Perhaps she could ask Olivia to extend this assignment by a few days, just so she could make sure Cindy's hypertension treatment plan was on solid footing. However, she swiftly abandoned the thought. Having not spent more than a few days in Austin since embarking on her nomadic career, she really was looking forward to spending a week in her hometown.

Sam motioned toward the handouts in Cindy's lap. "Do you have any other questions about those?"

"No, you've been very helpful." Cindy folded up the pages and tucked them into her purse. "So I'll see you for supper? I'm working again tonight."

Sam hadn't planned on going to the diner this evening. She figured she'd just grab something from the convenience store at the gas station, take it back to her motel room, and finish up the day's charts on her laptop. There were quite a few that she hadn't completed during a rush of patients earlier in the day.

But Cindy looked as if she'd be broken-hearted if Sam didn't show up.

Sam reluctantly nodded. "I'll be there."

THE AFTERNOON PASSED QUIETLY, yet Sam was ensnared in a continuous loop of patient appointments, leaving scant time for charting or pursuing the answers that her curiosity demanded. Her interactions with Bonnie were fleeting, limited strictly to patient care, with no chance to delve deeper into the mysteries exposed earlier in the day. At one point, she'd had a quick chat with Olivia, but Sam deemed it inappropriate to discuss the widow's recent loss. So by the end of the day, she hadn't learned any more about Cindy's revelations regarding Dr. Carlisle's death.

On the short drive to the diner, Sam contemplated Cindy's insistence that she stay in Dry Wells. There were plenty of good people here, from what Sam had seen during the past few days. They were hardworking, with many employed by the local lumber industry, since the town was nestled in the piney woods of east Texas. Sam liked it here. It reminded her of the forests in the fairy tales of her youth, not dark and scary, but magical and enchanting.

It was a nice place to visit. But she missed Austin.

Upon entering the diner, Sam was greeted with Cindy's warm welcome and guided to a booth. Now donning an apron over her outfit and her hair tied back in a ponytail, Cindy swiftly brought Sam an iced tea before cheerfully inquiring, "What's it going to be tonight, Doctor?"

"Please, just call me Sam."

"No, ma'am," Cindy said with a smile. "You earned that degree. You deserve to be called 'Doctor.'" She bobbed her head as if that was the end if that. "So, what do you want this time?"

Every evening at the diner, Sam had treated herself to a different southern specialty, turning dinner into an adventure that broke the monotony of Dry Wells. This had become a delightful escape into the flavors of the south amid the town's predictable rhythm. While she mulled over her dinner options on the menu, a law enforcement officer clad in tan strolled in, settling himself at the counter with an ease that spoke of routine. Cindy caught his eye and offered a friendly wave, to which he responded with a nod as he set his cowboy hat on the adjacent stool. The hat's removal unveiled his salt-and-pepper hair, closely cropped and perfectly edged against his dark skin, a stark contrast to the relaxed atmosphere of the diner.

Sam focused on the menu again. She wanted something lighter, but most of the items, while sounding delicious, were either fried or loaded with butter. She made her decision. "I'll try the catfish tonight."

"Ooh, you're gonna love it." Cindy grinned as she

scribbled on her order pad. "I promise you won't be disappointed. I'll bring it right out."

As Cindy walked off, Sam thought, *Still fried, but at least it's fish. And tomorrow, a home-cooked meal at Bonnie's.*

Before pulling out her laptop, Sam scanned the diner, noting a couple in the booth directly behind her and a woman seated a few spots down from the cop at the counter. Recognizing the public nature of the space made it less than ideal for working on patient charts, she decided instead to use the opportunity to catch up on reading clinical material, to address a few lingering questions from her day's patient visits.

But prior to beginning her research, she wanted to see if she could find anything on Dr. Carlisle's demise. A quick Google search only turned up one article from the local paper in Timmons with really no more details than what Cindy had already divulged. She'd just have to learn more about what happened to him somewhere else. She closed the page and logged into UpToDate, a website that summarized the latest diagnostic and treatment guidelines for doctors.

As she searched for articles on diabetes management, she saw Cindy go over to the officer—since it was a rural area, and since his uniform was tan, she figured he was either the sheriff or a deputy. He and Cindy chatted for a bit, and then he glanced over at Sam. She quickly looked down at her laptop and tried to focus on a section she'd been reading about the benefits and drawbacks of the newest diabetes drugs on the market, but it was hard to concentrate. By the time she checked the counter again, Cindy was scribbling on her order pad. She then disappeared into the kitchen as the officer picked up a newspaper from the counter and began to flip through it.

Sam went back to reading and was fully engrossed in

another article on endocrine disorders when Cindy reappeared through the swinging door and came over, with Sam's dinner in one hand and a pitcher of iced tea in another. Sam pushed her laptop to the side to make room for Cindy to set the oval plate down. It was filled with breaded catfish filets nestled amongst a pile of fries and two metal cups, one filled with tartar sauce, the other with coleslaw.

As she filled Sam's glass with more tea, Cindy asked, "Can I getcha anything else?"

"I'm good," Sam said. "Thank you."

While she ate, she continued to read, frequently wiping her fingers on her napkin to avoid getting grease on her trackpad as she scrolled. In the end, she finished only half her meal—it was delicious, with the filets flaky and the potatoes crisp, but it was just too much fried food. Thank goodness for the tart coleslaw; the vinegary dressing cut through the richness of the fat. But she would definitely need a Tums tonight.

Sam dabbed her mouth with her napkin, pushed her plate away, and began packing up her laptop. She looked around to get the check, but Cindy was chatting with the officer at the counter again. Mid-conversation, Cindy subtly tipped her head in Sam's direction. This prompted the man to turn his head, catching Sam in the act of watching them. Feeling her cheeks warm with a flush, Sam quickly diverted her gaze to her bag. Despite her attempt to look away, she caught a fleeting glimpse of the edges of his mouth curling into a slight smile. When she looked up again, he gave her a brief nod of acknowledgement.

Cindy emerged from behind the counter, scribbling on her pad as she approached Sam's booth. She ripped off the bill and handed it to her. "Here you are, hon."

As Sam pulled out her wallet to pay, Cindy said, "The sheriff wants to talk to you."

"What about?"

"Oh, I might have told him you're a wonderful doctor, and we want you to stay in our little town." Then she looked down sheepishly. "And . . . I might have said I wanted him to assure you that this is a safe place, even after what happened to Dr. Carlisle."

Sam glanced over at the counter. Having finished his meal, the sheriff tossed his napkin on his plate, stood up, grabbed his hat, and strode over to her booth. There was an understated power in the officer's demeanor, a blend of experience and restraint that spoke volumes about his authority.

"Evening, Doc." He extended his hand. "Ken Perkins. I'm the sheriff of Timmons County. Pleasure to meet you."

Sam began to stand as they shook hands, but he said, "Please, you don't have to get up." She released his hand and plopped back down on the seat.

"May I?" he said, motioning to the seat opposite her.

Sam nodded. "Of course."

As Sheriff Perkins slid into the bench across from Sam, placing his hat on the seat next to him, Cindy said, "Okay, I'll leave you two alone so you can get to know each other." Then she hurried off to tend to the customers in another booth.

"Cindy says you're considering taking over Dr. Carlisle's practice."

"Uh, not exactly," Sam said. "I'm just here temporarily, and then I have another assignment in San Angelo next month. But Cindy did ask if I would stay."

"I see." The sheriff nodded. "Well, I've heard great

things about you from some of the other folks around town. And, to be honest, we're in a bit of a bind here."

"Oh?" Sam's interest roused, both professionally and out of a growing concern for the community she had begun to appreciate.

Sheriff Perkins leaned forward slightly, his eyes reflecting the seriousness of the topic. "Since Dr. Carlisle's . . . untimely passing, we've found ourselves without a local doctor. The nearest clinics are over in the county seat."

"How far away is that?"

"About thirty miles. Of course, we're all used to driving far around here, but for some of our older residents, it can be somewhat difficult to get to their appointments." He shrugged. "We all help out though, running errands and what not for each other. You've probably also noticed we don't have a lot of the typical businesses you find in the bigger towns, so that adds to the burden and our need for community support."

"Yeah, since this is the only restaurant for miles, I've been eating almost all my meals here."

"My brother will thank you—he owns the place."

"Please give him my compliments. Everything I've tried has been wonderful."

"I will," the sheriff said with a brief nod. "Well, now that I better understand the situation, I won't bother you any longer." He picked up his hat and began to extract himself from the booth. "I think Cindy wanted me to give you a sales pitch about how safe it is here, to convince you to stay."

"Because of what happened to Dr. Carlisle?"

The sheriff stopped at the edge of the bench. "What happened to Dr. Carlisle is awful. It's still an ongoing investigation, but it appears that this was just an unfortunate random act." He stood up. "I assure you, though, this town is safe. We're a quiet community of hardworking folks."

"I can see that," Sam said as she slid out of the booth herself.

They both walked toward the door.

Sam decided to press a little more. "You said Dr. Carlisle's death was a random act—I heard that it was a home invasion. Is that true? How common is that around here?"

The sheriff frowned as he held the door open for her.

"It's not common at all," he said. "We've never had anything like that happen before. In fact, we called in the Texas Rangers to help with the investigation—that's how rare a homicide is around here." He donned his hat.

"When was the last homicide?" Sam asked. Since he'd brought it up, she was now curious, even though he'd already started to turn toward the SUV cruiser parked next to her car in front of the diner.

"In Dry Wells? Long before my time," he said. "And I've been sheriff for over a decade now." He pinched the rim of his hat and tipped his head. "Been a pleasure meeting you, Doctor. I'm sure I'll see you around."

He drove off as Sam got in her car. She started the engine and was just about to shift into reverse when a splash of bold black lettering caught her eye from a newspaper vending machine by the front door. The headline blared, "Doctor's lawyers file final motions before trial next week."

Cindy had mentioned that a doctor in Timmons was going on trial for some deaths at the hospital. Those would be considered homicides, wouldn't they? So why hadn't the sheriff mentioned them?

3

As soon as Sam returned to her motel room, she searched online for the case from the newspaper headline. Unlike the meager amount of information available on Dr. Carlisle's death, she found numerous articles about the upcoming trial of an anesthesiologist named Dr. Aaron Morton, charged with tampering with IV bags at the VA hospital in Timmons. The issue came to light tragically when another doctor, self-treating for dehydration with one of the tainted IV bags while on call, suffered a fatal cardiac arrest. Subsequent investigations revealed several suspicious incidents at the hospital over the previous year, all linked to routine surgeries involving Dr. Morton, with at least one ending in a patient's death. This connection pointed to a disturbing pattern of criminal activity.

The idea that a fellow physician could commit such crimes, in contradiction to the oath to "do no harm," was appalling. Why would he do this?

Perhaps Sheriff Perkins hadn't mentioned the case due to the differences in circumstances surrounding Dr.

Carlisle's death. Yet, as Sam reflected on their conversation, a detail stood out: the sheriff had specifically cited Dry Wells when claiming there had been no other homicides during his tenure. But considering his cruiser and uniform bore the insignia of Timmons County, shouldn't the town of Timmons, the county seat, also be within his jurisdiction? A quick search on her laptop confirmed her suspicion: Timmons indeed fell under his purview. This discrepancy raised doubts in Sam's mind. Was it possible that the sheriff was concealing something? Or had he omitted mention of the trial merely due to its peculiar nature?

THE FOLLOWING day unfolded with the usual bustle for Sam, who spent it attending to patients at the clinic until late afternoon. With just a handful of appointments remaining before it was time to head to Bonnie's house for dinner, Kelly, the medical assistant, gave Sam a sympathetic look as she quietly rolled the vitals cart out of an exam room and gently closed the door. "Good luck with your next patient, Dr. Jenkins," Kelly whispered, her tone conveying a mix of empathy and encouragement.

"Why's that?"

"Let's just say the family can be a bit . . . overbearing," Kelly replied. "Just look at these vitals."

She turned the cart toward Sam so she could see the readings on the display. Heart rate 110, blood pressure 145/100.

"This is for the daughter who's only fourteen," Kelly said. "I'd probably be jittery all the time too if I had a mom like that. Good luck!"

Upon entering the room, Sam was greeted by the sight

of a teenage girl sitting on the exam table, absorbed in her cell phone. In the armchair beside her, a woman sat, exuding an air of assumed importance. This woman, with her refined features, scrutinized Sam from head to toe. After a brief pause, as if having made a judgment, she nodded in approval. She introduced herself as Natalie Fontaine, in a tone that implied her name should carry significance. She then, with a gesture towards the girl, introduced her daughter Mia—Sam's patient. Mia, though barely glancing up, radiated a subtle unease, her feet restlessly tapping against the step stool below the table, overshadowed by her mother's commanding presence.

"Nice to meet you," Sam said, steadying herself in the face of the mother's conceit. She took her usual spot on the rolling stool and turned towards the quiet teenager, softening her voice. "So, what brings you in today?"

The girl continued to look at her phone while her mother answered the question. "Mia's been rather jumpy lately."

"How long has this been going on?"

"Oh, I'd say since the beginning of the school year. Mia's a sophomore, and she didn't make the cheerleading squad in the spring, but one of the girls got hurt, so they're having extra tryouts this afternoon. She's quite nervous about it."

"I see," Sam said. "And the school year began—?"

"Last month."

Sam glanced over at the girl, who still hadn't looked up from her phone. "So she's been jumpy, as you say, since then?"

"That's right."

"And when you say 'jumpy,' what do you mean, exactly?"

Natalie didn't respond immediately, as if she were

determining how much she should reveal. Finally, she said, "Well, I suppose 'jumpy' isn't precisely the right word. She worries a lot, and her grades, so far this year, haven't been as good." She glanced at her daughter. "Mia has lost some weight . . . which isn't such a bad thing. Especially with that opening on the cheerleading team."

"I see," Sam said again, then addressed Mia. "Do you agree?"

When the girl didn't look up from her phone right away, her mother snapped, "Mia! Put that down and pay attention!"

Mia bolted upright, dropping the phone next to her, causing it to thump on the paper covering the table.

No wonder she's jumpy, Sam thought. She turned to Natalie. "Would it be possible if Mia and I spoke in private?"

"Why on earth would you need to do that?" Natalie said indignantly. "Dr. Carlisle never asked that. And Mia has never kept anything from me."

"Well . . . you know," Sam said, "sometimes teenagers feel more comfortable sharing things without their parents around."

A scarlet flush spread from Natalie's neck to her cheeks, highlighting her fair complexion, as her eyebrows drew together, signaling an impending outburst. It seemed she was poised to unleash a torrent of words on Sam. However, before the situation escalated, Mia finally spoke. "It's okay. Mom can stay."

Her mother huffed with a sharp nod, as if that was the only acceptable answer.

Sam exhaled, realizing she wouldn't be able to understand the full extent of Mia's situation with her mother present. Nonetheless, she decided to proceed with the information she could gather. "Let me take a quick look at your chart," she said, gliding to the desk in the corner to access Mia's medical record on the computer. She was already aware of Mia's vitals from her colleague Kelly, yet she hoped to uncover any past incidents similar to the current one. The screen showed nothing out of the ordinary—just routine checkups and a few visits for minor illnesses. "I see you have no major medical issues, no history of surgeries. Is that accurate?"

"Yes," Natalie answered.

"Okay," Sam said, squaring her shoulders in determination before continuing. "I have a few questions that Mia needs to answer. Is that alright?"

"Yes," Natalie said again, looking annoyed.

Sam ignored this, turned to Mia, and repeated, "Is that alright?"

Mia gave a quick little nod.

Sam proceeded with the anxiety screening, tactically concentrating on Mia's symptoms to sidestep any sensitive topics Mia might be hesitant to discuss in front of her mother. The questionnaire delved into the previous two weeks, probing into symptoms like excessive worry, difficulty relaxing, and a tendency towards irritability. Mia responded to each query with obedience, helping to quantify the frequency of her experiences. Upon evaluating Mia's responses, Sam summed up her score. They fell into the moderate level of anxiety.

During Sam's focused exam, she confirmed Mia's heart rate was slightly elevated, along with sweaty palms and a mild tremor. To be thorough, she asked Mia to slide forward so she could stand slightly behind the girl. "I'm going to check your thyroid by placing my fingers over your neck. I need you to look up and swallow."

After Mia did as instructed, Sam sat back down on her stool in front of the girl. Mia's thyroid felt normal. No enlargement, no nodules, no goiters. But the thyroid exam could be normal even if there was an underlying condition.

"Have you had any diarrhea recently?"

Mia blushed. "A little."

"And have you felt too hot or too cold lately?"

"Now that you mention it," Mia said, "I've felt really hot at school. I thought it was just because they'd turned on the heaters since the cold front came through."

Sam turned to Natalie. "Has anyone in your family had thyroid problems?"

"No, not that I'm aware," Natalie replied. She narrowed her eyes. "Is something wrong with Mia's thyroid?"

"I'm not sure, but I'll order some labs to check."

Natalie looked put out. "We don't have time for that. Mia needs to get back to school for the cheer team tryout." She stood, motioning for Mia to do the same, then opened the door and left the room.

Sam followed them out into the hallway, just as Natalie said, "What a waste of time. I have something I'll give you."

"I would strongly advise you not—" Sam began, but a man poked his head out of the exam room next to her.

"Nurse," he barked. "How much longer do we have to wait?"

Sam looked down the hallway, but Natalie and Mia were already going through the door to the lobby. She started to chase after them, but the man grabbed her arm.

"Did you hear me?"

"Excuse me." Sam yanked her arm away and glared at him. "Please don't touch me again."

The man's towering height and wide shoulders dominated the doorway, nearly obscuring the view of a woman meekly seated on the exam table behind him. With a dismissive air, he crossed his arms and repeated his question, "How much longer do we have to wait?"

"As it turns out, I just finished seeing my previous patient." Sam looked down the hallway again, but Mia and her mother were now gone. "And you're next."

"Fine," the man said as he stepped aside. "You can come in."

4

As Sam entered the examination room, the man promptly followed, quickly shutting the door behind them. He then casually sank into the chair next to the exam table, nonchalantly draping an arm over the back and adopting a wide-legged posture, exuding a sense of ownership over the space.

Sam, however, paid him little mind, and instead turned her attention to the woman perched on the exam table. She appeared withdrawn, shoulders hunched and arms loosely folded in front of her, her hands settled timidly between her knees.

"Hi, I'm Dr. Jenkins. What brings you in today?"

"She says it burns when she pees," the man answered.

"Is that right?" Sam asked, addressing her patient.

The woman glanced up at Sam, eyes peeking through strands of frizzy auburn hair. She offered a small nod before lowering her gaze back to her lap.

"And how long has this been going on?"

The woman started to say something, but before she

could respond, the man interjected, "She says it started a couple of days ago."

Irritation fired up within Sam, but she paused for a second and managed to tamp it down. Forcing a smile as she turned to him, she said, "I'm sorry, Mr. …?"

"Clark."

"I'm sorry, Mr. Clark, but would you mind stepping outside for a moment?"

He sat up, bracing his hands on the arms of his chair, readying himself for a confrontation. "Whatever for? There ain't no secrets between me and my wife. Isn't that right, Luann?"

Luann nodded as she turned her head to look at her husband. He glared at her while she spoke. "That's right. I don't have any secrets. I share everything with Isaac. He can stay."

Isaac settled back in his chair with a smug look on his face.

"Okay," Sam said, "but it might be best if Luann answered my questions herself."

He scowled at her, but she pressed on.

"It's just that Luann might be able to tell me more details about her symptoms and what's bothering her," Sam said. "Things that will help me make sure I take the best care of her that I can."

She fumed inside, resentful of having to justify to this man her need to speak directly with her patient.

After a moment, he crossed his arms and gave her a curt nod.

Continuing with Luann's medical history, Sam discovered a previous urinary tract infection from several months back. With Luann unsure of the prescribed antibiotic, Sam consulted her electronic health record. There, she found that in addition to the occasional UTI, Luann had several other visits in the last couple of years, including a few for minor injuries. Sam didn't want to spend too much time looking at these while she was in the exam room, but it did give her pause.

She scrutinized the details of the most recent visit, discovering that Luann had been prescribed Bactrim—a go-to antibiotic for urinary tract infections. However, Sam's brow furrowed with concern; Bactrim, despite its popularity, was losing ground in the battle against UTIs. An alarming increase in antibiotic resistance among strains of *E. coli*, the usual suspects behind UTIs, had been undermining Bactrim's effectiveness, a trend that troubled Sam as she considered the best course of action.

"The last time you had a UTI, did the antibiotics work?"

"Yes," Luann replied. "Cleared it up in a day."

"Are you having any fever, abdominal pain, or back pain right now?" Sam asked. She glanced over at Isaac. He was focused on his phone now, apparently no longer interested in what was going on.

"No, just the burning," Luann said. "Oh, and feeling like I have to pee all the time."

Sam nodded and then began her exam. When she tapped Luann's back on the right side at the costovertebral angle, just under the ribs, Luann jumped.

"Why'd you do that?"

"I'm just checking to see if you're having any pain in your kidneys. You seem a bit sensitive there—did it hurt?"

"A little."

"But you said you haven't had any fever or chills?"

"No, not really."

Sam went back to the computer to check Luann's vitals on the chart. Afebrile.

"Have you taken anything recently, like ibuprofen or Tylenol?"

Luann shook her head. "My back hurting—what does it mean?"

Sam glanced over at Isaac again before answering. He was still engrossed in his phone.

"I'm a little concerned that you might also have a kidney infection." When Luann started to look worried, Sam said, "It's not a big deal, it just means we'll need to treat with different antibiotics than last time and for a longer duration." Then she added, "Is there any chance you might be pregnant?"

Out of the corner of her eye, Sam saw movement from Isaac. Luann gave a shy smile and looked over at her husband, who had dropped his phone in his lap and now was paying full attention.

"We've been trying," Luann said quietly.

"That's great," Sam said reflexively. "So, in addition to checking your urine for an infection, let's also do a pregnancy test. Is that okay?"

Luann nodded, and Isaac pursed his lips, his chin scrunched in agreement.

"Good," Sam said. She entered the orders in the computer before locking the screen.

As she guided Luann to the restroom with instructions for collecting her specimen, Sam wondered if a pregnancy was the best thing for the Clark's marriage. But who was she to judge? She'd only just met the couple.

While she waited for Luann, she worked on Mia's chart at the computer in the hallway. But Isaac's presence loomed through the open exam room door only a few feet away. His watchful manner suggested an unspoken vigilance, a silent assurance against any possible misconduct.

Just as Sam completed Mia's note and put in the order

for her blood work—with a twinge of uncertainty about whether Natalie would actually follow through—Luann reappeared and retraced her steps back to the exam room.

Sam informed the couple that the tests would require a few minutes and closed the door behind her, a welcome barrier between herself and Isaac's piercing scrutiny. She moved towards the small lab area nestled next to the restroom. Donning a pair of gloves, she retrieved Luann's urine sample from the discreet pass-through compartment built into the restroom wall.

As soon as she dipped the test strip into the specimen cup, two of the squares immediately turned pink and purple, indicating presence of nitrites and leukocytes—signs unmistakably pointing towards a urinary tract infection. The additional symptom of flank pain suggested the likely progression to pyelonephritis. She proceeded to dispense a few drops of urine onto a pregnancy test strip, then she set the timer.

After removing her gloves and washing her hands, Sam returned to her computer. She first issued orders for the remaining urine specimen to be sent to an external laboratory for a detailed bacterial culture and sensitivity analysis. Then, turning her attention to Luann's medical history, Sam discovered a note about a spontaneous abortion, more commonly referred to as a miscarriage, from the previous year. Dr. Carlisle's notes indicated the miscarriage had occurred at approximately eight weeks of gestation and confirmed that all pregnancy tissue had been expelled without any retained products of conception, eliminating the need for any further medical intervention.

Then there were the visits for the injuries. Nothing too serious, but either Luann was extremely clumsy, or someone was contributing to them. But there was no definitive evidence of abuse. If Dr. Carlisle had suspected something, he certainly hadn't mentioned it in his notes. Since Sam had just met Luann, and Isaac was with her, Sam knew this wasn't the best time to broach the subject with her patient.

The timer in the lab area beeped, so Sam locked the screen on the computer and checked the pregnancy test.

Positive.

Sam went back to the exam room and paused before she knocked on the door. She could hear Isaac's voice rumbling through the wood, with occasional higher-pitched responses from Luann.

She sighed.

Maybe she was overthinking the situation too much. But if not, she had a plan.

After lightly rapping on the door and receiving a combined "Come in," she entered.

They looked at her expectantly.

"I have some good news and some bad news," she said. "The bad news, you kind of already know—you definitely have a UTI. And it's likely spread to your kidney, since you have some tenderness in your back." Then she attempted a comforting smile, despite her suspicions. "The good news is . . . you're pregnant."

Broad grins splashed onto Luann's and Isaac's faces. He sprang from his chair and rushed to her, planting a quick kiss on her lips, then enveloping her with his long arms. She rested her head onto his shoulder, the sound of her sniffles softened by his shirt.

"Oh, baby," he said, rubbing her back, "this is what we've been waiting for."

5

Watching the couple melt into each other's arms, Sam reappraised her first impression of Isaac. Had she judged him too harshly? Maybe there was a reason beyond first impressions for his seemingly stern exterior and Luann's initial reticence. Could there be another side to the story she hadn't considered?

After a moment, Isaac released Luann, then hiked himself up onto the table next to her. She brought her right hand up to brush away tears from her eyes, joy emanating from her as Isaac grasped her other hand, caressing it.

They turned to Sam, expectant looks returning to their faces.

"What's next?" Isaac asked.

"First," Sam said, "we need to take care of this infection."

"Do I take the same medicine as before?" Luann's voice held a hint of worry.

"You took Bactrim, which is usually effective but not recommended during pregnancy due to risks to the baby. It blocks folate, which is very important for the baby's neurological development."

"My friend Nicole had to take folate supplements when she was pregnant," Luann said, tucking a strand of hair behind her ear. "Is that why?"

"Exactly," Sam replied. "We want growing babies to have as much folate as they need, because if they don't, they can develop birth defects. But we also need to use a different antibiotic that's better for treating kidney infections, and we'll need to treat you longer than we would for a regular UTI to make sure we clear it out completely."

Luann nodded and squeezed Isaac's hand. "Will the baby be okay?"

"This shouldn't affect the baby at all, but just to be sure, how about you come back in a couple of days so I can check on you?" *Without your husband*, Sam thought, but she didn't dare say this aloud. While the atmosphere had certainly improved since Sam had first entered the exam room, she knew that sometimes abusers could really switch on the charm.

Luann glanced at Isaac, who gave her a smile and patted her on the back. "I can do that," she said.

"Great," Sam said. "Just one more question: when did your last menstrual period start?"

Something—was it disgust?—flashed on Isaac's face before he turned his head away from the women and let go of his wife's hand.

Luann's cheeks turned a soft pink as she looked up at the ceiling. "I know I should be keeping track of these things, but . . . let me see . . ." She counted on her fingers. "It must have been about five or six weeks ago." She counted her fingers again. "Yeah, I think that's right, maybe six weeks ago. I guess I didn't realize I'm late."

"And are your periods regular?"

"Not always, but like I said, I haven't really kept track," Luann said, looking embarrassed.

"That's okay," Sam said. "It seems like it's pretty early, and while these pregnancy tests are quite sensitive, you'll need to have an ultrasound to confirm in a few weeks. Do you have an OB/GYN?"

"No, I've just been having my annuals with Dr. Carlisle. But now that he's gone . . ." Luann dropped her gaze to her lap.

"That's okay," Sam said again. "We have time to figure this out. For now, let's get you started on those antibiotics, and I'll send your specimen to the lab so we make sure we're treating you appropriately. How does that sound?"

Isaac, who was paying attention again to what Sam was saying, pushed himself off the table and stood. "That sounds great." He cupped Luann's chin, bringing her face up for another quick kiss. "Baby's gonna have a baby!"

Luann smiled, her eyes glinting with freshly formed tears. She slid off the table and wrapped her arm around his waist.

"Thanks, Doctor," she said, then the happy couple exited the room.

Alone at last, Sam returned to the computer in the corner. With Luann being the final patient of the day, Sam opted for sitting rather than standing at the computer desk in the corridor, giving her feet a needed rest. She methodically entered the results of Luann's UA dipstick and pregnancy test into the system, followed by the prescription details, which she promptly dispatched to the pharmacy. In this small community, the Dry Wells Pharmacy, located en route to Timmons, seemed to be the sole option—at least, it was the only one Sam had noticed in the medical records. Typically, in larger towns and cities, office staff would have to verify the patient's preferred pharmacy, but

Sam surmised that in this tight-knit setting, such a task was markedly simpler.

She then searched to see if there were any OB/GYNs nearby. Dr. Carlisle had been an old-style country doctor, taking care of everything, including delivering babies. While she felt fairly comfortable handling most of the medical conditions she'd encountered in this little town so far, she wasn't sure she'd want to deal with labor and delivery. She hadn't delivered a baby since medical school, and there were so many potential complications she knew she wouldn't be prepared for.

The nearest OB/GYN office was in Timmons. That figures. Like almost everything else, about thirty minutes away, with the hospital just beyond that. Not ideal, but Sam supposed that's just how it was in rural America.

A knock on the doorframe interrupted Sam's research and planning for Luann. She looked up to see Olivia standing there.

"I'll get these codes in as soon as possible," Sam said. "And I'll finish up all the outstanding charts tonight." She felt bad for taking so long to complete all of her work, since the clinic couldn't bill for anything she'd done until she'd at least documented ICD-10 and CPT codes.

Olivia held up her hand. "No worries. I know you're on top of it." She looked down the hallway and smiled. "The Clarks seem to be in an upbeat mood. Did you just give them some good news?"

"Well . . ." Sam hesitated. Even though, as office manager, Olivia had access to all of the patients' information and data, Sam was reluctant to discuss it.

"She's pregnant, isn't she?" Olivia came into the room, casually settling against the exam table's edge, holding up her hand again with a grin. "It's okay, you don't have to say anything. I saw the positive test on the lab bench."

Sam mentally kicked herself. She should've cleaned up everything before she came back into the room.

"And don't worry," Olivia reassured, resting her hands on either side of her as she leaned forward slightly. "It's no secret they've been trying. Luann was my neighbor growing up, but she was quite a bit younger—she was only a toddler when I was in high school. After I left home, I'd get updates from my mom about her—how she'd become a cheerleader and then homecoming queen." Her smile dissolved, replaced by concern. "But she's changed. She's been unusually quiet lately, not attending church as much. It's been worrying me." She paused, letting out a sigh. "Perhaps this baby will bring her the joy she needs."

A moment of awkward silence filled the room. Caught in uncertainty, Sam found herself at a loss for words. Meanwhile, Olivia's gaze lingered expectantly, as if urging Sam to reveal more about the couple's visit. Instead, Sam chose to stay mum, her resolve to keep the details confidential standing firm.

Finally, Olivia took in a breath with a subtle shake of her head. "Anyway, that's not why I'm here."

"What do you need?" Sam asked.

"We need a doctor capable of not just filling in, but fully taking over this practice. That's what we need."

"Have you tried finding someone permanent through the agency?"

"I have, but most of the candidates just don't seem right." Olivia looked directly at Sam and smiled. "I think we have the person we need right here."

"What? Me?" Sam swallowed against the tightness in her throat. Being asked to take over the practice felt like being asked to fill shoes much too large for her, a task both exhilarating and daunting. "I'm not qualified. I haven't finished residency, and it seems like Dr. Carlisle practiced the full range of family medicine."

With the mention of Dr. Carlisle's name, Olivia's smile faded. Her gaze became distant, with a subtle tightness around her eyes revealing a deep, lingering sadness.

"I'm so sorry. You miss him, don't you?"

Olivia nodded, her focus dropping to the floor momentarily. Her eyes, glistening with unshed tears, were quickly wiped with the back of her sleeve as she moved to an armchair beside the exam table. Observing this, Sam reached for a Kleenex and extended it towards her. Olivia accepted it gratefully, gently dabbing at the tears that streaked her cheeks. In a silent show of support, Sam wheeled the stool over to her and sat so their knees nearly touched.

"I do. I miss him so much." Olivia crumpled the tissue as she looked up at Sam. "You know, I'm the one who found him."

"You were?"

"Yes. And I felt awful that I hadn't been there. I'd been staying at my parent's house—we'd had a little spat that I . . . I wish hadn't happened. If only I'd . . ." Olivia furrowed her brows, her lips pursed slightly as if she could undo the past.

"It's alright." Sam squeezed her hand.

Olivia nodded as she took in a breath. "Anyway, I came home and found him. Right there. In the middle of the foyer." She closed her eyes, then covered her face with her hands.

Sam stood and grabbed another tissue from the desk, then perched herself on the edge of the exam table next to Olivia's chair, offering the tissue as she patted her shoulder. "I'm so sorry."

Olivia accepted the second tissue and blotted her eyes,

then she sniffed before blowing her nose. "I'm okay . . . I guess. It's made me a little more anxious, not knowing if it could happen again. I bought a gun for protection because if it. But I don't know what else I could have done."

Sam withdrew her hand and gave Olivia time to weep, to mourn. After a few moments, Olivia took a deep breath, trying to compose herself. She turned to Sam. "Thank you. You're so kind and caring. Which proves that you're just the type of doctor this town needs."

Sam shook her head. "But I'm not qual—"

"You *are* qualified. You've had more training than most doctors did a hundred years ago, right?"

"Things were different then. We have so much more technology—"

"Technology doesn't matter. People matter, and you care about people. You want to help them. Everyone has told me how much they like you."

"Everyone?" Sam was certain that wasn't the case for Mia's mother.

"I know. You're thinking about Natalie Fontaine." Olivia rolled her eyes, a smirk playing on her lips, breaking through the sadness. "Natalie was born with a silver spoon in her mouth and a stick up her butt. The only thing that would make her happy is flying to Paris for breakfast, just to have a croissant from her favorite bakery."

Sam laughed.

"Anyway, would you at least consider it? Our town needs you."

"I have an assignment in San Angelo coming up in a couple of weeks."

"If you're open to it," Olivia proposed, her expression thoughtful, "I could speak to the *locum* agency and try to find a way out for you. I know you're only scheduled to be here until the end of next week, but would you consider staying at least until your next assignment?"

Sam had been yearning to return to Austin, to unwind and reconnect with her friends before heading off to San Angelo. She'd been on the move across the Lone Star State since the startup company fiasco. But she had grown fond of the folks here. And working alongside Olivia, despite her being a tad too curious, had been enjoyable.

On top of that, she wanted to make sure Cindy got her blood pressure under control, so she didn't suffer the same fate as her father. Plus, Mia's case intrigued her, despite the challenge posed by Natalie Fontaine's attitude. And now, Luann had lodged herself into Sam's concerns.

But was she prepared to make that leap, to plant roots in this tiny town nestled amidst the sprawling piney woods of east Texas?

Sam drew a deep, steadying breath. "You've given me a lot to think about. Can I get back to you next week?" That way, she'd have the chance to go back to Austin on her days off, reset and rest at bit, talk things over with James, her best friend, and get a fresh perspective.

Olivia smiled. "Of course."

6

Olivia was on the verge of saying something else when her cell phone began buzzing. She excused herself and swiftly made her way down the corridor to the front of the clinic. Meanwhile, Sam gathered her belongings and headed out through the waiting room, spotting Olivia through the doorway of her office. She was barely visible, surrounded by stacks of boxes marked with the ZenithVita Essentials logo. Sam called out, saying she'd see her at Bonnie's house. Olivia, preoccupied with her phone to her ear and a concerned look on her face, simply nodded and waved in response.

Once Sam was in her car, she took a moment before starting the engine. The brief encounter with Olivia left Sam pondering her future. What if Sam were to take over this practice? Was she up to it? The stability of staying in one place with an established panel of patients certainly was attractive. As she pulled away from the office, her thoughts shifted towards the evening ahead.

The drive to Bonnie's house unfolded in silence, with the streets winding through the small community, feeling familiar despite her newcomer status. Sam found herself appreciating the simplicity of the town, a stark contrast to the bustling city life she had left behind. It was in these quiet moments, with the hum of the engine and the passing scenery, that Sam allowed herself to reflect on the possibility of moving here. The promise of a fresh start, a slower pace of life, and meaningful work was appealing, but it was the warmth of the people, like Bonnie and Olivia, that made her feel like she belonged.

As she followed Bonnie's simple and straightforward directions, Sam thought about the upcoming dinner. She didn't know what to expect from Bonnie's hospitality, but the casual invitation and the promise of a home-cooked meal felt comforting. There was something about sharing a meal that broke down barriers and forged connections, and Sam looked forward to it. Not only for the food but also for the chance to discover more about Bonnie and her friends, and potentially herself as she considered starting a new chapter in her life.

Pulling into the driveway of Bonnie's ranch-style home, Sam's reflections gave way to anticipation. The house was modest and well-kept, surrounded by a white picket fence, with a tire swing swaying gently in the breeze, hanging from a large oak tree in the front yard. She parked behind Bonnie's car under the carport and picked up her purse. She felt empty-handed. Usually, when she'd been invited to someone's home, she'd bring a bottle of wine or dessert. But, as the sheriff had pointed out, the town lacked many big city conveniences, where she could easily pick up a hostess gift on the way to a gathering. Certainly another thing to consider should she move here permanently. Even so, Sam had still offered to bring something, but Bonnie had insisted she needn't worry. With a deep breath, Sam stepped out of the car, ready to embrace the evening's possibilities.

Bonnie greeted her warmly and ushered Sam into the kitchen, where Bonnie was just finishing up her meal prep. Sam was immediately charmed by the rustic wood cabinets and the nostalgic aroma of something delicious simmering on the stove.

"Can I offer you something to drink? I don't have anything fancy, just box wine."

"That would be great. Thank you," Sam said.

Bonnie retrieved a small juice glass from the cupboard next to the fridge and filled it with white wine from a Franzia box stored on the fridge's top shelf, using her hip to keep the fridge door slightly open while she pressed the spigot. After handing the glass to Sam, she then picked up her own from beside the stove. Raising her glass, Bonnie proposed a toast, "Here's to a successful week."

Sam echoed the gesture, and they both sipped their wine. The tartness tingled her tongue.

"Of course, we still have tomorrow," Bonnie said, "but at least it's not a full day."

"Have you always shifted the week? Seems like Saturdays would be pretty busy."

Bonnie smiled. "You'd think, but most people don't want to spend any of their weekend in the clinic. If we were open on Mondays, I'm sure we'd be packed."

"Yeah, seems like everyone wants to have an excuse not to go to work or school."

"Exactly. They'll suffer through their minor afflictions over the weekend, since it's *their* time."

"Are Tuesdays usually busy, then?" Sam asked. "It didn't seem that way this week."

"This week was pretty typical. If people really need care on a Monday, they can always head over to Timmons.

Heck, I'm usually over in Timmons on Mondays myself. It's been great having a weekday off to get errands done." Bonnie took another sip of wine, then picked up a sheet pan with rolls on it. "Let me just pop this in the oven. Dinner will be ready in a jiff."

"Is there anything I can do to help?"

"Oh, no, but thank you for asking," Bonnie said as she bent over to put the rolls in the oven. "I just made some stew, nothing too special."

So that's the wonderful aroma, Sam thought. It smelled of warmth and comfort, and the stew would be perfect on this September evening, the first cold snap having come through town a couple of days before.

The doorbell rang, and Bonnie said, "That should be Sally. Would you mind answering it?"

"Sure thing." Sam went back through the living room to the front door and opened it.

A woman with dark hair who appeared to be around Bonnie's age stood on the welcome mat holding a tin of cupcakes. "You must be Dr. Jenkins," she said. "I'm Sally Hudson. It's a pleasure to finally meet you. I've heard so much about you!" She gave Sam a warm, conspiratorial wink.

"Nice to meet you too," Sam replied, wondering what had been said about her as she opened the door wider to welcome Sally inside. Moving with familiarity, Sally breezed past Sam and headed straight to the kitchen, where she found Bonnie busy stirring the stew.

"I brought these for everyone," Sally said, holding up the cupcakes.

"Wonderful! Just put them over there." Bonnie pointed to an empty spot on the counter as she replaced the lid on the stew pot.

Sally's presence added a new energy to the room. As

she set down the dessert, she teased, "Remember when we decided to have a bake sale for that fundraiser last year and had to stay up all night?"

Bonnie's laughter filled the kitchen. "How could I forget? We totally bit off more than we could chew. But at least it all turned out okay." She turned to Sam and explained, "For some crazy reason, we thought we could bake five hundred cupcakes all in one night, not thinking through the fact that we could only bake forty-eight cupcakes at a time."

"After that, I thought I'd never want to be around another cupcake again." Sally smirked. "But I'm over it now. I love frosting too much!"

Sam let out a gentle laugh, sharing in the camaraderie. It was clear these two had a long and storied friendship, their ease and banter hinting at years of shared experiences.

Looking around the living room, Sally asked, "Did Olivia ride over with one of you? I didn't see her car out front."

Bonnie's expression shifted subtly, the corners of her mouth turning downward as her eyes clouded with a mix of concern and disappointment. "Unfortunately, something came up and she won't be able to make it tonight."

"I hope it's not serious," Sally said, her brow furrowing with apprehension.

"I hope so, too," Bonnie agreed, her voice tinged with a note of worry. She paused for a moment, as if weighing her next words. "Apparently, it was some kind of family issue. I guess we'll find out more later." Her tone softened further, a warm smile slowly replacing the tension on her face as she sought to reassure her guests. "But I'm truly glad you and Dr. Jenkins could be here. The rolls are in the oven, so let's take a moment to relax." She gestured towards the kitchen table.

Sally took a seat and Sam followed suit, while Bonnie went back to the fridge to pour a glass of wine for Sally before joining them at the table.

Sam listened quietly as the two friends chatted about the goings on at the high school. After a moment, Bonnie put her hand on Sam's arm and said, "Sorry, our boys are sophomores and have been friends since—" She glanced at Sally. "When did Trevor and Brian first start playing together?"

"Oh, I can't remember," Sally said as she looked up at the ceiling, trying to recall. "Must have been first or second grade."

Laughing softly, Bonnie added, "It feels like they've been friends forever, just like us."

Sally gave a warm chuckle in agreement.

"Did you both grow up here?" Sam inquired.

"Yeah, we did. That's why I'm still here, I guess," Bonnie said.

"Same here. But we didn't really know each other when we were kids. Bonnie graduated from high school a few years ahead of me. Then, while she was off at nursing school, I graduated, went to the cosmetology academy, and opened my own hair salon."

"Sally's quite industrious," Bonnie said.

Her friend beamed at the compliment. "In fact, Dr. Jenkins," Sally offered, "you're welcome to stop by my place anytime, and I'll give you a special discount. It's the Knotty by Nature Salon on Spur 34, right next to the Dry Wells Pharmacy on the way to Timmons."

"Bonnie!" An older woman's voice came from the hallway off the living room. "Bonnie! I can't find my glasses!"

Bonnie's face momentarily stiffened, a flicker of frustration passing through her eyes before she masked it with a practiced smile. She placed her wine down a little too hastily, the clink of glass on the tabletop echoing in the now quiet kitchen.

"That's my mother," she said, her voice carrying a slight edge of weariness that hadn't been there before. She forced a smile, though it didn't quite reach her eyes, revealing the underlying tension she felt. "I'll be back in just a sec. Please, make yourself at home."

As Bonnie disappeared down the hallway, her steps a mix of reluctance and duty, Sam couldn't help but notice the subtle shift in the room's atmosphere.

7

"Poor Bonnie," Sally said, a tinge of sympathy softening her voice. "Her mother's developing dementia, which, I'm sure you know, can be quite challenging."

Bonnie returned just then, looking a little frazzled. "Can you believe it? My mother couldn't find her glasses because she was wearing them!" She sniffed, her nose aimed toward the kitchen. "Rolls are done."

As Bonnie pulled the tray out of the oven, Sam asked, "You don't need a timer?"

"No." Bonnie smiled. "I can tell when they're done by the smell. Something my mother taught me." The smile slipped from her face as she looked down the hallway. "I just want to let you know that my mother will be joining us for dinner, if that's okay with you." She looked at Sam and Sally in a way that almost made it seem like she wished they would say no.

"Of course," Sam said. It was Bonnie's home, after all. Why wouldn't she be okay with it? She looked at Sally, who just shrugged.

"Okay. I just want to warn you—and Sally already knows this . . ." Bonnie glanced down the hallway again. "My mother can be . . . a bit rough around the edges at times. She was diagnosed with Alzheimer's last year." She closed her eyes briefly before continuing. "We've seen some changes in her personality." She looked at Sam, forcing a smile. "She's really a lovely person . . . but she has her moments."

Sam nodded. "I completely understand."

"Thank you." Bonnie's shoulders relaxed as she turned to the cupboard, pulling out a stack of bowls.

Sam stood to join her in the kitchen, with Sally following.

"Are you sure you don't need help with anything?" Sam asked.

Bonnie grabbed a ladle out of a drawer and began scooping stew into the bowls. "Could you put these on the table?" She handed two piping hot bowls to Sally and Sam each. Sam was glad the rims on the bowls were large enough to keep her hands cool.

They set the bowls down on the table, and Bonnie followed with small plates and a basket filled with the rolls, their yeasty fragrance, along with the hearty stew, causing Sam's stomach to growl.

As Bonnie returned to the refrigerator to refill her glass of wine, her mother appeared at the entrance to the hallway, her posture slightly stooped with a confused look on her face. After a moment she glanced at Sally and gave a huff, then turned her attention to Sam, fixing her with a piercing stare. "Who are you?" she barked.

"This is Dr. Jenkins, Ma. Remember?" Bonnie said, looking slightly frustrated. "I told you there was a doctor joining us for dinner." She turned to Sam and smiled. "And this is my mother."

The older woman paused, eyeing Sam critically before responding. "You may call me Mrs. Wright."

"Pleased to meet you, Mrs. Wright." Sam extended her hand.

Instead of taking it, Mrs. Wright looked her up and down. "When you said a doctor was coming over, I thought it'd be a man. Someone to set a good example for Trevor." She looked around. "Where is that boy, anyway?"

"He's out with Brian and their friends," Bonnie replied.

"You shouldn't let him skip dinner with his family."

"Ma, it's Friday night. There's a football game, and he went to see it with his friends."

Bonnie's mother huffed again, then shuffled over to the table and took a seat at the place setting where Sam had her glass of wine. Sam quickly moved it to the adjacent spot, next to Sally. Bonnie was the last to join, with her wine and a glass of water for her mother.

As Mrs. Wright settled, she picked up a napkin, her fingers trembling slightly as she folded and refolded it, a meticulous yet aimless focus in her eyes. She hummed a fragment of a melody, her attention drifting from the napkin to the window and back again, encapsulated in a moment that seemed both present and far away. Then her awareness seemed to come back to the present, and she pointed to the empty place setting. "Who else is coming?" she demanded.

"Olivia was going to be here," Bonnie said, "but she couldn't make it."

If Olivia had made it to dinner, Sam wondered, would she and Bonnie have teamed up to convince her to stay?

But instead of bringing it up, Sam found herself engrossed in stories about the town's history, shared with enthusiasm by Sally and Bonnie. An amusing tale emerged about a miscommunication that led to the town's unique name: Dry Wells. Contrary to hopeful rumors after the success at Spindletop in 1901, no oil was ever discovered here. This anecdote made Sam think the duo had missed their calling—they could have been the perfect promoters for a local tourism bureau, had the town been large enough to support one. The conversation then shifted to the town's early days, when it was still called Fontaine after a French family from Louisiana, with the friends explaining how most of the current residents, including Bonnie's own family, were descendants of settlers who had arrived in Texas during the mid-1800s. They'd been drawn by the opportunities in the booming lumber industry, which thrived in the dense, piney woods surrounding the area.

At this point, Bonnie turned to Sam. "Hopefully you haven't encountered anyone from the Fontaine family yet. They can be a handful."

Sally nodded, adding, "They act like they're royalty, just because their family's been here so long, and they made a fortune with everyone moving to Texas, needing wood for their houses."

Sam smiled knowingly. "I met Natalie Fontaine earlier today."

"How did it go?" Bonnie asked.

"It was . . . fine, but now I understand why she acted the way she did."

Throughout the conversation, Bonnie's mother plowed through her bowl of stew, mostly ignoring the younger women, except for the occasional interjection to correct Bonnie regarding some fact or figure. Bonnie never reacted when this happened, other than saying, "That's right, Ma," letting her mother's statements, sometimes derogatory, slide off her back. Once her mother got to the bottom of her bowl, scraping it clean, she grabbed a roll, stuffed it in her pocket, and disappeared down the hallway.

After Mrs. Wright left the room, an uneasy stillness settled amongst the women.

Finally, Sam took a deep breath and ventured to ask the question that had been on her mind. "Bonnie, how have you been holding up since Dr. Carlisle's passing? It must be tough for you."

Swirling the wine in her juice glass slowly, Bonnie paused a moment before answering. "It's been . . . difficult. He was so much to me. A mentor and a close friend. We'd been through a lot together in this town." She took a long sip and sighed. "As for his death, I can't shake the feeling that something's off. I don't buy the whole 'random home invasion' story. But, I don't have any evidence to back it up. It's just a feeling."

Sam raised her eyebrows as her mind went back through everything she'd learned over the last few days. "What makes you think that?" she asked.

Before Bonnie could reply, her mother appeared at the entrance to the hallway again, her voice cutting through their conversation. "Bonnie! Why couldn't you be more like your brother? A real doctor!" She pointed at Sam. "Like her!"

Bonnie's face flushed with a mix of irritation and embarrassment, but she stood firm, meeting her mother's critical gaze. "Not now, Ma."

Sally began to speak, but a swift glance and a subtle shake of Bonnie's head silently conveyed her wish for this moment to pass.

Mrs. Wright, however, wasn't so easily deterred. "Your brother's so successful. If you were more like him, maybe you wouldn't be stuck in your situation. After that doctor friend of yours died."

Bonnie's eyes widened, and Sam could sense the sharp pang of pain those words inflicted. She glanced sympathetically at Bonnie, wishing she could intervene. But before Sam could say anything, Bonnie jumped up from the table, took her mother by the elbow, and turned her around to go back down the hallway. Over her shoulder she said to her guests, "Sorry, can you excuse me for a bit?"

Sam nodded, and Sally's face softened with compassion.

"You were smart enough," Bonnie's mother went on as they went down the hallway. "You should have been a doctor, too."

"I know, Ma. We talked about it many times."

"Your brother is a doctor. Why aren't you a doctor?"

"Ma, let's not talk about this now," Bonnie pleaded.

"You should be more like your brother. You should have been more like him."

"I'm not so sure about that."

"You could have been a doctor, too. Just like him. People respect him."

Bonnie snapped. "Not any—"

Her voice was cut off by the sound of a door shutting.

Sam's fingers tightened around her glass, the condensation leaving small droplets on her palm. There was an unspoken heaviness in the room following Mrs. Wright's departure, and Sam's thoughts began to whirl. The heat of embarrassment rose to her cheeks. To be a witness to such a raw, familial moment was unintentional, and she couldn't help but feel like an intruder in Bonnie's personal life.

After taking a sip of wine, Sally said, "Bonnie was hoping her mother would be friendlier this evening, but with dementia . . ."

"I know," Sam commiserated. "It can be touch and go at times, and sundowning can be an issue."

"What's that?" Sally asked.

"It's when dementia patients become more agitated

later in the day."

"Ah, makes sense. Sundowning. Bonnie had mentioned that her mom seemed to be more upset in the evenings." She turned to face Sam. "But Bonnie really wanted to have you over tonight. And she figured you would understand. She says you're wonderful with the patients, and she really enjoys working with you."

Sam blushed at the compliment.

"Bonnie says that ever since Dr. Carlisle passed away, it's been a roll of the dice as far as how the doctor who's filling in will be." Sally paused. "I mean, Bonnie says they've all been nice. It's just . . . you know, some people are easier to work with than others."

"I completely understand," Sam said. She looked around the table, trying to find some diversion, some distraction. The bowls were empty. "Why don't we help Bonnie out by cleaning up?"

"What a great idea."

They gathered up the bowls, took them to the sink, and then worked together, with Sam rinsing the dishes and Sally loading up the dishwasher.

Bonnie returned from the hallway and said, "Oh, please, don't worry about that."

Sam shut off the water. "We just wanted to help. I'm sorry your mom was . . ."

"A handful? I'm the one who should apologize, since you had to witness her behavior." Bonnie took a deep breath. "Like I said before, she has her moments."

"So you have a—" Sam began, but then she cut herself off. She wanted to ask Bonnie about her brother, especially since he was also in the medical profession, but it seemed to be a sensitive topic. It's always difficult when parents compare siblings, especially when they pick favorites.

"A brother?" Bonnie finished Sam's inquiry. "Yes. And

he is a doctor, just like Ma said." She finished her statement with a down note to her voice, suggesting she'd prefer not to discuss him any further.

"He's been dealing with some things," Sally said, "so that's another source of stress."

Bonnie nodded, looking grateful for her friend's intervention. She looked around the kitchen, then motioned for the others to follow her into the living room. "I can clean this up later. Can you stay a little longer? There's something I'd like to talk to you about."

"It wouldn't have to do with having me stay in Dry Wells, would it?"

"As a matter of fact," Bonnie said as they all sat down around the coffee table, "it does. So Olivia already asked you?"

"She did, but there's a lot to consider. It's too bad you couldn't just take over the practice. The patients have had great things to say about you."

Bonnie blushed. "That's wonderful, but I wouldn't feel comfortable without someone to back me up."

"So who's your supervising physician right now? Surely it's not a *locum*."

"No, a family friend in Timmons is supervising me. It's fine for the time being, but it's not a long-term solution. And he's already at his max on his prescription delegation, so that really limits what I can do."

Sam nodded. The whole time she'd been in Dry Wells, Bonnie had mostly been seeing patients independently. However, whenever she needed to prescribe certain medications, she relied on Sam to write the script.

"So, if I were to stay, that would really help you out, too."

Bonnie smiled, a hopeful expression coming across her face. "It certainly would."

8

The clinic on a Saturday morning bore little resemblance to its weekday hustle. The usual symphony of ringing phones and chattering voices was replaced by a serene quiet, punctuated only by the soft hum of the heat pump and the occasional shuffle of feet across the linoleum floor. Sam appreciated these slower starts, the gentle sunlight filtering through the blinds, casting a warm glow over the waiting area that seemed to relax even the most anxious of patients. Today, the chairs held fewer occupants, each spaced out as if the tranquility of the room demanded a respectful silence. There was a palpable sense of calm, a rare commodity in the otherwise frenetic pace of clinical life.

As she moved into the back hallway, Sam noticed everyone's subdued demeanor. They seemed more at ease, their faces softer, the lines of worry less pronounced than on busier days. This quietude allowed her a moment to observe, to really see her patients beyond their charts and ailments. It was on mornings like these that she felt a deeper connection to her work, a reminder of why she had chosen this path.

Sam approached Bonnie, who was busy typing on the computer, to express her gratitude once more for the dinner invitation. Bonnie, feeling no need to reiterate her wish for Sam to remain in Dry Wells, suggested they should definitely plan another gathering in the future.

Since Olivia wasn't around, Sam asked about her, hoping everything was alright.

"Olivia often stays late during the week, so she sometimes takes Saturdays off," Bonnie explained. "We did text, though. Turns out, her cousin's dealing with some crisis—nothing to do with health, just needed her assistance."

"Well, I'm glad everyone is okay," Sam said.

Bonnie nodded. "Same here."

Although there was a steady flow of patients, not all of the exam rooms were filled. However, the end of September had ushered in cold and flu season, and the two women saw mainly a mix of adults and kids with sniffles and coughs throughout the morning.

There really wasn't much to do in these cases other than provide the usual guidance of rest and fluids since the most common cause for these maladies were viruses. Sam did see one baby with a fever who kept tugging at his ear while his mother, a first-time parent, nervously bounced him in her lap. The mom was grateful for Sam's patience with the irritable infant, since it took a few attempts for her to finally get a good look at his affected ear. Sure enough, his tympanic membrane was an angry red, full and bulging. Sam sent off a prescription for antibiotics to the local pharmacy and reassured the now-relieved mom to return if her son's symptoms didn't resolve.

After the mom left, Sam mentally kicked herself. She'd

told the mom to come back on Monday out of habit, but since the clinic was closed then—precisely so it could be open on Saturdays—the poor mom would have to travel to one of the urgent care clinics or the hospital in Timmons if her little one had any issues. So before Sam moved on to see the next patient, she called the clinic's answering service and left instructions to patch the mom through to Sam immediately if she were to call.

When Sam entered the next exam room, Luann Clark sat on the table with her left leg propped up, a cold pack draped over her ankle. She was alone, to Sam's relief. Even though Luann's husband seemed very happy about the pregnancy, his initial controlling behavior still clouded Sam's view of him.

"Goodness, Mrs. Clark, what happened?" Sam asked.

Luann smiled meekly at her. "I just tripped. I can be pretty clumsy sometimes."

Sam thought back to the EHR, where she'd seen that Luann had repeated visits for injuries in the past. She went over to the table and gently lifted the cold pack off Luann's ankle. "Tell me about it."

"It's just one of those things, you know. Isaac was working on a project of his, rebuilding an engine with a buddy," Luann began, her voice trailing off for a moment as she glanced away towards the door, a subtle but unmistakable nervous tic. She forced a small laugh, her eyes darting back to meet Sam's before quickly looking down at her hands, folded in her lap. "He's always got something or other spread out in our living room." She paused, the laughter fading as she seemed to weigh her next words with some regard. "Of course, he's real careful, puts out newspaper so as not to foul up the carpet." Her fingers twisted the hem of her shirt, betraying her attempt at nonchalance. "Says it's the only place he can work on it 'cause we don't have no garage, and if he left it out on the back patio, he reckons some critter or 'nother would make a nest in his stuff. So, he puts it in our living room." She gave a shrug, a bit too quick, her gaze flitting to the side, avoiding Sam. "I just tripped over his toolbox. Twisted my ankle." Luann's voice tightened, her words rushing out as if she was avoiding a tenuous truth.

It seemed like Isaac's choice to use the living room as a place to work on his car parts had been a point of contention.

Sam decided not to push into it further at this point. At least Luann was opening up, sharing a little more.

Instead, Sam switched her focus to the injury. She asked Luann to try moving her ankle, but Luann was limited by pain. Sam watched Luann's face as she gently pressed on the ligaments, starting with the ones away from the swollen area, careful to stop when Luann grimaced. "When you tripped, did your foot turn inward or outward?" Based on the location of the swelling, she already had an idea what Luann's answer would be, but she wanted to keep her talking, to distract her while Sam performed the exam.

Luann looked up at the ceiling for a second. "It turned inward."

Sam nodded. Indeed, the swelling was right over the anterior talofibular ligament, the one most commonly injured with sprained ankles. When she gingerly palpated it, Luann winced. "Sorry about that," Sam said. "I just need to check one more thing—it might be a little uncomfortable."

"Do what you need to do, Doctor," Luann said as she braced her arms on either side of her, readying herself for the oncoming pain.

Sam put her left hand on the lower part of Luann's leg,

above the ankle, and cupped Luann's heel with her right hand. She then moved the heel from side to side, checking for stability. Luann winced again, but she didn't seem to be in extreme pain, and there was minimal laxity.

"Good," Sam said. "It seems like it's just a sprain and not a tear. Should heal up just fine."

"That's good to hear," Luann said as she relaxed a little.

"And how are you doing with the antibiotic?"

"I started it last night, and already, the burning is gone."

"Great," Sam said. "Do you mind if I check your back, again?"

"Sure." Luann leaned forward for her.

Sam made a fist and gently tapped Luann's back just below the rib cage on both sides of her spine. Luann flinched, but not as much as she had the day before.

"Did that hurt?"

"Only a little."

"Good. It seems like you're improving. Just make sure that you keep taking those antibiotics until you run out."

"Will do, Doctor."

Just then, Sam noticed the bruise.

It wasn't very big, but it stood out like a warning on Luann's left arm.

"What happened here?" She leaned closer to inspect it.

The bruise was on the inside of the forearm, like a dark purple thumbprint, surrounded by Luann's pale flesh. A strange spot, not where someone would normally have bumped themselves. Usually the extensor surfaces, on the outside of the arm or the elbow, were more prone to these kinds of contusions.

Luann quickly placed her right hand over the bruise, covering it with her palm, rubbing back and forth.

She seemed to sense Sam wouldn't accept a typical excuse, that she just ran into something, so she mumbled, "It's nothing, really. When I tripped, Isaac grabbed me. That's all." She hung her head, her shoulders folding forward. She was closing down.

Sam sat on the stool and slid it over to the table near Luann. She placed her arm next to where Luann sat, not touching, but signaling she was available. She peered up from where she sat, looking into the cave formed by Luann's hair, shadowing her face. "You can talk to me, if you want," Sam offered gently, sensing the layers of unsaid words hanging between them.

Luann glanced at Sam briefly, her eyes a pool of unshed tears, before she shook her head, a fragile whisper escaping her lips. "No, it's alright. Everything is better now." The words felt heavy, laden with a sorrow yet to be voiced. She nodded. "The baby's what we've wanted."

Sam waited a few moments, hoping Luann would say more. It was a delicate situation. If she pressed too hard, too quickly, Luann might withdraw. But she sensed there was more Luann had to say.

She just needed to give her some space.

Let it come out when Luann was ready.

Without a word, Sam wheeled her stool over to the computer. After unlocking the screen, she pulled up Luann's chart, clicked on the current visit, and began typing her note, much more slowly than usual, trying to give her patient as much time as she needed to open up. That is . . . *if* she'd open up.

A few more moments passed, then Luann said quietly, "I just told him he couldn't be working on his car in our living room no more."

Slowly, Sam swiveled her chair to face Luann, aiming to project an aura of nonjudgmental openness.

Luann met Sam's gaze, peering out from under her bangs, her eyes imploring Sam to understand. "You know, 'cause of the baby."

Sam nodded.

"We can't have that greasy mess around with a baby."

Sam waited, giving Luann time, in hopes she would continue. Then, she gently probed, "So, there was an argument?"

Luann gave a tiny nod. "That's all."

"And this is your first baby?"

Another tiny nod. "We've been tryin'."

They sat in silence again.

"Are you worried?" Sam asked.

Luann blinked, then nodded, a bigger affirmation. "Last time I thought I was pregnant, it didn't take."

"I'm so sorry to hear that," Sam said, her voice filled with compassion. She leaned in a bit closer, as if sharing a confidential secret. "It's okay to feel worried or scared. But remember, you're not alone. We're here to support you in every way we can."

Luann let out a breath, seeming to relax a touch. Then her eyes grew wider. "But don't tell Isaac. He never knew."

"Don't worry," Sam assured her, her tone gentle yet firm. "Everything you tell me is confidential. I won't share it with anyone, not without your consent."

Sam's promise seemed to offer Luann a semblance of solace, a momentary respite in the storm of her fears. However, another worry struck Sam. She was about to leave town for the rest of the weekend. What if something happened to Luann while she was gone?

She spun her chair to face the desk and scribbled her cell phone number on the note pad next to the computer. Tearing off the top sheet, she spun back to face Luann and extended the paper towards her. "Here's my number. You can call or text me any time."

Luann nodded, a silent acknowledgment of the bond they had formed. She accepted the slip of paper, caressing it as if it were a precious gift.

9

The rest of Sam's shortened day in the clinic passed in a blur, with her hands moving automatically as she tended to the few patients who came in, but her mind was elsewhere, tangled in thoughts of Luann. After the last patient left, she found herself alone in the exam room, and a memory surfaced unbidden, sharpening her unease into a keen edge of frustration.

Last year, she had encountered a similar situation at the clinic where she'd practiced in Austin. A woman, eyes downcast, voice barely above a whisper, her story not quite aligning with the bruises that painted her arms in shades of pain. Back then, Sam had known exactly whom to call, which advocate would respond with the right blend of warmth and steel.

Now, as she stood by herself in the quiet room, that certainty eluded her. She pictured Luann's hesitant smile, the way her fingers twisted together as she spoke of her husband. The parallel was too stark to ignore, but here in Dry Wells, Sam's toolkit felt empty.

She sighed, a sound that filled the empty room and

echoed back to her, a reminder of her isolation. "I need to do something," she murmured to herself, "but what?" The question hung in the air, unanswered. She reached for her phone, then hesitated. In Austin, a quick call would summon a network of support. Here, her contact list was barren of such resources.

Sam's feelings of powerlessness mounted as she slid the phone back into her pocket. She wasn't just out of her geographical element; she was out of her depth in ways that city life had never prepared her for. The thought of Luann, possibly waiting for a lifeline that Sam didn't know how to throw, gnawed at her.

What else could she do? She grabbed her things and stopped to say goodbye to Bonnie in the hallway.

"Heading out?" Bonnie asked.

"Yep," Sam said, glancing at her watch. "Since we're done pretty early, I'm planning on heading back to Austin." As she prepared to leave, a thought struck Sam. Perhaps Bonnie could offer some insight. "Say, are you familiar with the Clarks?" she asked.

"Of course. In this town, we all know each other." Then, with a gleam in her eye that betrayed her usual composure, Bonnie leaned closer. "Olivia told me Luann's pregnant! How wonderful!"

Sam forced a smile as she began to have second thoughts.

Bonnie continued, apparently not noticing Sam's reticence. "Luann's always been Dr. Carlisle's patient, and I've only seen Isaac a few times, but they seem like a lovely couple." An inquisitive look came over her face. "Is there something you wanted to ask me about them?"

Even though Bonnie was a fellow clinician, her idle chatter about the couple concerned Sam, reminding her of Olivia's push to gain information from her. Plus, she knew

Bonnie had her own issues in dealing with her mother, and Sam didn't want to burden her further, especially without solid proof of anything. Just a suspicion.

Sam shook her head. "No. It's nothing."

"Well," Bonnie said, "it's been great working with you this week. Thanks so much for helping us out."

"Sure thing," Sam said.

Bonnie picked up her own bag, and the two headed into the parking lot to their cars.

"Have a safe drive to Austin. So we'll see you Tuesday?" Bonnie asked, with a touch of uncertainty.

"Yep," Sam said, her voice reassuring. "I will be here Tuesday."

It was a beautiful autumn day, and with Austin just three hours away, the drive promised to be pleasant. She anticipated being back in her hometown by early evening, leaving her enough time to catch up with friends. But first, she needed to refuel.

On the way to her motel, she pulled into a weathered Texaco, its peeling paint and the bold "Get your bait here!" sign, seemed stuck in time. The sharp, almost nostalgic scent of oil and rust lingered in the air, mingling with the distant, earthy promise of rain.

There wasn't a reader at the pump, so she had to go inside. A clerk sat behind the counter and only glanced up briefly when she entered. He was too busy playing a game on his phone, barely paying attention to her as she handed him her card.

She stepped back outside, opened her car's gas cap, slid in the nozzle, and lifted the old pump's holder. The sharp odor of gasoline filled the air, its scent making her eyes water, as the pump chugged rhythmically.

Seeking relief from the overpowering fumes, she took a step forward, moving toward the front of her car where the air felt somewhat less toxic. Leaning against the cool metal of her car's hood, she found a brief respite while she waited for the tank to fill.

She was tempted to pull out her phone, just like the clerk, to pass the time. However, a warning sign prominently displayed on the side of the pump caught her attention, urging customers to keep their cell phones off. The reminder of the potential danger made her think twice. The last thing she wanted was to trigger a spark and end up engulfed in a terrifying ball of flames.

A couple of cars passed by on the lonely rural road, and then an SUV cruiser painted in law enforcement two tone with a seal encircled by the words "Timmons County Sheriff's Department" turned into the station lot and pulled up on the opposite side of the pump from Sam. Ken Perkins stepped out and nodded at her.

"Afternoon, Doctor. How are you doing today?"

"Hello, Sheriff," Sam said as she pushed off her hood and stepped closer to him. "Just filling up before I head back to Austin."

A surprised look crossed his face. "You aren't leaving us already, are you?"

"Oh, no. I'm not leaving the clinic for good, at least not yet. I'm just heading home for the next couple of days." She winced inwardly when she said the word "home" — she didn't really have a home in Austin. Not anymore. She put on a smile. "But I am considering Olivia's offer to stay."

"That's good to hear." He shook his head. "You know, the more I thought about it, maybe Cindy's right. That what happened to the good ol' doctor could have been keeping some of the prospective replacements from staying." He looked at her directly in the eyes. "So I want to assure you again, this town is safe."

Sam waited a beat, then, in a softer tone laden with curiosity, she probed, "What about the case in Timmons?"

The sheriff's face, which had been an open book before, shuttered for the briefest of moments. It was so fleeting that Sam almost missed it. A depth of emotion flashed in his eyes. Was there a personal connection?

"That's . . . an unusual case, with very unusual circumstances," he finally said, his voice sounding slightly strained. "What I meant was, violent crime isn't a common thing around here. That case in Timmons is . . . different." He looked away, avoiding Sam's direct gaze, before focusing on her again with a more composed demeanor.

While Sam sensed some evasiveness, her gut told her that the sheriff was a good man. She switched gears, because she wanted to maintain a good rapport with him, no matter how long she stayed in Dry Wells. And she might need his help, so she changed her tone.

"You mentioned you've been in your position about a decade the other night. Did you always want to be sheriff?"

Sheriff Perkins hesitated a moment, then said, "That's right." He looked at her and smiled. "But no, I never expected to be back here. When I was young, I wanted to get out of here as fast as I could." He looked off in the distance as he recalled that version of himself. "I joined the Army after high school. My folks couldn't afford to send me to college, so I figured it was the only way to keep from ending up at the mills like my dad."

The pump clicked off, but Sam ignored it, wanting to know more.

"So how did you become sheriff? Was it difficult?" Sam wanted to keep him going so she could ask the questions that truly mattered to her.

"Let me guess what you're really thinking: how did a man like me become sheriff in a county that's just a stone's throw from where another Black man was dragged to death only twenty years ago?"

Sam was taken aback by his assumption. She supposed that was something she was curious about, but she'd spent most of her life in the bigger cities of Texas and had had many diverse friends and colleagues over the years, people of all types. She hadn't really thought of it, but obviously it was something that was on the sheriff's mind.

He seemed to sense her surprise at his comment, so then he continued, "I was in an MP in the Army—that's the military police. When the old sheriff passed away, and . . ." He pursed his lips and flared his nostrils. "Well, let's just say I was needed around here."

Sam was going to press him further, but the radio in his cruiser squawked.

"Excuse me," he said as he leaned into the vehicle to answer.

Sam pushed the pump's lever down, pulled out the nozzle, and tapped it to avoid dripping gas on her car and her shoes before placing it back in the holder. While the sheriff continued talking on the radio, she entered the store to pay and retrieve her card.

When she returned outside, she found the sheriff leaning on his cruiser, the gas still flowing into his tank. Although Sam was eager to head back to Austin, she couldn't shake off a twinge of guilt for merely leaving her cell number with Luann and not doing more. Plus, she hadn't considered what her next steps would be if Luann actually called. Being one hundred and fifty miles away, how could she possibly help her? Now was the time to see how much she could depend on Sheriff Perkins.

"I was wondering, Sheriff, what kind of social services are available in this county?"

He raised an eyebrow. "Why do you ask?"

"Well, let's just say—hypothetically—that I see a patient whom I suspect may be the victim of domestic abuse. I was just wondering if there were any social services available for them."

He took in a deep breath and paused before answering. "Well, Doctor, you'd want to talk to the Health and Human Services Department over in Timmons. They could send someone out to talk to this patient of yours." He gave her a knowing look as he said this. "But you can always give me a call." He reached into one of the chest pockets on his uniform and pulled out his card. "Here you go. Just in case you need it."

Sam took the card, and as she studied it, he added, "You can always call the main number and dispatch will know how to get through to me."

"Thank you. Timmons is the county seat, right? Is that where your office is?"

"Yes, but I live out in this direction. My folks aren't far, and as you know, my brother owns the diner, so I'm around. Plus we have a deputy who's assigned to this sector of the county." He paused a beat, then said, "Now, is there anyone you might want me to check on while you're away?"

Sam smiled guardedly. "I'm sorry, Sheriff, but you know how it goes with patient confidentiality." She hesitated, aware that, without definitive evidence, her concerns remained just a strong hunch. "But really, I was just speaking hypothetically."

"Of course," the sheriff said, his eyes gleaming with unspoken comprehension. "I will say, however, these cases can be difficult." He shook his head. "I've been called out to quite a few domestic dispute reports over the years, but it's really hard to do much, even when signs of problems are apparent. The victim usually doesn't want to make a statement once I show up. If they do, they change their story or recant a few days later, after they've thought about it." He used air quotes with this last statement.

He shook his head again, frustration evident. "It's heartbreaking. My authority to act is limited by the law, despite my desire to help."

10

Following her discussion with the sheriff, Sam felt a bit more at ease about leaving town, but her concern for Luann remained. On the short drive to her motel, she crafted a plan: if Luann were to reach out for help in distress, Sam was confident she could call upon the sheriff or one of his deputies through the county dispatch for support. She felt there was an unspoken understanding between her and Sheriff Perkins about which patient she'd been referring to, though Sam couldn't be entirely certain. Then again, it dawned on her that the unfortunate reality was the sheriff likely had his hands full with similar cases of domestic issues plaguing other families across the rural expanse.

While she packed, she thought about where she'd stay in Austin. She could always go to her parents' house. Well, technically, it was now her father's and stepmother's house. She'd left some personal items there, mainly for easier access than her storage unit offered. So it ostensibly remained her "home." But it didn't feel like home. Not really, since it wasn't the house she'd grown up in.

Returning always resurrected a familiar pang of judgment, an unwelcome shadow over her visits.

Sure, Millie was nice enough, and they'd connected on some level. But Millie wasn't her mother, and she seemed more like a diplomat trying to keep all sides at peace as opposed to the nurturing type.

Sam's father had made his disdain for her career choice painfully clear, viewing *locum tenens* doctors as the profession's underachievers. This judgment often made Sam reflect on the broader perception of temporary medical staff, particularly traveling nurses. Her experience, however, painted a different picture. Having worked alongside numerous traveling nurses, she found them to be exceptionally capable, often surpassing their permanently stationed counterparts in both skill and adaptability. This insight not only deepened Sam's respect for them but also reinforced her belief in the value of *locum tenens* roles—roles like her own, which her father too hastily dismissed.

The bottom line was, Sam wanted to go back to Austin this afternoon, but she didn't want to deal with her father. So she texted her friend James as she continued gathering up her things, letting him know she was headed his way. She wanted to know if he and Kevin would mind having her crash on their couch for a couple of days.

Catching her reflection in the bathroom mirror as she packed her toiletries, Sam noted the weary eyes that stared back at her. Did she really look that exhausted? Plus, she really needed a haircut. Sure, she could get away with letting it grow a little longer. She could always put it up in a bun or ponytail. But her locks hung in uneven waves around her shoulders, the ends frayed and betraying signs of neglect. As long as she was in Austin, she might as well fit in an appointment at her favorite salon. So she pulled out her phone and booked one for Monday.

While she had her phone out, Sam sent a message to Renee, a friend from medical school who now worked in family medicine at a large clinic chain in Austin. Their friendship had deepened after reconnecting when Renee moved to Austin for her job, shortly before Sam departed. Initially acquaintances during their medical studies—Sam in her fourth year and Renee as a third year—they truly bonded when Renee joined Sam's team for an elective rotation her fourth year, with Sam then serving as a surgery intern. With Sam currently traversing the state for *locum* assignments, often dealing with cases typical of family medicine, she frequently sought Renee's advice for complex cases beyond the reach of online resources. In her text message, Sam mentioned she'd be in Austin for a few days, hoping they could arrange a meet-up.

Sam zipped up her duffel bag, now full with a couple of changes of clothes and some toiletries, then she locked up the motel room, and threw her things in her car. She'd left most of her clothes tucked away in the closet in her suitcase, which she lived out of full-time now. The room was paid up through the end of the following week, since that was the planned end of her *locum* assignment.

But perhaps Dry Wells would be her home a little longer. With all of these cases causing some concern for Sam, maybe she would ask Olivia to extend her assignment. She was still not seriously considering accepting Olivia's proposal to take over the practice, though. One of the many reasons she wanted to see James was to talk through her options with him and get his opinion.

She started up her car, backed out of her space, then turned onto the farm-to-market road heading toward Austin. Tall pines lined each side of the road for a ways, but once she got closer to the highway, there were more clearings for farmland. Right after she turned onto the highway, her phone rang. She answered it on speaker without looking.

"Heya, Sam," James said. "I was just about to call you when I saw your text."

"Oh, really? Why?"

"You won't believe it, but I'll be in your area tomorrow."

"What do you mean?"

"I got a great assignment! I'm covering the angel of death case in Timmons!"

"Angel of death?" Sam asked. "You mean the one with the doctor? I just learned about it a couple of days ago."

"Yeah, that's it. And, well, he's not technically an angel of death—someone told me that term's mainly used for nurses who purposely kill patients surreptitiously."

"I read that he tampered with IV bags, and that maybe at least one patient died directly as a result, with several having complications—as far as they can tell."

"I know," James said excitedly. "Can you believe that?"

"It's really pretty awful," Sam said.

"Right. Sorry." The zeal fizzled out of his voice. "All of this is pretty horrible, isn't it? Look at me, getting worked up over a killer."

"No, it's okay," Sam said. "Even though the subject matter is a bit macabre, it's great that you got this assignment."

"Thanks for understanding," James said. "So, what I was calling to tell you is that I'll be there in the morning. Timmons isn't that far from you, right?"

"It's about thirty minutes away, but it's in the same county."

He went on to describe the details of his assignment, how he'd be in the courtroom during the trial each day, sending reports back to the newspaper in Austin. It was certainly a big deal for James, and she was happy for him.

While he talked, Sam turned off the highway and pulled over onto the shoulder. She needed to figure out what she was going to do, since he'd be leaving in the morning.

As much as she missed Austin, the thought of not seeing James there dimmed her enthusiasm. Sam mulled it over, as the cars zoomed past her. Was the lengthy drive worthwhile if the one person she was eager to see wouldn't even be in town? Maybe this unexpected change in plans was an opportunity in disguise. A chance to support James and explore the area more, especially with the offer to stay here permanently. Plus, it would give him more context when he offered his advice to her.

"Anyway," James said, his voice pulling her from her reverie. "I'm leaving in the morning so I can get some local color over the next couple of days. Jury selection begins Monday, and the trial is supposed to start Tuesday. Could you show me around?"

The question snapped Sam back to the present. "Sure, but I don't know if I'd be much of a tour guide. I've only been here a week, and most of that time has been in the clinic."

"I'll bet you've met plenty of people there. Maybe I could talk to them, learn more about life in east Texas and what they think about this case."

Sam thought about Cindy, how she'd be more than happy to chat with James. "There are a couple of people I could introduce you to."

"That'd be great!" James said. "It's always easier when there's a warm lead. And then I'll need to talk to the local law enforcement."

"I've met the sheriff. He seems like an upstanding guy."

"Awesome! So are you still coming here? You're more than welcome to stay at our place, and then we could drive back in the morning."

The thought of spending so much time in the car, driving back and forth for so many hours in less than a day was not appealing. "No," Sam said. "If you're coming here, there's no point in my going there."

"Makes sense. Where should we meet tomorrow?"

They hashed out plans for the morning, and after Sam hung up, she turned her car around and drove back to the motel.

11

The following morning, Sam found herself perched on the edge of the motel bed, idly clicking the remote as she awaited James's arrival. Strips of sunlight sneaked through the thin curtains, bathing the room in a soft, muted light. With the volume low, the early Sunday programs became mere background noise as she aimlessly cycled through channels on the chunky old TV. Typically, she'd be absorbed in her phone or laptop, easily tuning out the pundits' political debates. However, having already sifted through her emails and social feeds, boredom had firmly set in. This left her feeling somewhat anxious, especially regarding how James might approach the townsfolk.

Right as she was about to switch channels to escape the impending on-screen shouting match, the sound of a car pulling up caught her attention. Peering through the curtains, she spotted James in his worn-out sedan. She turned off the TV, grabbed her bag, and made her way outside to greet him.

"Hey, Sam!" James called out, his voice carrying

through his open window as she stepped outside, the morning chill brushing against her skin.

"How was the drive?" She climbed into the passenger seat next to him.

"Great! I'm itching to get going on this story," James said.

"Where are we headed?"

"I set up an interview with the local sheriff, so we'll start there."

"On a Sunday?" she voiced aloud, immediately recognizing the folly of her comment. First responders, she well knew, are seldom truly off duty—a reality likely even more pronounced for a sheriff covering a large county.

"He said today would be better than tomorrow."

A tightness cinched Sam's stomach. While Sheriff Perkins had seemed friendly enough the day before, she worried that he might not be as open with information as James hoped.

"I don't know, James. I don't want to impose on him."

"Don't worry about it." He grinned confidently. "I've got it covered."

Sam couldn't shake off her restlessness as they pulled away from the motel. Her mind was caught in a loop, replaying the nuanced exchange with Sheriff Perkins at the gas station the day before—a conversation heavy with shared worries about Luann. Then, thoughts of James overstepping boundaries emerged, fueling a silent plea for moderation. She found herself hoping against hope that his tendency to chase a story with too much zeal wouldn't sour her relationship with the sheriff. It was important for her to keep a positive rapport with him, considering she might require his assistance later on.

As James navigated the winding country roads through the dense pine forest toward Timmons, his chatter filled the car. Occasional breaks in the tree line revealed farmland clearings, allowing weak autumn sunlight to flicker across the interior. He was full of news, painting a vivid tapestry of Austin's ever-shifting landscape, sharing gossip about a few of their mutual friends—and former friends. Notably, he brought up Claire—someone they had both been close to until a horrible event disrupted what was meant to be her wedding day the previous year. "Seems like Claire's finally moved on," James remarked.

"You talked to her?" Sam asked, surprised he was still in contact with Claire.

"No, but I heard she took a job somewhere in New England."

"Good for her," Sam said. And she truly meant it. "I wanted to talk to her after . . . after all that's happened, but, you know . . ."

He reached over, squeezed her hand, and said, "I know."

Twenty minutes later, they reached the sheriff's office on the edge of the county seat. Nestled among similar one-story brick buildings, the modest structure bore a sign above the entrance proclaiming, "Timmons County Sheriff's Office." Mature oaks dotted the street and the square, lending a serene atmosphere to the surroundings.

Upon entering the building, they stepped into a cozy lobby. To the right, a woman in her fifties, her face welcoming, was busy at a computer desk. The walls, bathed in pale yellow, hosted a bulletin board next to her, adorned with flyers announcing upcoming community events. The lobby's gray linoleum flooring stretched into a hallway on the left, carrying the sound of distant conversations into the space.

The woman greeted them with a smile. "Can I help y'all?"

James stepped forward, holding out his press credentials. "Yes, we're here to see Sheriff Perkins."

"Is he expecting you?"

James presented his business card, and the woman took it. She checked a clipboard and nodded. "Alright, I'll let him know you're here. Just have a seat, and he'll be with you shortly."

They settled into a pair of stiff chairs by the window that offered a view of the street. Sam was enveloped in an aura of awkwardness as she anticipated another encounter with the sheriff. Just yesterday, she had informed him of her brief return trip to Austin. Yet, here she was, in Timmons unexpectedly, and accompanied by a reporter, no less.

After a few minutes, the phone on the desk buzzed. Following a quick conversation, the woman gestured for them to approach. "Sheriff Perkins will see you now. His office is just down the hallway on your left."

They proceeded along the corridor and paused before a door, left slightly ajar, marked by a plaque bearing the sheriff's name. James rapped on the door, eliciting a deep voice from within. "Come in."

They entered a compact office, its window offering a view of the front parking lot. A wooden desk dominated the space, cluttered with a computer and several file folders, and was flanked by two chairs for visitors. Sheriff Perkins stopped typing and greeted them with a smile as they walked in.

His initial surprise at seeing Sam quickly transformed into a wider smile as he stood. "Well, well, look who's here. Dr. Jenkins, it's good to see you. I was under the impression you were leaving us for a few days."

"My plans changed," Sam said as she glanced at James.

"I see," the sheriff said, with a curious look on his face. "And you must be James Lewis."

James stepped forward, extending his hand. "Yes, sir. It's a pleasure to meet you."

The two men shook hands, and then the sheriff gestured to the chairs in front of his desk. "Have a seat, both of you, and tell me how you know each other."

Sam explained how she and James had been friends in high school, then lost touch as they went off to college. James then took over the story and explained how he and Sam had reconnected when she'd moved into his apartment complex in Austin a couple of years before.

"And we've been in touch ever since," James said. "Since Sam happened to be working nearby, she agreed to tag along while I got a feel for the local color, so I can paint a more complete picture for my stories."

"I'm glad you want to put in the legwork to see what life is really like around here and not just focus on the sensational aspects of the trial," Sheriff Perkins said amicably. "I'm sure you'll find our neck of the woods is normally quiet and peaceful, filled with hardworking folk." His expression became more serious. "Now, how can I help you?"

James began his interview by asking basic questions about the investigation. Sam quietly observed, listening as he probed to establish a timeline of events.

Sheriff Perkins replied with calm professionalism, providing succinct answers. When James inquired about the IV bag laced with a paralytic agent discovered after the on-call doctor's death, the sheriff shifted forward in his chair.

"That was the key piece of evidence," he explained. "We knew something was off about the case, that there was no way a healthy woman in her early forties would just stop breathing. Especially since the initial tox screen showed no opiates on board. However, once we analyzed the IV bag's contents, it became clear we were dealing with a homicide."

Now James leaned in. His eyes sparkled with a curiosity eager to dispel any shadows of deceit. "Sheriff, there's something I need to address," he began, his tone critical yet inquisitive. "In the course of my research for this story, I've encountered rumors concerning your department's conduct during the investigation—specifically, accusations of evidence tampering. Could you comment on these allegations?"

The sheriff's demeanor changed immediately. His brow furrowed, and he sat back in his chair, folding his arms across his chest. "I don't know who's been spreading those rumors, but they're not true," he said. "Our department conducted a thorough investigation, and we worked closely with the Texas Rangers and the federal authorities to ensure that everything was done by the book."

James raised his eyebrows, undeterred. "But there have been reports that evidence was mishandled, that the investigation focused on the defendant too quickly. Can you speak to that?"

Sheriff Perkins leaned forward, the edge of his desk pressing against his abdomen, fixing James with a stern gaze while maintaining an even tone. "Mr. Lewis, I won't entertain groundless accusations. Our investigation followed every protocol to the letter, strictly adhering to the established procedures and regulations. If you have any specific concerns, I'm more than willing to discuss them. However, I will not respond to unsubstantiated rumors."

As the tension in the room escalated, it felt as if the walls were closing in, intensifying Sam's unease. She shifted uncomfortably, caught between James's investigative zeal and the sheriff's pivotal role in upholding public safety. The balance was delicate; she worried James might overstep, risking her rapport with the sheriff—a connection she valued, particularly as she pondered making this town her permanent home.

James pressed on, his tone respectful but firm. "I understand that, Sheriff. But the public has a right to know that the investigation was conducted fairly and without bias. If there were any missteps, it's important that they be addressed."

"I assure you, Mr. Lewis, there were no missteps." The sheriff leaned back, waving his hand as he sighed. "I'm sure the defense spewed forth these claims to discredit the investigation and sow doubt amongst the jury pool."

James, still eager to explore every angle, ventured into another provocative line of questioning. "Sheriff Perkins, some people in the community have mentioned that there were a few incidents where the anesthesiologist had behaved erratically in the past. Some say he was even reprimanded by the hospital administration. Do you think his prior behavior is relevant to the case? Was your department aware of any concerns raised about him?"

Sheriff Perkins closed his eyes briefly. It was evident that the question had struck another sensitive chord, and the irritation that had receded moments earlier returned with renewed intensity.

"Mr. Lewis," he said, his voice strained but still controlled, "I must reiterate that there are aspects of this investigation that cannot be discussed openly. Furthermore, it's not my place to comment on matters concerning hospital administration. Our primary focus is on the facts surrounding the death of the ICU doctor and ensuring that justice is served."

An edgy wave washed over Sam. James's questions

were pushing the sheriff's patience to its limits. As much as she wanted to support her friend, should she intervene and attempt to diffuse the situation?

Yes. It was time to step in.

Before James could ask another question, Sam put her hand on his arm and said gently, "I think Sheriff Perkins has been very helpful in providing us with what information he can. We should respect the boundaries he's set for this interview. Plus, can't you always follow up with other sources for more information on the anesthesiologist's background?"

James glanced at Sam, his features easing into a gentler expression. "You're right," he acknowledged. Then, turning back to the sheriff, he added, "I appreciate your time and the particulars you've provided, Sheriff. Thank you for your cooperation."

The lawman gave a curt nod, his features relaxing ever so slightly. "You're welcome. I understand your job is to report the truth, but it's important to remember that we all have specific roles and responsibilities to uphold."

With the interview concluded, the air, once thick with tension, felt lighter. Sam and James offered a final word of thanks to Sheriff Perkins and took their leave. The moment they stepped outside, a thought clung to Sam's mind, unshakable and persistent. Did James's probing have any basis in fact? Or were Sheriff Perkins's deflections meant to conceal something deeper?

12

No sooner had they stepped outside than Sam punched James in the shoulder. "What the heck was that all about?"

James acted coy, unlocking the car and sliding into the driver's seat. "What was *what* all about?" he asked, feigning innocence.

"You know what I mean." Sam slid into the passenger seat and slammed the door a little harder than she'd intended. "What were you trying to do? It seemed like you were accusing the sheriff of wrongdoing. Do you have proof?"

"Well, no," James said as he started the engine and pulled out of the parking lot. "But he's hiding something. I mean, I totally understand all the garbage the defense is throwing out there to sow doubt, but I still think he's hiding something." He glanced at her. "Don't you think so? I mean, he became quite defensive when I questioned his early focus on the anesthesiologist as a suspect in the investigation."

Sam couldn't really argue with that. From the beginning, it had seemed like Sheriff Perkins had not necessarily been lying, but he'd certainly been omitting something. Like when he'd told Sam that other than Dr. Carlisle's murder, the town of Dry Wells was perfectly safe, even though there was a murder trial going on down the road here in Timmons.

James turned the corner, and they were now on the town square. The sudden shift in scenery took Sam by surprise, momentarily drawing her out of the whirlpool of her thoughts. The quaintness of the Timmons town square was disarmingly picturesque, a stark contrast to the tension in their conversation. The square itself seemed like a haven of peace: at one end, the old courthouse, its stone façade basking in the sunlight, stood with majesty, while small shops and cafés dotted the perimeter, their welcoming fronts seeming to encourage passersby to leave their concerns behind, if only for a moment. This fleeting display of tranquility provided a glimpse into a potentially different life, one that might await if Sam decided to take Olivia's offer.

The more she'd thought about it, and how nice it would be to stay in one place instead of bouncing around the state, the more it seemed attractive. She was being given the opportunity to put her career back on path by taking over Dr. Carlisle's practice. And yet, there was so much she didn't know about these communities.

"You're being awfully quiet," James said after a few moments. "What's on your mind? Didn't you get the same vibe I got, that Sheriff Perkins wasn't being forthcoming with everything?"

"It does seem like he's not being completely forthcoming . . . but he *is* a law enforcement officer, and there's only so much he can tell us. I can kind of understand, though. As a doctor, I'm bound by confidentiality, too."

Her mind drifted back to the conversation she'd had with the sheriff, specifically his concerns about handling domestic violence cases. Sam had believed their mutual worry was for Luann, yet she couldn't be entirely sure. Even though she could tell he was holding back—heck, she herself had been holding back when she'd indirectly discussed Luann's case with him—she sensed that he was a man of integrity.

"Is that why you stepped in and shut things down?" James asked, annoyed.

Sam shifted in her seat so she could face him as he drove. "That, and I just want to maintain a good relationship with him."

"Why do you need to do that? It's not as if you're staying here permanently."

"Well, I could be," Sam said sheepishly.

"Hold on, what? Unpack that for me."

Sam looked at her watch. Lunchtime.

She wasn't really hungry, but part of the reason she'd wanted to see James was to discuss Olivia's offer. It was something better done face to face instead of in the car. Besides, Timmons, with its authentic town square and grand courthouse, beckoned for a bit of exploration. Spotting an inviting café, she said, "Why don't we grab something to eat?"

Over lunch, Sam briefed James on Olivia's proposal, pausing as James interjected in with questions now and then. She'd mentioned Dr. Carlisle's death to James but left out the details, especially the fact that he'd been murdered. She wasn't ready to field the difficult questions she knew he would have upon learning the truth. At the moment, she needed his support as a friend more than anything, to help her decide if accepting Olivia's offer was the right move.

James sat back in his chair, looking thoughtful. "So, it

kinda makes sense, then, that you don't want to get on the sheriff's bad side. But you wouldn't need to interact with him much, would you?"

"I might," Sam said, "especially if there's a patient who could be in danger."

He raised his eyebrows at this. "Do you have a patient in danger?"

Blowing out her breath, she said, "I can't discuss anything about my patients."

"Now *you're* stonewalling, just like Sheriff Perkins."

"I know it seems that way, but like I said, I understand where he's coming from, since we both deal with situations that require sensitivity."

After lunch, they took their time wandering through Timmons, pleasantly surprised to find the town more sprawling than Sam had initially imagined. Their walk led them by an assortment of charming shops and inviting storefronts, each proudly displaying the vibrant local culture and craftsmanship through their windows, offering a vivid snapshot of the town's life.

As the afternoon wore on, the setting sun dipped lower in the sky, draping the streets in long, theatrical shadows. The buildings basked in a golden and amber glow, transforming the town into a pleasant scene straight out of a painting. James, always attentive to details, pointed out the unique quirks of the local architecture. Every building seemed to narrate its own history with its weathered bricks and the stories etched into its faded signs.

Sam, however, found herself drawn to the townspeople. She observed their interactions—simple nods, knowing glances, and whispers that seemed to vanish just as quickly as they appeared. It was evident that the upcoming trial was at the heart of all conversations, creating a buzz that vibrated through the community, pulling at its seams.

The air was saturated with the delicious aroma of brisket, a scent that defined the town, wafting from hidden barbecue spots. This smoky fragrance mixed with the streets' atmosphere, offering a warm welcome that stood in stark contrast to the palpable sense of anticipation for the trial. This blend of warmth and suspense gave Timmons an enigmatic charm, as though beneath its welcoming exterior, it harbored a vibrant tale, like a slumbering giant on the verge of awakening.

Their exploration brought them to a small, antiquated bookstore that seemed to lean slightly to one side, its windows adorned with an array of colorful local history books and worn-out novels. The bell above the door chimed merrily as they entered, announcing their presence to the solitary figure behind the counter. Inside, the air was thick with the musty scent of old paper and leather, a comforting aroma that spoke of countless stories waiting to be told.

As they perused the tightly packed shelves, they overheard snippets of conversation from a group of locals gathered around a table at the back of the store. "Did you hear about the evidence they found at the scene?" one whispered, her voice barely audible over the rustle of pages. "It's going to be a real spectacle," another added, the corners of his mouth turning down in disapproval.

Sam and James exchanged a glance, their curiosity piqued. They knew that the upcoming trial would be more than just a legal proceeding; it would be a revelation that could shake the very foundations of Timmons. But for now, they were content to lose themselves in the simple pleasures of the town, a brief respite before the storm that was sure to come.

~

The next day was Monday, so Sam didn't have to work at the clinic. And since reporters weren't allowed in the courtroom during jury selection, she joined James again as he continued exploring the area. They started by visiting the Veterans Affairs hospital, on the far side of Timmons from Dry Wells, where the accused anesthesiologist had worked. James aimed to glean insights from the staff, seeking to grasp the case's impact on the hospital.

As they approached the building, Sam couldn't help but feel a sense of apprehension. The hospital staff must be shaken by the accusations against their colleague, and she wasn't sure how they would react to outsiders asking questions.

The sprawling two-story building, cloaked in sun-bleached brown bricks, stood as an unassuming guardian at the town's edge. It had a utilitarian feel to it, with no decorative flourishes or landscaping to speak of. Inside, harsh fluorescent lights bathed the hallways in a sterile, impersonal glow.

Stepping into the familiar setting, Sam was suddenly awash with vivid memories of her grueling residency days at the nation's largest VA hospital in Houston. It had not been spectacular. The severe staff shortage forced residents to undertake basic patient care tasks that were typically handled by nurses and support personnel. For instance, if Sam didn't input a blood draw order into the outdated computer system by 4:30 am for the hospital's sole phlebotomist to collect the sample, she would have to perform the task herself. Even though it wasn't the most efficient system, it was a good learning experience. But she often wondered if it really delivered the best patient care.

As they wandered around the hospital, they occasionally stopped to ask staff members for their thoughts on the upcoming trial. Whenever they raised the topic of the case or the accused doctor, staff members became reticent, their lips pressing into tight lines, wary of unfamiliar visitors.

The pair traced a shadowy path through the labyrinthine corridors of the hospital, passing the stronghold of the ICU—a fortress of modern medicine where lives hung in a precarious balance between hope and despair. At the VA hospital in Houston, the ICU was the one place that did seem to run well, from Sam's perspective. She wondered if that was also how things were here. The automated doors opened as they walked by, with the sterile smell of disinfectant clinging to the frigid air like a ghost of the many battles fought here against death, and the constant beeps of ventilators and telemetry monitors spilling out into the corridor. Just beyond the ICU entrance, they located the call room, and a sudden cold shiver traced a malicious path down Sam's spine. It was there, in that claustrophobic box, that the victim had breathed her last, forever etched into the history of the institution.

Even so, it was disconcertingly business as usual in the thriving behemoth of a medical institution, a demonstration of the relentless pace of healthcare. The orchestrated chaos of doctors, nurses, and technicians swirled around them, their faces solemn, voices muted, eyes averted. Life went on, immune to the undercurrent of morbidity that had seeped into the foundations of the building. There was an eerie disregard for the chilling reality that had unfolded.

Sam frowned, her eyes taking in the distant gaze of a passing nurse and the stoic resignation of a busy doctor. Death, she knew, was a regular guest in this realm of white and steel. It walked the sterile halls hand in hand with life, a grotesque dance between light and shadow. But this . . . this was different. This wasn't the noble death in battle against disease or old age, but a life snuffed out prematurely in the name of a perverse desire for dominance.

A fellow doctor—a protector turned predator—had committed the unfathomable. He had succumbed to his festering need for control, turning his Hippocratic Oath into a macabre joke. Sam had anticipated a shift in the hospital's atmosphere—a subtle change in the static charge of the air, a whisper of shared grief or shock. But instead, she was greeted by the hardened face of professionalism, the eerie calm of routine. The layers of stoicism, however, did nothing to hide the faint tremor of unease that rippled beneath the surface.

James tried the door to the call room, but it was locked.

When Sam gave him a disapproving look, he said, "What? I just want to see what it looks like in there."

"I can tell you, call rooms in hospitals are nothing special. They're very spartan. Just another hospital room, usually with a couple of beds, sometimes bunks. Maybe a bathroom and a TV, if you're lucky."

"Sounds like a prison cell."

"Yeah," she said, remembering the countless nights she'd spent on call. "It can feel that way."

Sam heard her name called from behind her. They turned to find a middle-aged woman in scrubs coming towards them.

"Dr. Jenkins! So good to see you! Are you visiting a patient here?"

It took a moment for Sam to place the woman. Then she remembered: the woman was a patient she'd seen toward the beginning of the previous week, but she couldn't remember her name. Sam did remember that she'd mentioned she was a nurse, and fortunately, the woman had a VA badge and introduced herself to James.

"Hi, I'm Vivian McCormick. I was one of Dr. Jenkins's

patients last week, and she was great." She leaned closer to James as he reflexively shook her hand. "Are you her boyfriend?"

"Oh, no," Sam said. She glanced at James as he frowned and took a step back. "He's just a good friend of mine, and he happens to be in town for an assignment."

"Really?" Vivian asked. "This place doesn't exactly draw a business crowd. What line of work are you in?"

"I work for a newspaper in Austin," James said.

At that, Vivian's eyes lit up. "You're here for the trial, aren't you?" She lowered her voice. "You know, I always thought Dr. Morton was a little too arrogant."

"So you worked with him?" James asked as he took a closer look at Vivian's badge. Under her picture, it stated she was part of the Medicine Service Line.

"Yes, I work in the ICU, so Dr. Morton often had to help out with intubations, central lines…" She looked at Sam. "You know, the usual procedures we deal with."

Sam nodded.

James asked, "You mentioned you thought Dr. Morton was arrogant. Did you notice anything else about him before all of these things came to light?"

"Nothing really specific, honestly. I just got a bad vibe from him. You know, one time—before we learned how evil he was—Sheriff Perkins had come to visit one of his old Army buddies who'd been a patient here. He and Dr. Morton had some sort of disagreement, and I heard them shouting at each other out here in the hallway."

James looked meaningfully at Sam, then asked Vivian, "Did you hear what it was about?"

"No. As soon as they saw me, they shut up. But it seemed pretty intense. I don't know if it had to do with the sheriff's friend or not. As far as I recall, his friend's stay here was pretty uneventful. But Dr. Morton and the Sheriff looked like they were about to get into fisticuffs until they saw me."

"What happened after that?" James asked.

"Sheriff Perkins said something under his breath, shook his head, and stormed off."

"And what did Dr. Morton do?"

"He just acted like nothing happened . . . except he did have a smug look on his face, like he'd scored some points during the argument."

"That's very interesting," James said.

"Anyway, a few months later, Dr. Perry died, and then the investigation started. That's when we truly found out what an awful person Dr. Morton is."

Sam and James remained silent.

Then Vivian said, "So rumor has it, you might be taking over Dr. Carlisle's practice."

Sam flushed. "Well, I haven't made any decisions yet."

"So it's true, then!"

Sam nodded. "Olivia has asked me to stay."

Vivian turned to James. "She's a very good doctor."

"So I've heard," he said.

The doors to the ICU opened, and another woman in scrubs peeked out. "There you are. Can you help me turn Mr. B—I mean, one of my patients?"

"Sure thing," Vivian said. She turned back to Sam and James. "It was good seeing you, Dr. Jenkins, and nice to meet you, James. Hope to see you again soon."

13

Upon entering the clinic the next morning, Sam was enveloped by the welcoming scents of freshly brewed coffee and the soft murmur of patients chatting in the cozy waiting area. Just a week after her arrival in Dry Wells, what had once felt alien was now warmly familiar. The atmosphere was buzzing with a gentle anticipation, underscored by friendly exchanges, signaling a day bustling with activity in this close-knit community. But despite the inviting environment, Sam felt a nagging weariness that fogged her mind. This fatigue starkly reminded her of the rejuvenation she had missed by foregoing her visit to Austin. Even though her time spent with James provided a temporary respite, she remained haunted by the feeling that she might not be in the optimal condition to meet her patients' needs effectively.

It was then that her gaze landed on the new addition to the lobby—a sleek display of ZenithVita Essentials' products, conspicuously set against the left wall, absent just days before. The display included a range of offerings, from vibrant bottles of supplements to neatly stacked packages of herbal teas, each promising wellness and vitality. Above the shelves, a digital screen played serene landscapes, intermittently swapping with testimonials from satisfied customers. This unexpected sight stirred a mix of curiosity and skepticism. She was familiar with the trend of clinics diversifying into retail, such as OB/GYNs offering skincare products, recognizing it as an additional revenue stream for healthcare providers. However, she harbored doubts about the appropriateness of selling such products within a healthcare setting, questioning whether it truly served the best interests of the patients. It was something else to ask Olivia about.

As Sam entered the back hallway, she observed Bonnie guiding a patient, a woman roughly her own age, into an exam room. The patient inquired, "How are you holding up?"

"About as well as you'd expect," Bonnie responded. Then, catching sight of Sam, her expression shifted to a frown before she quickly shut the door.

Bonnie's reaction seemed a bit odd, but Sam just attributed it to the stress of caring for her mother and her evolving dementia. Understanding the toll such a situation could take, she dismissed the incident and turned her attention to the computer, checking the schedule for her first patient.

As the hours ticked by, Sam found herself immersed in a whirlwind of appointments, consultations, and paperwork. The relentless pace of the clinic left little room for rest or reflection. Each patient brought their own set of challenges and concerns, demanding her full attention and expertise. The morning's fatigue gradually morphed into a deep-seated exhaustion as the day progressed. Yet, amidst this bustling routine, Sam occasionally found her focus wandering to the decision looming over her—the possibility of taking over the clinic.

It was mid-afternoon when a brief pause in her schedule offered a moment of respite. The clinic's corridors, usually echoing with the day's activities, felt momentarily serene. Sam was collecting her thoughts, preparing for the next round of patients, when Olivia found her.

She approached with a sense of purpose, her timing impeccable as if she had waited for this quiet moment to speak. "Dr. Jenkins, have you given any more thought to my offer to take over this practice?"

"I've considered it, Olivia, but . . ." Sam paused, her mind meandering. Over the last couple of days, she and James had delved deeply into the subject. As they explored the area, the idea of calling this slice of Texas home had often crossed her mind. Dry Wells, with its charm nestled amongst the piney woods, held an undeniable allure. Still, she found herself wavering at the notion of laying down roots in this place permanently. She had always lived in larger cities, never in a place smaller than Austin—a point James had repeatedly emphasized.

"Well, how about this?" Hope flickered in Olivia's eyes. "What about extending your assignment here? You said your next one isn't for a couple of weeks. Couldn't you at least stay a little longer?"

Sam hesitated again. Maybe she'd feel a little differently if she'd gone back to Austin for the weekend. Of course, there was one patient she was concerned about, which kept her from flat out refusing to stay.

"I'll let you think about it," Olivia finally said, apparently sensing Sam's reluctance to answer. "We can always discuss it later. And I'd be happy to call the *locum* agency if you change your mind about staying even longer." Then, as if she'd read Sam's mind, she added, "You know, Luann really seemed to like you. She wouldn't stop talking about you when I checked her out after her visit last week. It's the most she's opened up in a while, like she was her old self again. But I saw that she came in again on Saturday—is everything okay?"

Sam's heart tightened as she replayed the visit, the image of the suspicious, deep-purple bruise marring Luann's arm haunting her. Olivia would have seen the diagnostic code, likely read Sam's note, and begun piecing things together.

The older woman watched her expectantly, waiting for an answer. But an unspoken apprehension echoed within Sam. She couldn't discuss Luann's medical issues with anyone without Luann's consent. An ethical lapse could potentially harm her patient's trust in her.

"I'm sorry, Olivia. You know I can't talk about her visit with you. It's confidential," Sam said firmly.

Olivia's face momentarily clouded with disappointment, yet her resolve remained unshaken. "I understand that, but I'm just worried about her. She's been through so much, and I haven't been able to talk to her as much as I used to. I wonder if her husband is being too controlling," she said, her voice trailing off.

A whisper of doubt began to dance around the edges of Sam's consciousness, a subtle misgiving that refused to be silenced. Olivia was obviously trying to trade information, and Sam wasn't sure she wanted to engage in that kind of conversation. It went against her morals to talk about a patient's condition, even if that patient was a personal friend, as Olivia claimed. But Sam couldn't shake the thought that maybe Olivia had some details which might be helpful, so she decided to probe a little herself.

"What do you mean, too controlling?" Sam asked cautiously. "Has Luann said anything to you about it?"

Mr. Harrison, whom Sam had just seen, emerged from the restroom, each movement heavy with the unbearable weight of years marred by pain. Bent like a question mark, he leaned laboriously on his cane, as he wrestled with his chronic arthritis. His feet, in a rhythm dictated by caution and control, slid across the linoleum, slowly and carefully. With each step forward he fought back a grimace, revealing the depth of his discomfort.

As he drew closer, the two women instinctively separated, creating a path between them. His nod, as he edged past, was a soft glow of sunset, appreciating their respect for his journey, one he wished to navigate with his own compass of independence. During her visit with him, Sam had offered to help him out to the lobby several times, but he'd stubbornly refused, as if he wanted to maintain at least a small semblance of dignity.

His struggle under the relentless siege of chronic arthritis was as tangible as the cold aluminum cane he gripped. Sam's therapeutic efforts felt like a drop in an ocean of his suffering—a shot of toradol, a temporary reprieve from the onslaught of pain.

He'd assured her that it was Dr. Carlisle's usual treatment, but now she considered the potential lying dormant. If she remained here, she could pierce the veil of routine care, delve deeper into the man behind the patient. She would have the chance to explore the uncharted territories of other possible remedies, a chance to potentially mitigate his pain more effectively. Mr. Harrison was more than a case; he was a challenge she could truly immerse herself in, a person she could help—if only she chose to stay.

After he disappeared into the front office, Olivia closed the gap between her and Sam, her voice dropping to a whisper. "You know how it is in small towns. Word gets around. And I've heard things, Dr. Jenkins. Things that make me worry about Luann's safety."

Olivia's words cascaded over Sam like a cold shiver, each one a chilling affirmation that her deepest suspicions were far from unfounded. "What kind of things have you heard?" she asked. "Anything specific?"

"Well, no, nothing specific. But when you met with them, didn't you see anything?"

Was she just fishing for information? "I'm sorry, Olivia, but I really can't discuss *any* patient's condition," she said, maintaining her professional stance.

A shadow of frustration crossed Olivia's face. "My husband never had such reservations with me."

Sam raised an eyebrow, not quite believing Olivia's claim. It was conceivable Dr. Carlisle had shared more than he should have, under the guise of marital privacy, yet she remained wary. "The principles of confidentiality aren't negotiable," Sam countered, her tone firm yet empathetic.

Undeterred, Olivia leaned closer, her eyes searching Sam's. "I know you're worried about Luann, too. She trusts you. Isn't there anything you can share? Anything that might help?"

Sam found herself torn, caught between her duty and the pressing concern in Olivia's plea. After a brief, contemplative pause, she conceded, albeit cautiously. "There are indeed aspects of Luann's situation that concern me," she confessed, her voice a blend of reluctance and resolve.

Olivia's expression softened. "I see it too. But I just don't know what to do. She's always so loyal to her husband, even when he's not treating her right. It's like she can't see what's happening."

Sam frowned, not liking the sound of that at all. "How did they meet?" she asked.

A flicker of relief passed over Olivia's face at the opportunity to share. "They were in high school together," she said. "And Isaac was really charming. But after they got married, my parents said he wouldn't let Luann go anywhere without him. Seems like he's almost too obsessed with her."

"How do you mean?" Sam asked.

"I heard from Sally—oh, and she really enjoyed meeting you the other night. Sorry I couldn't make it."

"It was a nice time. Is everything okay?"

Olivia waved her hand. "Yes, we're all okay. It's just my cousin—he's dealing with some issues right now, but we're all fine." She lowered her voice again. "Anyway, Sally says Isaac controls everything and always wants to know Luann's passwords."

"How does Sally know this?"

"She's Luann's neighbor, and they talk when Isaac's not there." Olivia shrugged. "He can't always be around, after all."

Before Sam could ask anything else, Tanya, the office receptionist, appeared, telling Olivia that Mr. Harrison wanted to speak with her up front, and that the ZenithVita rep was there as well. Olivia excused herself, leaving Sam alone in the hallway with her thoughts.

She'd wanted to ask Olivia if she or Sally had seen any signs of abuse without revealing more than she should.

But could she really trust Olivia?

While Sam could tell Olivia really was concerned about Luann, she suspected Olivia might also be leveraging Luann's situation to persuade her to stay in Dry Wells. She knew she had to be careful with Olivia, but she couldn't dismiss the thought that she'd need to skirt some of her own rules if Luann really needed her help.

14

Sam took a deep breath, allowing the clinic's sterile scent to momentarily wash away the tension from her exchange with Olivia, before she stepped into the next exam room. Upon entering, she was taken aback to see Cindy Bergstrom in the chair next to the exam table. Cindy's follow-up appointment for her hypertension treatment was set for after Sam was due to leave Dry Wells. But Cindy wasn't alone. Sitting on the table was a teenage girl bearing a strong resemblance to her.

Sam gave them a welcoming smile. "Hi, Mrs. Bergstrom. What brings you in today?"

Cindy's gaze shifted to Sam, worry creasing her brow and tightening the corners of her eyes. "Good afternoon, Doctor Jenkins." No insistence on having Sam call her by her first name this time. "This is my daughter, Sarah. She's been having trouble sleeping."

Turning to the teen, Sam said, "Hi, Sarah. Nice to meet you. Can you tell me a little more about what's been going on?"

Sarah looked up at Sam, her expression guarded. "I

don't know. I just can't seem to fall asleep at night. And when I do sleep, I wake up feeling tired."

Cindy nodded in agreement. "It's gotten to the point where it's affecting her mood during the day."

As kindly as she could, Sam asked, "Has anything changed in your life recently? Any new stresses or worries?"

Sarah looked down at her hands in her lap, her forehead furrowing. "I don't know . . . School, I guess. It's just hard, you know?"

Cindy gently took her daughter's hand, offering a silent promise of comfort and unity—a sharp contrast to the distant interactions Sam had seen between Mia and her mother. In that simple touch, a world of maternal love and worry was conveyed, bridging the gap of unspoken anxieties.

"It seems Sarah's been having a hard time with some of the other girls at school." Cindy paused. "Plus, it's been a little difficult at home, too."

Sam's eyes flickered between mother and daughter. "Difficult?"

Cindy hesitated, her eyes darting away for a moment before meeting Sam's again. "It's just been a little rough lately. Her dad's been working long hours, and we're both trying to make ends meet."

Although she'd only had positive encounters with Cindy before, Sam's shoulders tensed, bracing a touch for the same pushback she'd received from Mia's mom as she asked her next question. "If you don't mind, it might be best if I talk to Sarah by herself. Is that okay?"

But Cindy's face showed only compassion and empathy as she bobbed her head in understanding, silently rose from her chair, and exited the room.

Once they were alone, Sam focused on the teenager

perched on the exam table. The girl tried to mask it, but her demeanor was a delicate balance of determined poise and thinly veiled nervousness. Bright, vigilant eyes revealed a weariness far beyond her years, while her hands, slender and trembling slightly, whispered tales of inner turmoil. She sat with her back erect, a portrait of readiness against whatever diagnosis Sam might offer, yet her shoulders dipped ever so slightly.

Her complexion, a shade too pale, contrasted subtly with the faint blush on her high cheekbones, while her hair, despite being neatly arranged, carried a certain brittleness. Sam watched as the girl absently smoothed her clothing, a comforting action amidst her unease. Her eyes darted to the door and then back to Sam, revealing the storm of thoughts racing through her mind. It was evident she was striving to project a sense of normalcy, yet the telltale signs were there for Sam to see—the slight puffiness around her eyes and the quickened pulse throbbing at her throat—hinting at something beyond the usual teenage angst.

"So, Sarah, can you tell me more about what's been bothering you?" She asked this gently, aiming to make the girl feel comfortable.

The teenager looked up at Sam, a mixture of apprehension and exhaustion evident in her eyes. "Yeah, it's just hard to fall asleep sometimes. I have these thoughts that don't shut down. All the work I need to do for school. And Mom and Dad. I know they're doing their best. But I worry about them too," she replied, fidgeting with her hands.

"I see," Sam said. "And your mom mentioned something about having issues with the other girls at school?"

The teenager hesitated, then let out a small sigh. "It's . . . you know . . . just the normal stuff with friends."

"Like, what kind of stuff?"

"You know," Sarah replied with a shrug. "Just stuff."

Obviously, this was a sore point for the teen, and Sam decided not to press any further for the time being. "Okay. Let's take a look and see what we can find."

Sam began to examine Sarah and couldn't help but notice the similarities between mother and daughter. They had the same bright blue eyes and curly brown hair. As she listened to Sarah's heart, she noticed the rate seemed a little high. Sam placed her fingers on Sarah's wrist, palpating her pulse in the radial artery, counting the beats as the second hand ticked away on Sam's watch. Just over one hundred ten beats per minute. And that tremor became more evident as Sarah brushed the hair out of her eyes.

A thought flickered into Sam's mind. Could it possibly be hyperthyroidism, just as Sam suspected with Mia? She felt a sense of foreboding, that there was something more going on here. How could there be two teenagers with possible hyperthyroidism in just a few days? She still didn't know definitively what was going on with Mia—she hoped Natalie Fontaine had allowed Mia's blood to be drawn and sent to the lab. She'd have to look into it. For now, she'd need to do the same workup for Sarah.

With the exam complete, Sam summoned Cindy back into the room with a reassuring smile that masked her own brewing suspicions. Cindy took her seat in the chair again, looking worried. "Is everything okay, Doctor?"

Sam hesitated a moment before responding. "Well, I'm a little bit concerned about Sarah's symptoms. I'd like to run some blood tests to make sure everything looks good before we discuss how we want to address Sarah's problems sleeping."

Though Sam believed she had delivered her plan in a calm and sensible manner, Cindy looked even more unsettled at the mention of blood tests. "Do you think something is wrong with her?" Her voice broke, revealing a mother's deep-seated fear barely held at bay.

Sam maintained eye contact, her tone steady but infused with empathy. "Let's just get the tests done as soon as possible and go from there."

Cindy bit her lip, her hands clasping and unclasping in her lap. "But you think something is wrong, don't you?"

"I don't want to jump to any conclusions," Sam replied, leaning slightly forward to bridge the space between them. "However, understanding your family history could give us some valuable insights." Her voice was calm, encouraging Cindy to see this as a step forward rather than a verdict.

Cindy nodded, taking a slow, steadying breath as she seemed to draw courage from Sam's composed demeanor. "Okay," she finally said, the tension in her shoulders easing slightly, accepting Sam's efforts to soften the blow of uncertainty.

Sam started with some general questions about anxiety and depression, but she also asked about endocrine disorders, including thyroid problems. Cindy answered that no one, as far as she knew, had had any of the conditions in her family.

"That's good," Sam said. "Let's just see what the blood work shows." She looked back and forth between mother and daughter, and they both seemed to be slightly more placated.

Sam walked them out of the exam room and found Kelly. To speed things up, Sam explained which labs she was going to order, and that she'd put them into the computer while Kelly was drawing Sarah's blood.

"Just so you know, Dr. Jenkins," Kelly said, "we had to

switch the laboratory we send our specimens to. Could you make sure the req goes to Quest?"

"Sure," Sam replied. "Not a problem." She didn't know exactly how to do that, but she'd figure it out. There was probably a drop-down menu somewhere in the EHR.

After saying goodbye to Cindy and her daughter, Sam watched as Kelly guided them towards the hallway's phlebotomy nook, its shelves lined with meticulously organized supplies around a padded chair. She went back into the now-empty exam room and unlocked the computer so she could put in the orders. It was then she noticed that the EHR system automatically sent requisitions to a local lab unfamiliar to her. Sam, with her extensive experience from *locum* assignments, was well-acquainted with major labs like Quest Diagnostics and LabCorp, as well as numerous smaller regional labs across the state. The preferred lab in Timmons made sense, given its proximity compared to the nearest Quest facility in Nacogdoches, a good hour's drive away.

With a pragmatic shrug, Sam entered the lab orders, changed the destination to Quest by selecting it from the drop-down, and moved on to her next patient.

But later in the day, when Sam finally got a chance to catch up on some of her charting, and she got to Sarah's note, her intuition suggested there were hidden layers to the situation. How could there be two teenagers with similar symptoms in such a short span of time? Yes, anxiety and teenage angst were common, but the physical signs for both girls were suggestive that there was an organic cause. It seemed to be too much of a coincidence.

What could link these cases? And what if the answer lay hidden, not within the clinic's walls, but amidst the town's secrets?

Perhaps there was an environmental factor causing this.

With the logging industry in the area, along with the pesticides and other chemicals used by local farmers, perhaps she'd find an explanation.

She just didn't know, but she was determined to find out.

15

Following a short break, the next patient Sam saw was Mrs. Firth, a widow in her sixties struggling with COPD. In reviewing her previous visits, Sam noticed her condition seemed to be worsening. She wished she could offer more than just a steroid injection and a prescription for antibiotics. However, Mrs. Firth assured Sam she was fine with coming in every few weeks to deal with her COPD exacerbations since Dr. Carlisle had passed away. There was just one problem: the interval between Mrs. Firth's visits was decreasing. Sam knew she needed to adjust Mrs. Firth's medications, even though she was already on some pretty high dosages, but the pattern was concerning. It looked like Mrs. Firth would soon end up in the emergency room . . . or the morgue.

As Sam stepped out of the room to fetch supplies for the injection, her mind circled back to Olivia's proposition to take over the practice. The offer held the potential to continue caring for patients like Mrs. Firth and enhance their quality of life. The decision loomed over her like a dark storm cloud, casting a shadow on her ability to truly aid each patient in need.

After retrieving a bottle of Depo-Medrol and a syringe from the supply closet, Sam headed back to Mrs. Firth's room. Along the way, she noticed a man in a suit standing at the end of the hallway. His posture suggested he was waiting for someone or something. With a serious look etched on his face, his presence stirred a sense of unease within her. The way he lingered there, almost lurking, ignited Sam's interest in his intentions.

The man's tall, sturdy frame, short hair, and chiseled jawline made him conspicuous in the clinic's humble setting. His attire, a decent but clearly off-the-rack suit complemented by polished shoes, seemed out of place. Sam speculated he might be a pharmaceutical sales representative, although his outfit lacked the usual branded polo shirt.

However, something about him hinted more at a lawyer's air than a salesman's charm. Was he connected to the trial James was covering? Perhaps. It was certainly possible that some of Dr. Carlisle's patients had ended up under the care of the defendant. But surely, with the trial starting today, any lawyers associated with the proceedings would be at the courthouse, not at this clinic.

Sam walked closer to the man, realizing that he seemed to be waiting outside Dr. Carlisle's old office. His alert, piercing eyes were scanning the hallway, seemingly on the lookout. As he caught sight of her advancing, his attention sharply shifted to Sam.

"Can I help you?" Sam asked, her tone professional yet cautious.

Their eyes met, a tense pause filling the moment before he finally spoke. "I'm waiting for Olivia Carlisle," he said. His eyes briefly dropped to her embroidered name on her white coat: Samantha Jenkins, MD. It had been a gift from her mother when she'd graduated from medical school, but now it felt like a shield.

"How long have you been working at this clinic?" he inquired.

"A little over a week," Sam replied.

"And are you the only doctor here?"

"Yes." Sam's professional mask didn't falter, but internally, alarm bells were ringing. His questions were too pointed, his presence too imposing. This felt like an interrogation, and she couldn't help but wonder what he was really after. She took a step back, putting some distance between them.

The man nodded, with his gaze staying on her, sharp and assessing, as if he was piecing together a puzzle she didn't know she was a part of. "Interesting."

"I'm sorry, but who are you?" Sam asked, eyeing him warily.

Before he could answer, Olivia appeared out of nowhere, looking flustered. "Oh, hello." Her eyes ricocheted between Sam and the man. "I'm sorry to keep you waiting." She turned and gave Sam a brief, forced smile. "It's nothing. You don't need to worry about this." She escorted the man into Dr. Carlisle's office and closed the door, leaving Sam alone in the hallway.

What was that all about?

"Dr. Jenkins?"

Sam turned to find Kelly looking at her somewhat anxiously.

"Do you know who that man was?" Sam asked.

Kelly gave her head a little shake. "I'm sorry. I don't know. But your next patient, Mr. Tramble, is ready for you. He says he needs to leave soon, so he can pick up his son."

Sam nodded, then looked down at the bottle and

syringe in her hand. "Could you give Mrs. Firth a Depo-Medrol shot?"

"Certainly."

"And tell her I'll come back in to speak with her after I'm done with Mr. Tramble," Sam said as she handed Kelly the supplies.

"Of course, Dr. Jenkins."

Sam headed towards her next patient's exam room, but she couldn't ignore the unsettling feeling that something at the clinic was amiss. The encounter with the man in the suit had sparked her curiosity while leaving her with a niggling discomfort. She felt compelled to uncover the reasons behind his visit and Olivia's apparent distress. As a medical professional, Sam had always been wary of becoming too involved in office politics, but this was different—could this be related to Dr. Carlisle's murder?

If she was serious about taking over the practice, she needed to know exactly what was going on.

16

The rest of the afternoon whirled around Sam in a blur of activity, and her brief encounters with Olivia were limited strictly to discussions about patients. She was itching for a chance to talk to Olivia alone, curious to learn more about the mysterious man in the suit. But it wasn't to be. Instead, for her last appointment of the day, Sam found herself drawn into the world of Mrs. Preston, a widow whose tears over her beloved Bichon Frisé, Daisy, painted a poignant picture of loss. Each photograph she shared was a window into a life filled with love and now, profound emptiness.

With no one else waiting and nothing better to do than head back to her lonely motel room, Sam was glad for the distraction. Earlier, James had sent a text canceling their evening plans, having met other reporters from Dallas and Houston, also covering the trial, who'd invited him to dinner. Even though she'd been looking forward to seeing him, she knew it was the perfect opportunity for him to network, to build the foundation needed for his career.

At half past six, well after the clinic had closed, there

was a brief rap on the door, and Olivia stuck her head in. She saw Mrs. Preston, all teary-eyed with a wad of tissues in her wrinkled hands, and nodded knowingly while looking a little relieved that Sam was deeply occupied.

"I'm sorry to interrupt," Olivia said, "but I've got to head out, and everyone else has already taken off. Would you mind locking up when you're done?"

"Sure," Sam said, "I can do that. What do I need to do?"

"Great. The front door's already locked, so just exit through the side door in the break room—it'll latch behind you," Olivia explained. "Oh, and hit 'Arm' on the security pad. You'll have one minute to leave."

"Will do," Sam said, and Olivia vanished.

After a few more pictures and memories, Sam finally gathered her things and escorted poor Mrs. Preston through the break room, leaving the clinic together. Outside, on the sidewalk, the old woman thanked Sam profusely for spending so much time with her before finally going to her car.

As Sam paused in the tranquility of the empty parking lot, the day's psychological toll wrapped around her like a dense fog. But as she stood there, enveloped in the stillness of the autumn evening, with the air crisp and leaves quietly rustling, a subtle shift began. Slowly, the emotional mist dispersed, allowing room for introspection. Away from the relentless pace of her medical duties, the profound essence of her work became clear. It wasn't just about diagnosing illnesses or prescribing treatments; her role wove deeper into the fabric of human connection, offering solace and a listening ear on days laden with the world's burdens. In the quietude, with nature's gentle reminder of life's cycles, Sam's appreciation for her ability to provide comfort in the midst of chaos grew, anchoring her in the profound impact of her care.

Feeling uplifted from her time spent cheering up Mrs. Preston, Sam headed to the diner for another meal. As the diner's neon sign flickered into sight, Sam's thoughts transitioned from the deep feelings surrounding Mrs. Preston's grief to the intellectual challenge of diagnosing the two teenagers. This represented a distinct kind of problem-solving—one that fully engaged her mind, contrasting sharply with the heartfelt connections formed in her daily clinical work.

Determined to solve the puzzle, Sam decided to delve further into hyperthyroidism research, aiming to uncover any clues about the girls' condition. While she couldn't be sure they were both suffering from the same ailment without lab results, the coincidence of two cases in a small town seemed too peculiar. Perhaps, she reasoned, they shared a common cause. If Cindy was on duty tonight, Sam planned to probe deeper, inquiring about Sarah's routines and any potential exposures she and Mia might have in common.

However, as Sam entered the diner, a different waitress greeted her. She was a young woman, her blonde hair pulled back into a tight ponytail. "Is Cindy here?" Sam asked.

"She's off tonight," the waitress said, grabbing a menu out of the rack. "Where'd you like to sit?"

As Sam scanned the diner for a quiet corner, her search abruptly stopped. There, in a booth with a view of the entrance, was the man in the suit from the clinic. Her pulse quickened, a tangled dance of surprise and apprehension tightening its grip around her stomach.

He looked up, his eyes briefly locking with hers in a moment of unspoken recognition. Sam shivered as he nonchalantly turned his attention back to his companion across the table, as if their earlier encounter at the clinic was mere coincidence. She could only see the back of the woman he was with, her wavy dark hair cascading down her back, yet something about her posture stirred a sense of familiarity.

Sam selected the booth near the door, positioning herself so she faced the street, with an empty booth behind her serving as a buffer between her and the man in the suit. This way, she wouldn't catch sight of him every time she looked up from her meal or browsing on her laptop.

She ordered the meatloaf on the recommendation of the waitress and began researching different etiologies of hyperthyroidism on her laptop. She found that there were several causes, including hereditary predispositions as well as environmental concerns such as exposure to radiation or toxins. Sam delved deeper, reading about other risk factors and symptoms associated with hyperthyroidism. She took notes on her findings in a Google Doc, trying to piece together a potential cause for her patients' symptoms. As she read, she couldn't help but think about the teen girls. Were their cases related? Or was she just trying to look for a connection where there was none?

She'd been so focused on her work, that she jumped when she heard someone next to her say her name.

Sam glanced up to see Miranda Curran. Despite the months since their last get-together, their effortless rapport remained intact. From the beginning, they'd clicked, although their mismatched schedules had allowed them to hang out only a few times. However, in this small town, catching a glimpse of Miranda felt like a comforting link to her past life in Austin.

"I'd recognize that focused frown anywhere," Miranda

teased, her eyes lighting up with the warmth of genuine delight. "Are you working at a clinic here?"

Sam couldn't help but return the smile, feeling a surge of comfort in Miranda's presence. "Yeah," she responded. "Been here since last week. What brings you here?"

"I don't know if you've heard about that trial over in Timmons—I'm here to testify."

"Really?" Sam asked, surprised. "I thought you were with the Travis County Medical Examiner's Office." They had met and hit it off earlier in the year while both were entangled in a few murder cases back in Austin. Sam had been involved inadvertently, having known the victims, while Miranda's role was more direct, serving as a forensic nurse and investigator.

"I help out with other cases around the state when the Texas Rangers get involved. These smaller jurisdictions just don't have the resources for a thorough investigation."

"But doesn't the state provide those resources?"

"They do, and they have forensic investigators like me, but they sometimes get swamped and ask some of the larger jurisdictions to help out." Miranda glanced back at her dinner partner. "Anyway, I came over to Dry Wells after sitting around in the courtroom all day because Agent Harper is here on a case."

The mention of Agent Harper sent a jolt through Sam, her casual demeanor evaporating in an instant. "Agent Harper?" Her heart skipped a beat, the implication of his presence in Dry Wells weaving a thread of tension through her thoughts.

"Yeah, he's the one that recruited me to the FBI—oh, wait. You don't know, since it's been a while." Miranda grinned, her voice tinged with a mix of pride and anticipation. "I got in!"

"What? You got in to the FBI Academy?" The last Sam

had heard, Miranda had applied, but she'd been waiting for a response.

"Yes!" Miranda's eyes sparkled with excitement.

Sam lit up with genuine happiness upon hearing the news, her enthusiasm mirroring Miranda's as if the achievement were her own. "Congratulations!" She scooted out of the booth to give her friend a hug. "That's awesome! I'm so thrilled for you!"

"Thanks," Miranda said, her eyes now moist.

"When do you start?"

"In January. Hey," Miranda said as she tipped her head toward Agent Harper again, "why don't you join us?"

"Oh, I don't want to impose."

"No, you wouldn't be. In fact, you should talk to him. Like I've said before, I think you'd be a great agent."

Sam looked over her shoulder to meet Agent Harper's piercing gaze. "Okay," she said, a little reluctantly. This was going to be awkward, but she couldn't stave off her curiosity—why was the FBI at Dr. Carlisle's clinic?

It must have something to do with his death.

She packed up her laptop and followed Miranda to their booth.

17

As Sam cautiously slid into the plush confines of the red vinyl booth beside Miranda, Agent Harper hastily tucked a file folder, stamped with the FBI seal, into his briefcase. The snap of the lock cut through the otherwise hushed diner. Sam's gaze clung to the briefcase for a beat longer, a slight furrow creasing her brow, before she looked away, her fingers absentmindedly tracing the table's edge.

Oblivious to the undercurrents, Miranda made brief introductions and then shared a little about how she and the FBI agent met during the investigation in Timmons. Sam nodded along, her focus sharp, absorbing every detail, every shift in Harper's demeanor.

Finally, the silence from the agent stretched too long for Sam's comfort. "So, Agent Harper, what brings you to Dry Wells?" Her voice was light as she fiddled with the corner of her napkin.

Harper shifted, briefly clenching his jaw before he met her eyes. "Just some routine FBI business," he replied, his words smooth but his posture rigid.

Sam leaned back, her eyes narrowing just a fraction. "Is it related to Dr. Carlisle's death?" she prodded, her curiosity a palpable force between them.

He frowned, a crease forming between his brows. "What makes you ask that?"

"I'm just curious," Sam replied, her voice steady but her hand subconsciously running along the edge of her bag on the seat next to her. "I'm working at the clinic temporarily, and I'd heard his murder case is still unsolved."

This piqued Miranda's interest. "The doctor where you work was murdered?"

"Yes," Sam said. "It sounds like he was killed during a home invasion. I was told they think a drifter passing through town followed Dr. Carlisle into his home."

"That's awful," Miranda said. "You haven't come across that before, in your travels to these clinics around the state, have you?"

"No. Usually I'm just filling in because the doctor at a solo practice wants to go on vacation or just needs some time off. When I got here and found out the doctor had died, I'd just assumed, since he was a little older, that he'd had a chronic condition or illness which had caused his death. Not that he'd been murdered."

An uncomfortable silence settled over the trio as the waitress came over to their table and set two plates down, meatloaf with mashed potatoes for the agent, a green salad with grilled chicken for Miranda.

She smiled at Sam. "I see you've moved. I'll have your dinner out to you in a bit." She looked back and forth between the others. "Can I getcha anything else?"

The agent shook his head, while Miranda said, "I'm good."

The waitress nodded and disappeared into the kitchen.

The silence continued as neither of Sam's companions started eating. To break up the tension, Sam said, "You don't have to be polite. Please, go ahead and eat."

A moment passed, then Miranda and Agent Harper relented.

"You said you're starting at the academy in January?" Sam asked, then felt bad that she'd said this right as Miranda put a forkful of salad in her mouth. "I'm sorry. I caught you at just the wrong time."

Miranda nodded as she chewed, waving her hand to indicate it was okay. After she swallowed, she said. "It's all thanks to Agent Harper." She beamed at him.

He returned her acknowledgement with a short nod. "You deserve it."

Suddenly, the questions bubbled up in Sam. "How long will you be there? Is it really like the TV shows and movies?"

Before Miranda could answer, the waitress arrived with Sam's order, placed it in front of her, then retreated to her spot behind the counter when everyone seemed satisfied.

Between bites of her salad, Miranda launched into a detailed description of the rigorous training program, and Sam peppered her with more questions. Occasionally, Agent Harper provided limited commentary when Miranda checked with him on a few facts.

Sam listened in awe. She'd always admired Miranda's intelligence and tenacity ever since they'd first met, and it was inspiring to hear about her accomplishments.

The conversation naturally shifted to the trial in Timmons, with Miranda explaining their presence in the area. She revealed that both she and Agent Harper were there to testify. She went on to explain that because the crime had occurred on federal property, specifically the VA hospital, it necessitated FBI involvement, although local and state authorities had spearheaded the investigation.

"Contrary to popular belief, the FBI doesn't investigate homicides," Agent Harper clarified, "unless it's specifically not covered by another jurisdiction."

Sam continued to listen intently as Miranda detailed how she'd met Harper during the investigation and how he'd persuaded her to join the FBI.

"Now, I'm headed to the academy," Miranda declared. "It's been a dream of mine for years, and I couldn't be more excited." She turned towards the agent, gratitude accentuating her face. "Without your encouragement, the thought of applying would have never crossed my mind."

Harper nodded, a small smile playing at the corners of his lips. "You'll do well."

Miranda turned to Sam, her voice filled with fervor. "Can you believe it?" she said. "I'm going to be an FBI agent!"

Sam smiled, happy for her friend. "That's amazing, Miranda. You've worked so hard for this." Then she spotted the engagement ring on the chain encircling Miranda's neck. "I'm sure Dylan's very proud of you, too."

At the mention of Dylan, Miranda's face lit up like dawn breaking over the horizon, infusing the booth with a warmth that transcended its physical confines.

Meanwhile, Sam wrestled with a sharp pang of regret, a silent echo of what might have been. She shook her head subtly, as if to dispel the fleeting images of high school—those brief, intense moments of attraction with Dylan, all snuffed out by her own choices.

She suppressed those old emotions, tucking them beneath the undeniable joy visible in Miranda's eyes and the unmistakable chemistry she had witnessed between the couple, which confirmed they were perfectly suited for each other. Their happiness was authentic, and Sam understood her place was to safeguard it, not to unearth past errors. Despite the relative newness of their friendship, Sam cherished her bond with Miranda deeply, unwilling to jeopardize it for fleeting memories of what might have been.

"So, how do you two know each other?" Agent Harper asked.

Miranda delved into the story of how she and Sam had first crossed paths, highlighting the pivotal role Sam had played in cracking a couple of challenging cases back in Austin. She painted a vivid picture of Sam's keen intuition and resourcefulness, attributes that had been instrumental in their success. With a tone of admiration and conviction, Miranda shared with Harper her belief that Sam possessed the qualities and acumen that would make her an excellent fit for the FBI.

Harper raised an eyebrow, clearly interested. "Is that so?" he said.

Sam shrugged, feeling a little self-conscious. "I don't know about that."

"I think you'd be great," Miranda said, nudging Sam with her elbow.

Agent Harper's stoic façade seemed to soften a little as he gave her an appraising look. Was now the time to ask him why he was at the clinic?

She paused, torn between her reluctance to intrude and the pull of her curiosity. She couldn't help but speculate whether his visit to the clinic was connected to Dr. Carlisle's untimely demise or if it pertained to unforeseen aspects of the Timmons trial. It crossed her mind that Dr. Carlisle and the anesthesiologist facing trial might have shared patients, weaving their professional paths together in ways she was blind to.

But before she could gather the nerve to ask, Miranda interjected. "Hey, have you guys tried the pies here?" she said, her gaze fixed on the dessert case near the front of the diner.

Sam looked over at the rotating display, her mouth watering at the sight of the freshly baked pies. She'd been able to use her will power to avoid ordering a slice for the past week, but now she felt it faltering. "I haven't," she said. "But they sure look good."

"I'm gonna get a slice of apple," Miranda said. "What about you guys?"

Harper shrugged. "I'm good," he said. "But you go ahead."

The waitress noticed the group eyeing the pies, so she came over, cleared their plates, and asked if they'd like anything else.

Sam hesitated, unsure if she should indulge in dessert. But the temptation was too strong, and she found herself nodding. "I'll have a slice of cherry," she said. She couldn't let Miranda be the only one to enjoy a piece of pie.

As the waitress delivered their desserts to the table, Sam felt her nerves tighten, her eagerness for answers gnawing at her. She resolved to question Agent Harper about his visit to the clinic. All she needed was to muster a bit more courage.

Sam bit into her cherry pie, relishing the tangy sweetness. Across the table, Miranda eagerly tackled her apple slice, and Agent Harper, lost in thought, nursed his coffee. As she enjoyed her dessert, Sam became aware of an enigmatic depth to Harper that intrigued her. With his cautious posture and watchful eyes, he exuded a guardedness that only deepened Sam's curiosity. Despite her initial reservations, she was increasingly drawn to him, captivated by the complexity hidden beneath his gruff exterior.

Finally, Sam decided to take the plunge. "Agent Harper," she said, prefacing her question with a deep breath, "I hope you don't mind my asking, but why were you at the clinic earlier today?"

Harper didn't seem surprised by the question. "I'm afraid I can't talk about ongoing investigations, Doctor," he said, his voice low and even.

Sam nodded, and although she was a little disappointed, she had expected a response like this. She'd assumed that Harper was looking into something related to Dr. Carlisle's death, but she couldn't be sure.

Miranda, sensing the tension, chimed in. "You said Dr. Carlisle's death seemed to be the result of a home invasion? What was the mechanism?"

"He was bludgeoned in his front hallway," Sam replied.

"Did they find the weapon?"

"I don't think so, but I only know the very basic details."

As the women talked, Harper's attentive observation of the women resembled a scientist in a laboratory, meticulously analyzing them. Sam found herself wondering what he was thinking, but he remained a closed book, his expression revealing nothing of his inner musings.

Miranda looked confidently at Sam. "You're going to solve his case too, aren't you?"

Harper cleared his throat. "You know, Doctor," he said, "the FBI is always looking for applicants from a variety of backgrounds—including medical professionals." He tipped his head in Miranda's direction.

"But Miranda's trained in forensics," Sam said. "I'm not."

Harper shrugged. "You don't need forensics training.

In fact, you don't need any kind of law enforcement background at all. That's what Quantico is for." He pursed his lips for a moment in contemplation, then nodded, almost to himself. "You know, the more I think about it, for some of our cases, someone like you would provide a unique perspective and be a valuable asset."

18

Sam in the FBI?

Hearing Miranda's encouragement was one thing—inspiring, yet easily dismissed as the optimism of a loyal friend. But hearing it from an actual FBI agent? That nudged it into the realm of possibility.

The truth was, however, that Sam was rooted in a moment of choice, her options unfurling like the sprawling branches of a venerable Texas live oak, each one pointing toward a unique destiny. Should she accept Olivia's offer to stay in Dry Wells and continue caring for the townsfolk? Or should she keep traveling around Texas at the whim of the *locum tenens* agency, never knowing where she'd end up more than a month or two in advance?

The stability Olivia offered was attractive, but Sam wasn't certain she wanted to stay in this quaint town. There was another option, and that was to get back on the "normal" medical career track, find a residency that would accept her so she could finally complete a program and become board certified. That would be the most reasonable path for Sam to take, so she could escape the unpredictability of a *locum* doctor's life.

Despite grappling with these stark realities, that night, Sam's dreams whisked her away to the FBI Academy, a world far removed from her daily struggles. The dreams, in their usual defiance of logic, placed her alongside Miranda as cohort members and roommates, a scenario that defied feasibility. Yet, even within the dream, Sam's rational mind would occasionally surface, recalling the years and numerous attempts it had taken Miranda to achieve her acceptance.

As dawn's light awoke Sam the next morning, her dreams dissipated, their ephemeral fantasy leaving a strange longing deep within her.

As the clinic settled into its familiar, uneventful rhythm over the following days, a sudden confrontation shattered the calm. Sam was working in Dr. Carlisle's office, a gesture from Olivia, perhaps aimed at persuading her to feel more at home and consider staying. Suddenly, she was interrupted by the sound of an angry voice from the hallway. Curious, Sam stepped out to investigate and found Bonnie in a tense standoff with an irate patient, who was aggressively pointing her finger. Bonnie, trapped and looking overwhelmed, was backed up against an exam room door, her expression a mix of confusion and alarm, as if she wished she could disappear into the woodwork to escape the heated accusations.

"What did you mean by putting 'denies recreational drug use' in my file?" The middle-aged woman's voice quivered with indignation, capturing the attention of others in the clinic. Her handsome features were contorted, her face flushed with anger. "You think I'm lying to you?"

Bonnie, taken aback, tried to respond, "Mrs. Vesper, I didn't mean to imply—"

But the patient cut her off. "I saw it in that . . . that portal or whatever you call it! How dare you question my integrity?!"

Sam stepped closer, the tension in the air prickling her skin. She fought the urge to soothe Mrs. Vesper with a calming touch, fearing it might only fan the flames of her rage. Instead, she held up her hands with her palms open. "Ma'am, I understand your concern, but let me clarify. In medical jargon, 'denies' simply means that you answered 'no' to a particular question. It doesn't imply that we believe you're lying."

Mrs. Vesper's face reddened. "When I saw it, it felt . . . accusatory."

Sam nodded, softening her eyes with empathy. "I can see how it might seem that way without the context. But we always write our notes in a standard way to ensure consistency. It's purely clinical and not personal."

The woman dropped her hands, a contemplative look coming across her face as she processed Sam's explanation. After a moment, she said, "I guess I understand."

Sam, trying to lighten the mood, offered a small smile and asked, "Would you like to hear a funny story?"

Mrs. Vesper cautiously said, "Alright." Her face showed a blend of intrigue and uncertainty.

"A friend of mine had one of her patients ask her why she'd put him in 'time out' before his colonoscopy. Just like you, he'd read his procedure notes and wanted to know why an adult would be put in 'time out.'"

"Time out?" Mrs. Vesper blinked in confusion.

By now, the strain that had gripped Bonnie had

dissolved, leaving her looking much more at ease. "It's a requirement to maintain accreditation," she said. "A 'time out' is like a safety huddle—a quick pause to ensure everything's set for the right person, right place, right procedure."

The woman's features relaxed, a gentle smile touching her lips. "Time out," she chuckled, finding humor in the moment.

Now that the winds had shifted with Mrs. Vesper, Bonnie ventured, "That reminds me of something that happened when I was rotating as a nursing student in the OR. Want to hear it?"

Sam watched as Mrs. Vesper nodded in agreement, a sense of relief washing over her. She was glad to see the previously tense atmosphere of the hallway was now infused with a shared moment of levity.

"Along with the 'time out' requirement in the OR," Bonnie began, "we're constantly triple- and quadruple-checking everything. There was a patient I'd been assigned to who was waiting for surgery, and I was asked to verify the patient's information. You know—name, birthday, type of surgery, whether it was the left or right side . . ." She paused and smiled at the memory. "She gives me this serious look and says, 'I'm beginning to think no one knows what they're doing around here.' So I asked her, 'Why's that?' And she says, 'Because all of you keep asking me the same things over and over!"

The women all broke into laughter, including Mrs. Vesper. After a moment, she stopped, her earlier anger having melted into regret. "I'm sorry. It seems I . . . I just misunderstood," she admitted.

"It's okay," Sam said. "The things we do can be confusing, even for *us* sometimes. But we're always here to answer any questions you may have."

After the patient left, seemingly satisfied, Bonnie turned to her, relief evident in her eyes. "Thanks for stepping in."

"You're welcome." Sam let out a small laugh. "That's what we get for writing our notes defensively."

Bonnie nodded assent. "We just report the responses they give us. But I suppose we need to be more careful." A contemplative look came across her face. "Letting patients have access to their medical records can sometimes have unintended consequences."

Sam gave her a comforting pat on her shoulder. "Just another day in the life of the clinic, right?"

"Right," Bonnie replied with a chuckle. But it seemed like something else was bothering her.

"Is everything okay?" Sam asked.

"Yeah," Bonnie said, "just trying to keep up with everything. Thanks again." She gave Sam a weak smile, then turned to enter an exam room.

Checking the time on her phone, Sam noted she was nearly caught up on her charting, with just one more patient expected in fifteen minutes. This rare downtime in the office meant she could finish up her documentation without having to extend her work into the evening. It had freed her up for dinner with James the previous night, where he discussed the trial's progress. To Sam, his recount felt somewhat tedious, as the prosecution meticulously presented evidence that, according to James, offered no new revelations beyond what was already public. Having friends nearby was an unusual change from the solitude that typically accompanied her assignments in small towns, but she was grateful.

Tonight, Sam planned to meet up with Miranda, while James spent time in Timmons with his newfound journalist acquaintances. Having testified earlier in the day, Miranda was set to return to Austin in the morning. Eager for the catch-up, Sam anticipated hearing about the trial through Miranda's eyes and intended to probe to see if Miranda knew anything about Agent Harper's mysterious visit to the clinic. Since their initial encounter, Harper seemed to have stayed away, but Sam's duties had kept her mostly confined to the exam rooms, limiting her observations. On the few occasions she attempted to discuss Harper's visit, Olivia's attention was invariably diverted by clinic matters. Sam considered briefly seeking out Olivia at the front desk to ask her once more, but she quickly shelved the idea. Prioritizing the completion of her charts, she opted instead to focus on her work, ensuring she could fully enjoy her upcoming dinner with Miranda without any lingering concerns.

OLIVIA INTERRUPTED Sam during her last scheduled appointment of the day, a diabetes checkup for Mr. Gonzales.

"Dr. Jenkins," she said, her voice urgent, "I'm sorry to intrude, but there's an emergency, and I need you in exam room two."

Sam apologized to her patient and excused herself, glad that she didn't need to make any changes to his meds—they were pretty much done with his appointment anyway.

Once Sam stepped outside the door, Olivia whispered, "Luann is here, and she's in pain."

While Olivia followed Mr. Gonzales out to the front office, Sam rushed to Luann's room.

Luann rocked back and forth on the exam table, her hands gripping her abdomen tightly, her face ashen and etched with lines of distress. "I'm bleeding," she whispered, tears streaming down her face. "I think it's happening again."

"A miscarriage?"

Luann nodded and began to sob.

Sam wrapped her arms around Luann, who collapsed into the embrace, finding solace and strength. As Luann's sobs intensified, Sam held her closer, providing a steadfast presence through the storm of emotion, until at last, the waves of grief began to ebb.

Sam handed Luann a few tissues. Patiently, she watched as Luann gently wiped her eyes and cleared her nose.

"Okay," Sam said, her voice calm and steady. "How much have you bled?"

Luann scrunched her eyes as she recalled. "I used what was left in the box of pads I had."

"How many was that?"

"I don't know. Maybe four or five."

"And when did you start bleeding?"

"Last night."

Sam absorbed the information, fully aware of the seriousness of the situation. She knew that in early pregnancy, any bleeding beyond mere spotting warranted immediate attention. "Can I take a look at you?"

Luann nodded as she lay back on the table. During the exam, Luann winced when Sam palpated her lower abdomen. Sam double-checked Luann's vitals: temp was normal, but blood pressure and heart rate were slightly elevated. At least the BP wasn't low—if Luann had significant blood loss, a low BP would have been concerning. But as Sam performed the exam, she felt she wasn't equipped to deal with this. She didn't have everything she needed in this small clinic to do a proper workup, and she wondered how Dr. Carlisle did it all. But he was of a different generation.

Sam said, "We need to get you to the hospital."

"No, no." Luann shook her head vehemently. "I can't go."

"But I don't have the tools I need to take care of you here. And I'm worried about you and your baby."

"No. I can't." Luann continued to shake her head.

"Why?"

"Isaac can't find out. He'll be so angry with me."

Sam's heart twisted in response to Luann's anguish, a silent echo of the pain etched across Luann's face, resonating deeply within her. Her words seemed to affirm Sam's suspicions, prompting her to discreetly scan Luann's face and the visible skin on her arms and legs for any signs of new bruises—yet, she found none. This absence of physical evidence did little to ease Sam's worry; if her instincts were correct, Luann's fear was all too real and justified.

Sam took Luann's hands and squeezed. "Please," she said, her voice gentle. "We can help you. We can make sure that you're safe."

But Luann straightened up, with the air of resolution. "I'll be okay," she said, her voice barely above a whisper, betraying her words. "Just give me something for the pain, and I'll go home."

Sam closed her eyes. What could she do? She had to figure out how to get Luann to the hospital. "Would you go if I took you?"

Luann hesitated, on the verge of answering, when a soft tap interrupted them at the door. Sam, unwilling to part from Luann's side, remained steadfast, fearing that releasing her hands would mean losing her altogether.

The door slowly creaked open, revealing Sally's

concerned face. Upon seeing Luann, she hurried inside and enveloped her in a comforting embrace. "I've cleared my appointments for this evening," Sally announced, her voice a blend of concern and determination. "We're going to the ER in Timmons. I'll take you there myself."

"What will I tell Isaac?"

Sally released Luann and stood up straight. "We'll think of something, right?" She glanced at Sam. "There's got to be a good reason for Luann to go to the hospital."

Sam racked her brain for a moment, then said, "You could say you've been nauseous and vomiting, and I insisted you go to the hospital because you're dehydrated."

Sally nodded. "That's it. He can't argue with that."

"But what if . . . what if the baby . . .?" Luann's voice broke, fresh tears pooling in her eyes. "What if I lose the baby?"

Sally patted Luann's hand. "Let's not think about that now. Let's just get you to the hospital."

19

Sam offered to go with them to the hospital, but Luann declined, worrying it might look suspicious if she were to come along. Instead, the three women swapped cell numbers, setting up a line of communication for any updates. Before she left the clinic, Sam quickly relayed the essentials of the situation to Olivia, opting to keep the specifics to a minimum. Fortunately, their conversation was cut short by the ringing of Olivia's phone, which allowed Sam a timely exit.

She drove to the diner and took the same booth where she'd sat with Miranda and Agent Harper just a few nights before. Cindy must have had the night off again. Chatting with her would have offered Sam a much-needed distraction. Instead, while she waited, she nervously checked her phone, even though she knew it would be too soon for any updates.

Miranda arrived a few minutes later, sliding into the booth across from Sam. "Hey, what's up?" she asked, appearing to notice the look on Sam's face.

Sam smiled, feeling the tension in her body dissipate.

"Oh, nothing," she said. "I just had a bit of excitement today with one of my patients, but I think everything's going to be okay."

"Anything unusual?"

"Unfortunately, no. But still worrisome. I had to send a pregnant patient to the hospital," Sam said, stopping short of going into detail. While she'd wanted to discuss her suspicions of domestic abuse with Miranda—hoping for advice on handling the situation—Sam hesitated, fearing she might have already shared too much in a public setting, especially in a small town. She cast a glance around; fortunately, no one else in the diner seemed to be eavesdropping.

Miranda nodded, looking at her friend with admiration. "You're a good doctor, Sam," she said. "You really care about your patients."

Sam blushed at the compliment, grateful for Miranda's words. The life of a doctor brimmed with challenges, yet moments like these infused it with worth.

"So, how did your testimony go?" Sam asked, eager to hear about Miranda's experience in court.

Miranda's face lit up with a satisfied smile, reflecting the pride of a job well done. "It went smoothly," she said, her voice carrying a note of professional accomplishment. "I detailed the process of collecting evidence for the case, including the IV bags and the victim's blood samples, and how I submitted everything to the lab. Then, the prosecution had me walk them through the results."

Sam listened intently, impressed by Miranda's expertise. "What about the defense?" she asked. "Did they try to poke holes in your story?"

Miranda nodded, a flicker of annoyance crossing her features as she recalled the defense's probing. Despite this, a confident undertone laced her words. "Yes, they had their questions, but I stood my ground," she affirmed. "The chain of custody, my documentation—everything was ironclad."

Sam's smile widened, brimming with pride for her friend. It sounded like Miranda, with her expertise as a forensic nurse, had made a significant impact in the courtroom. Her knowledge and meticulousness must have left a lasting impression.

"Seems like you did a great job," she said.

Miranda's grin was quick and grateful. "Thanks," she said. "But enough about me. How are you liking things here?"

Sam offered a noncommittal shrug, her feelings about her time in Dry Wells mixed. "It's been both challenging and rewarding," she explained. "In fact, the office manager, who happens to be Dr. Carlisle's widow, has asked me to take over his practice."

"Really?" Miranda's eyebrows lifted in surprise.

"Yeah, but I don't know . . . I'm not really qualified."

Miranda looked puzzled. "How can you think you're not qualified? You're an excellent doctor."

Sam sighed, her doubts surfacing. "My training wasn't in family medicine. Heck, I didn't even finish residency. And I'm not sure I want to spend the rest of my life here, even if I can make a difference in my patients' lives."

Miranda responded with a sympathetic nod. "I get it. You don't have all the extra training, but all this post-graduate work and specialization—look how far it got Dr. Perry. Think about it this way: you've already made a difference in the short time you've been here, and you really *care* about these people. Imagine what you could accomplish in the long term."

Sam considered this. "That's true," she said slowly.

"But what about my career? I don't want to get stuck here and miss out on other opportunities."

"I might be a bit biased," Miranda said, her eyes crinkling knowingly, "but truthfully, I see you as an excellent fit for the FBI. However, accepting this offer doesn't mean you'd be trapped. You can always choose to move on later if it feels right. This could very well be the opportunity you've been waiting for."

The idea of Sam pursuing a career as an FBI agent brought back remnants of the dream she'd had the other night, stirring a mix of emotions. She nodded, her uncertainty still lingering. "Perhaps. It's just such a significant decision." She shifted in her seat. "Speaking of the FBI—I was wondering, do you happen to know anything about what Agent Harper is investigating? I mean, if I really want to consider taking over this practice, I need to know why he was at the clinic."

"Honestly, I have no idea," Miranda replied, looking thoughtful. "But you bring up a very good point. You don't want to be walking into a bad situation." She shrugged. "Maybe you should just ask him."

Sam frowned. "I can't really ask him about an investigation, can I?"

"Well, no," Miranda acquiesced. "But he could give you a hint as to whether you'd want to stay away or not. At least it would be another data point to help you make a big decision."

"Would he really do that?" Sam was skeptical.

"Yes, I think he would. He's a good man, and he has an amazing sense for distinguishing good from bad." Miranda leaned forward across the table, resting her hand on Sam's arm for emphasis. "In fact, after we were here the other night, Agent Harper showed a keen interest in you. He wanted more details about the cases in Austin, how you managed to solve them."

"Stumbled into them is more like it," Sam said.

"No, that's not true. You can tell when things don't add up, and you keep digging until you get to the truth."

"Even if the truth destroys my career," Sam mused as she recalled the aftermath of those cases in Austin.

"But that's exactly my point," Miranda interjected, her eyes alight with enthusiasm. "In the FBI, your relentless determination could be channeled into working on cases just like those in Austin, and it wouldn't just be commendable—it would propel your career forward. So, as you contemplate your long-term goals, why not consider applying to the FBI Academy? After all, what do you have to lose?"

20

Resuming her patient care duties the following morning, Sam found the zeal kindled by Miranda's encouragement to apply for the FBI Academy had faded, rendering the goal seemingly out of reach. Her focus shifted towards Luann's plight, which whispered as a constant murmur of concern in her mind, even amidst the bustling clinic environment. She frequently checked her phone for any news, yet there had been no updates. The last report she'd received was a late-night text from Sally, informing her that Luann had been admitted to the hospital.

Then, just before lunch, Sam's focus shifted again upon seeing that the lab results had come in for Mia, the teen with the domineering mother. A moment of hesitation gripped her before she clicked to reveal the data, feeling a wave of dread in her stomach. This hesitation stemmed not only from the anticipation of the lab results but also from concern for Mia, whose weary eyes seemed to plead for an ally against her mother's overbearing presence.

Sam's heart ached for her. Memories of her own childhood, overshadowed by a parent's demanding nature and the feeling of being unheard, flooded back. She harbored hope that the results would be normal, which would create an opportunity to address Mia's mental health more openly. Therapy might offer her desperately needed support, a possibility that sparked a glimmer of optimism in Sam. Natalie Fontaine's behavior certainly appeared to exacerbate her daughter's anxiety symptoms, and a referral to a therapist to learn coping skills seemed like the most beneficial next step. There was a chance, however slim, that Natalie might be receptive to this approach. After all, she'd brought Mia back to have the blood drawn for these tests.

But the results unveiled a startling surprise. Mia's thyroid function tests showed evidence of hyperthyroidism, which was as Sam had suspected. The high levels of T4 and T3, the two forms of thyroid hormone that circulate in our blood, made sense. However, Mia's levels of thyroid stimulating hormone, or TSH, were also elevated.

Sam frowned as she studied the results again, her mind racing through the possibilities. Normally, when T4 and T3 levels are high, TSH should be low, as it's the body's way of telling the thyroid to slow down production. The unexpected elevation hinted at a medical anomaly, a puzzle that could unravel into something both rare and grave.

There could be a couple of reasons to explain this pattern, one of them being a pituitary tumor secreting too much TSH, which Sam certainly hoped wasn't the case. And there was always the possibility that the lab results were just wrong.

Or could it be something else?

Closing her eyes, Sam delved deep into her memory, pulling from her medical training to recall the endocrine feedback loops that regulate thyroid hormone levels. She remembered reading a paper on this very topic at the diner, a moment interrupted by Miranda's arrival at her table. Realizing there might be another explanation for her observations, Sam knew she needed certainty. She needed more information.

The lab results had been sent directly to the EHR, leaving her unsure who she should contact for verification. She noticed Kelly at the end of the hallway, assisting an elderly man into an exam room. So she headed to the front office. However, upon looking through the door, she saw Tanya, the receptionist, engaged in conversation with a patient, and Olivia occupied with a call in her office.

She was struck by how much Olivia was constantly tied to the phone. When Sam once brought it up, Olivia explained that her life revolved around endlessly pursuing insurance companies to reimburse the clinic for patient services. Often, they would only receive a fraction of the billed amount, usually several months late, if they were paid at all.

Olivia caught Sam's eye and gestured with a finger, signaling she would be off the call shortly. However, just then, Kelly emerged from the nearby exam room. Sam shook her head at Olivia, silently communicating, "Never mind." She quickly followed Kelly, catching up to her just as she reached for the vitals cart.

"I have a question about some lab results," Sam said. "Do you know who I can call?"

"Sure. Let me find that number for you." Kelly left the cart where it was and went to the counter across from the computer Sam had been using in the hallway. She picked up a stack of business cards, shuffled through it, and selected one.

"Here's the lab director's phone number," Kelly said as

she began to hand the card to Sam. But she stopped and pulled it back. "Wait, when was it sent out? Because we had to switch labs."

"That's right," Sam said, "you mentioned it the other day." She stepped over to the computer, unlocked it, and found the collection date. "Day before yesterday."

Kelly nodded. "Okay, so that would be Quest." She looked through the cards again. Then she stepped closer to Sam, lowered her voice, and said, "Olivia's cousin runs the lab in Timmons where we usually send everything, but for some reason we had to stop. I know she's sensitive to what goes on there, but she's not sayin' why we can't use them right now. I heard some guys in suits showed up there last week."

This piqued Sam's interest. "Really?"

"Yeah, but that's all I know." Kelly shrugged. "Well, that, and some talk about billing and what not." She shook her head. "I don't know. I shouldn't be sayin' nothin' else." She picked out a different card from the stack. "Here's the number for our account manager at Quest. She's fine, but she doesn't give us nearly the same personal attention as Olivia's cousin."

"Thanks," Sam said as she took the card.

"No problem," Kelly said, then she walked down the hall to retrieve the cart and headed back into the exam room.

Sam traced the embossed lettering on the Quest business card before her gaze drifted to the first card Kelly had selected and left on the counter. She moved closer to examine it in greater detail. It was for East Tex Diagnostics & Lab Services, with Craig Lombard listed as the Director.

Could this be the reason Agent Harper had visited the clinic? Kelly had mentioned billing issues. Considering the extensive prevalence of Medicare fraud across the country, she wondered if that had sparked the FBI's interest. Maybe Agent Harper was there to meticulously examine the records for their accuracy—or inaccuracy.

No matter. Sam's main concern right now was getting to the bottom of Mia's labs. She went back to the computer desk, picked up the phone, and called the number for the Quest account manager. It was a Houston area code. The call went to voicemail, but Sam didn't leave a message. From her experience, an account manager was usually more like a sales person instead of the clinical expert she needed to answer her questions.

She visited the Quest website and clicked on the "Contact" icon, only to be met with a lack of phone numbers. Instead, she had to navigate through a series of dropdown menus, trying various combinations of selections, but ended up still with no useful information—only aggravation.

Why couldn't she just find a phone number so she could talk to someone?

Kelly was certainly right about the big lab companies not having personal service.

Now it looked like the website was trying to get her to log into some system, and she had no idea how to do that.

Sam sighed. She opened a new web browser window and Googled "Quest customer service phone number." An 800 number popped up, followed by common questions people searched for, including "How do I talk to a real person at Quest Diagnostics?"

Sam couldn't help but laugh. At least she wasn't the only one who was frustrated.

She dialed the 800 number, and after punching a couple of options to navigate through the phone system menu, she was put on hold. Figures.

While she waited, she searched for the paper she'd

been reading at the diner the other night. She'd saved a copy on her laptop, which was locked in her car, but she thought she remembered which website she'd found it on. With the phone wedged between her ear and her shoulder, she typed and clicked, but then the intercom buzzed and Tanya's voice came through the tinny speaker on the phone base. "Dr. Jenkins, you have a call on line three."

Sam hung up the phone—she'd have to call Quest later. She pushed the intercom button and asked, "Who is it?"

"It's Mrs. Fontaine. She saw the lab results on the portal, and she wants to talk to you about them."

Sam felt unprepared, on the brink of a conversation that was as delicate as a house of cards. "Could you tell her I'll call her back?"

"She insists on speaking to you now."

What kind of patient insists on talking to the doctor right away when they call? Don't they know that we're usually seeing patients all day long?

Kelly came out of the room where she'd taken the elderly gentleman and signaled to Sam that he was ready to be seen.

Sam let out a small sigh of relief. "Let her know I'm with another patient, and I'll get back to her as soon as possible."

"She's not going to like it . . . but okay."

"Thanks," Sam said, and then went in to see her next patient.

WHEN SHE CAME out of the exam room twenty minutes later, Sam knew she was obligated to call Natalie Fontaine back, but she wasn't exactly eager about it. The woman had been tough to deal with during the previous visit, and Sam didn't relish the thought of having to explain what the results might mean about her daughter's condition. On top of that, in order to get a definitive answer, Sam would probably have to send Mia for a series of studies to determine what was going on.

Seeking some privacy, Sam slipped into Dr. Carlisle's office and settled behind the desk. She took a deep breath to steady herself, her fingers trembling a touch as she dialed the number. The phone rang a few times before switching to voicemail. As she listened to the outgoing message, Sam felt her tension ease slightly. She left a brief message, deliberately keeping the details sparse, simply requesting for Mrs. Fontaine to contact the clinic for a follow-up appointment to discuss the lab results. This approach not only bought Sam some time to strategize but also seemed the most tactful way to handle the situation with Mia.

After she hung up the phone, she took a moment to regroup. A photo sat on the side of the desk, and Sam hadn't really paid much attention to it before. It showed Olivia with a gray-haired man, arms around each other's waists, along with two young women on either side. They were standing at the edge of a cliff overlooking a turquoise sea. Sam assumed the man was Dr. Carlisle, and the women their grown daughters, each looking like younger versions of Olivia, but with a hint of their father in their features.

The photo likely captured a moment from a family vacation, taken before Dr. Carlisle's passing. Despite the subsequent tragedy, the image suggested that the family had cherished times of joy and togetherness. Sam found herself yearning for such moments of happiness in her own future.

Before leaving the office, she paused to check her phone and noticed a missed message from Sally. It informed her that Luann had been discharged and was now heading home with her mother. Sam tapped out a quick thank you to Sally before moving on to her next patient, a woman struggling with asthma flare-ups due to the dry autumn air. Fortunately, the visit was fairly straight forward, and when Sam came out of the room, Olivia stopped her in the hallway, handing her a message slip.

"Natalie Fontaine called while you were in there." Olivia rolled her eyes. "She wants you to call her back immediately."

"I just left her a voice message to make a followup appointment for Mia, so we can discuss her lab results."

"Well, she's not happy with that. She wants you to explain why she needs to bring Mia back in."

Sam sighed as she briefly closed her eyes. "Okay, but it's an interesting situation."

"Really?" Olivia's eyes widened. "Do tell."

Sam shook her head. "I'm sorry, but . . . you know . . . patient confidentiality."

Olivia nodded, but disappointment flashed across her features. As she pivoted to make her way towards the front office, she called over her shoulder, "Good luck!"

After returning to Dr. Carlisle's office, Sam paused for a moment to center herself, closing her eyes briefly to marshal her thoughts before dialing Natalie's number. As she listened on the line, each ring seemed to echo louder in the quiet room, amplifying her nerves as she waited for Natalie to answer.

Finally, Natalie's sharp voice crackled on the other end of the line. "Hello?" She sounded impatient with just that one word.

"Hi, Mrs. Fontaine. It's Dr. Jenkins," Sam said, trying

to keep her voice steady despite the thumping in her chest. "I just received the lab results for Mia's blood work, and I'd like to have her come in for another appointment so we can discuss the results."

"Yes, I saw them on the web portal. But you need to explain to me what it all means."

Natalie's demanding tone was almost palpable through the phone. No matter how many challenging individuals she'd dealt with in the past, the apprehension never waned when it came time to face them again. She took a deep breath and willed her heart to slow down. "I would prefer to discuss this in person," she said cautiously. "And I would also like to speak with Mia."

"Why can't you just tell me over the phone?" Natalie barked. "What are you trying to hide?"

Sam clenched her jaw, a familiar tightness reminding her to choose her words carefully. "It's not something that can be properly explained over the phone," she said firmly. Then she repeated, "And it's important that I speak with Mia alone as well."

Natalie snorted. "We have no secrets from each other."

Sam wasn't sure that was true, and she felt like anything she said in response to this statement would not help build rapport, rapport that she'd need to figure out what was going on with Mia. Instead, she tried a different tack. "It's always better to discuss medical information in person," she said. "That way, we can take our time, and I can thoroughly answer any questions you might have, to make sure you're comfortable and fully understand everything."

There was a pause on the other end of the line, and Sam could hear Natalie breathing heavily. Finally, she spoke. "Fine," she said. "But you're being very obstinate about this. I'll let Olivia know."

Sam bit back a retort and instead took a deep breath. "Thank you," she said. "I think it's best if we schedule an appointment as soon as possible."

As Sam transferred the call to the front office, she felt a touch of relief that the episode was over. But she knew that she still had to deal with this woman, and that it wasn't going to be pleasant. She could only hope that the next encounter would be on her own terms, but she couldn't shake the feeling that things were about to get even more complicated.

21

The rest of the day unfolded in a monotonous rhythm, with each patient's arrival and departure ticking away like the precise movements of a well-oiled clock. At one point when she was alone in an exam room, Sam lingered at the computer, her concern for Luann gnawing at her. With a hesitant glance toward the door, she found herself typing Luann's name into the EHR, seeking her address—a silent admission of her deep-seated worry. She knew that accessing an address for somewhat personal reasons may be crossing a boundary. The principles of patient privacy and confidentiality were drilled into her during her medical training, principles she had always upheld with the utmost respect. Yet, the unsettling feeling in her gut, fueled by her genuine care for Luann's well-being, made her question the rigidity of those rules in this moment.

After the final patient of the day departed, Sam gathered her things, then headed to the now-quiet waiting room toward the exit. Olivia was there, crouched next to the ZenithVita display, absorbed in rearranging the shelves stocked with products. Sam paused, observing the scene.

"That's quite a selection," she commented, her voice even, masking any judgment. She had been eager to discuss this display with Olivia, and now seemed like the right moment.

Olivia looked up, her smile steady, yet her eyes flickered briefly with an undercurrent of apprehension or perhaps anticipation—Sam wasn't certain. "We're broadening our offerings. Wellness isn't just about what happens in the exam room, don't you think?"

"Addressing wellness is valuable," Sam started, her tone deliberate, "but what about the potential for conflicts of interest?"

"I get where you're coming from." Olivia stood and extended her hand toward the shelves. "But having these products here can make things easier for our patients, especially since a lot of them are buying them from other places already."

Sam nodded, still cautious. She measured her words, aware of the potential impact on her job prospects. Despite her wavering with the decision, she recognized that Olivia could rescind the offer. "I see the convenience," she admitted, "but as a physician, I feel we have to watch out that we don't turn medicine into just another business. We should always back our recommendations with solid evidence, to keep our integrity and earn our patients' trust."

Olivia scrunched her lips and didn't respond immediately, but then her expression warmed, with what might have been a hint of respect in her eyes. "I appreciate your dedication to ethical standards." Then, reading between the lines, she offered, "If you do decide to join the practice, we can explore this topic further. And if you're strongly opposed to selling these products, we can figure something out."

While Olivia's response seemed somewhat reassuring, Sam remained a touch ambivalent. Even though Olivia could be a busybody, perhaps this would be a collaborative and respectful working relationship should Sam take over the practice. But she just wasn't sure.

"Which, by the way, you still haven't given me an answer. And you're leaving tomorrow," Olivia pointed out.

Guilt tugged at Sam. The week had flown by, and Olivia was right—Sam had been avoiding making a decision. But this decision impacted the rest of her life, and relocating was not something to take lightly. Moreover, she still had many questions about the practice, such as why Agent Harper had visited the clinic earlier in the week. She could ask Olivia about it now, but her priority was to check on Luann.

"I'm sorry," Sam said. "It really is a big decision, and I just need more time to think."

Olivia nodded. "I understand. Well, the offer still stands, even after you move on. I've got someone lined up for the next couple of weeks, and the couple after that." She smiled. "But it would be nice to have someone I trust working here all the time."

Sam returned her smile. "Thank you, Olivia. I appreciate that."

They said their goodbyes for the evening, with Olivia saying she'd be by in the morning for a final farewell, and Sam left through the front door.

As she turned out of the parking lot, dusk had settled, with the sky deepening into a rich indigo, punctuated by the early glimmer of stars. This stunning scene, though beautiful, cast a subtle darkness over the moment, altering Sam's mood from cautiously optimistic to introspective. It suggested the looming challenges that might lie ahead.

On the way to Luann's house, her immediate world seemed to blur. The once familiar and comforting fragrance of moss and pine now felt foreign in the dim light of evening, with each turn creating spectral silhouettes at the periphery of her headlights. Sam's grip on the steering wheel grew tighter with every mile. It wasn't until the outline of Luann's home came into view in the dwindling light that Sam realized her drive had been nearly subconscious, propelled by a profound sense of duty and worry.

Nestled among sprawling fields and whispering evergreens, the neighborhood's modest homes stood apart, their flickering lights casting long shadows in the tranquil yet slightly eerie twilight. Sparse streetlights barely pierced the deepening blue of the evening sky, lending a rustic charm that was both comforting and isolating. The air, crisp with the scent of woodsmoke, seemed to slow time itself, enveloping the area in a quiet anticipation of nightfall.

The short driveway to the Clark residence displayed a patchwork of grease stains and cracked concrete, leading to a carport that sheltered more than just vehicles. A rusty pickup truck, its paint faded and peeling, was parked halfway under the canopy, alongside a compact sedan that had seen better days. The carport itself was a makeshift workshop, cluttered with tools dulled by time and neglect, along with pieces of equipment that lay scattered like forgotten puzzles, all revealing a history of numerous unfinished projects. As Sam neared the house, the combined odors of motor oil and rusting metal enveloped her, evoking the sense of a silent force, as if the very air was charged with the presence of unseen, dormant energy.

With a steady hand, Sam knocked on the door, despite the flutter of nerves within her. Unsure of what was in store, she remained resolved to offer whatever help she could. While waiting, she stepped back and took in the nearby houses, speculating which one might belong to Sally. Not recognizing any vehicles in the neighbors' driveways, she supposed Sally might be at her salon that evening.

Isaac answered the door, his posture rigid, eyes narrowed. "Doctor."

Sam, maintaining her composure, inched forward slightly, her voice a blend of professionalism and genuine concern. "I just came by to check on Luann," she said. "Is she okay?"

"She's fine," Isaac said curtly. "She doesn't want visitors." He crossed his arms, his chest expanding as his frame filled the doorway menacingly.

Sam's unease deepened at Isaac's cold dismissal. His indifference was palpable, heightening her apprehension. "I understand," she said, trying to keep her voice calm. "But if there's anything I can do . . ."

"Oh, I think you've done enough for her already," he said sharply.

Shock rippled through Sam at Isaac's words, coldness creeping down her spine. Questions spiraled, unspoken and heavy. What did he mean? Had Luann told him about the bleeding, or did a deeper rift lie beneath? Her heartbeat quickened, facing the frost in Isaac's look. "I'm sorry," she steadied her voice against the turmoil. "I'm here to help." Her determination flickered back to life, a silent defiance against the haze of doubts.

With a scowl, he said, "She don't need your help."

Sam paused, uncertainty etching her features as she weighed her next move. The last thing she wanted was to complicate matters for Luann, yet her instincts screamed that something was amiss. Isaac's guarded stance and brusque manner hinted at his desire to keep her at bay. But for what reason? Just as she was gearing up to probe further, a voice cut through her contemplation.

"Isaac, who is it?"

Luann emerged in the dim hallway behind her husband, her complexion pale and features weary. It was clear she was still grappling with the aftermath of her hospital visit.

"Just the doctor," Isaac muttered.

Surprise and a hint of nervousness widened Luann's eyes. "Doctor Jenkins! What brings you here?"

"I wanted to check on you, to see how you're doing," Sam said, her voice gentle.

Luann offered a faint smile. "Thank you," she murmured. "Please, come in."

As Sam approached, she scanned Luann's face for any signs of distress or injury. Although there were no visible bruises or marks, the dullness in her eyes spoke volumes.

When Sam got to the door, Isaac stepped in her way, blocking her path.

Luann reached out, placing her hand on his shoulder. "Isaac, please," she implored, her voice trembling.

He turned, shifting his gaze back and forth between the two women.

As the atmosphere grew tense, Sam quietly deliberated her next move, her mind teeming with possible scenarios. Should she leave? But the thought of Luann held her there. What would happen to her?

Finally, after a lengthy pause, he stepped aside and muttered, "Fine, go ahead."

Sam entered into the cozy living room, but it was tinged with discomfort due to Isaac's imposing presence nearby. With a huff, he shut the front door behind her and retreated into the kitchen beyond a dividing wall separating it from the living room.

Sam looked around, noting a scattering of family photos on a shelf above a TV and a well-worn couch tucked into the corner. Luann settled into an old wingback chair next to it, gesturing for Sam to join her.

In the background, the sounds of Isaac's movements in the kitchen filtered into the room, followed by the clatter of keys and the slam of a door. Soon after, the truck's engine roared to life before gradually fading away as Isaac drove off, leaving Sam and Luann alone.

The silence that fell after Isaac's departure was heavy, almost tangible in its weight. Sam watched as Luann tried to compose herself, the air between them charged with unsaid words and raw emotion. She knew she needed to bridge the gap, to offer support without pushing too hard.

"Luann," Sam began, her voice gentle, threading through the quiet like a lifeline. "I can't even begin to understand what you're going through, but I'm here for you. Can you . . . would you feel okay telling me about what happened at the hospital last night?"

Luann's eyes met Sam's, a storm of pain and vulnerability swirling in their depths. She drew a shuddering breath. "It was . . . it was all so fast, Dr. Jenkins," she whispered, the words catching on her sobs. "One moment, I was scared but hopeful, and then . . ." Her voice trailed off as she gathered the strength to continue her story.

Sam moved closer, her presence a quiet assurance. She listened with an aching heart, carefully tucking away her own reactions to remain fully present for Luann. As Luann's narrative unfolded, revealing the stark and painful details of the night before, Sam's admiration for her patient's courage grew. Despite everything, Luann was here, sharing her most vulnerable moments.

While Luann spoke, her narrative settled into a rote recitation of events. Sam began to separate the clinical details in her mind, trying to piece together the care that Luann had received. Based on her descriptions, it sounded like she had been examined in the ER, then taken for a transvaginal ultrasound. The doctors concluded that Luann had suffered a miscarriage, a diagnosis drawn from her recounting of the events leading up to her hospital visit and the ultrasound's inability to confirm any signs of pregnancy. They held her overnight for observation, and then they released her this afternoon, telling her she needed to follow up with her OB/GYN.

Sam took all of this in, offering words of comfort, and when Luann finished speaking, Sam asked the question that had been troubling her.

"Does Isaac know?" She glanced nervously toward the door even though she knew he was gone.

Luann shook her head. "No," she said. "Since Sally took me to the hospital, we told him I just had some bad food poisoning, like you suggested." She dropped her head into her hands. "I don't know how I'm going to tell him the truth."

Sam put her hand on Luann's shoulder. "You don't have to do it alone," she said. "I'm here for you, and we'll figure it out together."

22

Once she was in her car, Sam closed her eyes. Did she just lie to Luann? She was supposed to go back to Austin tomorrow, after the half-day shift, back to her hometown. How could she keep her promise to be there for Luann if she was gone?

Glancing back at the house, Sam felt it might be safe to leave Luann alone, though she harbored some doubts. Luann had assured her of her safety, hinting at the option to stay at her mother's if needed, without explicitly mentioning spousal abuse. She'd mentioned staying with her mother previously when Isaac had lost his temper, only to return once he'd calmed down and pleaded with her to come back. "Everything will be okay," Luann had insisted.

Sam closed her eyes once more, then she gazed through her windshield at the dusky street. The evening breeze gently rustled the neighborhood's trees, casting movements that played between the amber glow of street lamps, culminating in dancing shadows. What should she do?

Originally, she'd planned to stay with James and Kevin

at their condo for a week after this assignment, before heading to San Angelo in west Texas. But so much had changed since Sam had first arrived in Dry Wells.

With James staying in Timmons for the ongoing trial next week, Sam felt it would be awkward to stay with Kevin in his absence. Sure, Kevin was awesome and wouldn't think twice about letting his boyfriend's best friend stay for a week, but she didn't want to impose. The other option was that she stay with her father, but she didn't really feel like dealing with his passive aggressive comments aimed at making her feel like she hadn't lived up to her potential.

She started her engine and pulled out of the neighborhood, heading toward her motel. She hadn't eaten dinner, but she wasn't hungry. Instead she was just plain exhausted. If she didn't stay, she felt like she'd be leaving a mess.

The responsibility for Natalie and Mia's follow-up appointment would fall onto the shoulders of the next *locum* doctor, who'd likely be unprepared for what awaited. Plus, she still wondered if there was a connection between Mia's and Sarah's symptoms.

Poor Cindy. Sam felt guilty, like she'd be leaving Cindy hanging, the person who'd first asked Sam to stay. Sam wanted to see what her daughter's lab results showed, to see if they matched the unusual pattern that came up in Mia's labs.

There was a lot of work to do, and not all of it would be pleasant. She would need to explain to Natalie Fontaine precisely why Mia required additional tests—expensive ones that necessitated a trip to Timmons for completion. Likely, one of these tests would involve the use of radioactive iodine, a detail she was sure would freak Natalie out.

Finally, Sam had just promised she'd help Luann figure

out how to deal with Isaac. Not something to be taken lightly. Luann really needed her.

Deep down, Sam knew the decision she had to make.

Once she pulled into the motel parking lot, she texted Olivia.

"I'll stay for another week."

Moments later, Olivia responded. "Great! Any chance you'll stay longer?"

Sam replied back, "Still thinking about it."

She regretted the short notice she gave Olivia, knowing it would force her to cancel the *locum* scheduled for Tuesday. However, it wasn't like Sam hadn't been in a similar position before, having received last-minute cancellations from the agency herself. No matter how much you prepare, plans change.

THE NEXT MORNING, with the first light of dawn coming through the clinic windows, Sam felt a mix of anticipation and relief. It was in this early hour, as the day was just beginning to stir, Sam shared her decision with Bonnie. She waited for a lull between patients, the soft hum of the clinic around them serving as a backdrop to her news. "I've decided to stay a bit longer," she told Bonnie. "Another week."

Bonnie, who was in the midst of organizing a stack of fax printouts, paused mid-motion, her hands stilling as she processed Sam's words. Her face lit up with a bright smile. "Really? That's wonderful! I can't tell you how much this means to us—to me," she said, her warm tone making Sam feel welcomed and appreciated.

As the day went on, the news of her decision brought an ease to her interactions with everyone. Olivia dropped by for a couple of hours and was just as enthusiastic about Sam's extended stay. Near noon, with the clinic quieting down, Bonnie approached Sam while she was finishing up a note.

"Since you're staying," she said, "how about dinner at my place again? I could whip up something special, a little celebration for your decision."

Sam turned to face Bonnie and smiled as she gently declined. "I'd love to, really. But I've already made plans." After making her decision the night before, she'd let James know, and they'd agreed to meet later that afternoon.

Bonnie's expression softened, a mix of disappointment and acceptance. "Of course, I understand. Rain check, then?"

"Definitely," Sam assured her.

As Sam gathered her belongings and stepped out of the clinic into the bright light of the early afternoon, the weight of her decision to stay in Dry Wells felt a little lighter. The path ahead was uncertain, but for now, Sam was exactly where she needed to be.

BACK IN HER MOTEL ROOM, Sam glanced at the clock, calculating the hours she had before her rendezvous with James. Determined to make the most of this time, she reached for her phone and dialed Renee. They had exchanged a few texts during the week, as they had planned to meet if Sam had returned to Austin the previous weekend, but Sam had canceled. Now, she hoped Renee would be willing to give her a curbside consult.

Once Renee answered and they exchanged a few pleasantries, Sam said, "I've got a puzzling situation I need some help with."

"Give it to me," Renee replied, her tone shifting to one of focused interest.

Sam detailed Mia's case, describing the symptoms and the lab results that had left her intrigued. "Both T4 and T3 are elevated, along with TSH. It's not adding up, and I'm considering whether it might be exogenous. You know, since hyperthyroidism is pretty rare, and unless there's a pituitary tumor, I don't really know what else could explain that high TSH."

Renee paused, then said, "With those labs, it's certainly a possibility."

"Of course," Sam said, "maybe I'm just hoping it's not a tumor, and I'm stretching for another explanation."

"Could be, but you've got to work the differential," Renee said. "Have you considered any environmental factors, or perhaps access to medication that shouldn't be there?"

Sam nodded to herself, her brain ticking through the possibilities. "I have, but I'm not even sure where to start. I suppose I could visit the local pharmacy to see if there's a pattern of thyroid medication prescriptions that stands out."

"Or, you could check the EHR," Renee said.

"You're right, I should do that." The idea sparked a renewed vigor in Sam; while sifting through the EHR data might not provide clear answers, it was a step forward, illuminating her path. "Thanks for the suggestion."

"You're welcome," Renee said. "So when are we getting together again? Didn't you say you'd be back this weekend?"

Sam explained how she'd be staying in Dry Wells another week, and then she mentioned that Olivia had asked her to take over the practice.

"Really? Sam, that's amazing!" Renee exclaimed.

"Small town medicine? You're perfect for it. Think of the impact you'll have."

"It is, but I'm not sure I'd want to live here permanently."

"Boy, I'd jump at that if I had the chance."

"I thought you liked the practice you joined."

"I did, at first. But these large groups are all focused on tracking key metrics and hitting milestones," Renee said, exasperation creeping into her voice. "It's not what medicine should be about. And Austin . . . it's changed. It doesn't have the college vibe anymore." She sighed. "I dream of moving to a smaller town someday. It's what I'm used to." After a pause, she said, "You know, I grew up in Longview, not far from Timmons."

"That's right. I'd forgotten." A notion struck Sam. "Maybe I should tell Olivia *you* might be interested in the job."

"Oh, Sam," Renee said. "You don't have to do that. This is *your* opportunity."

They chatted a little more and promised to get together when Sam drove through Austin on her way out to west Texas. After hanging up, Sam pulled out her laptop and logged into the EHR with a fresh sense of direction. She began her search for connections that might explain Mia's unusual lab results.

She ran a report on the diagnostic codes and studied the results. There were only three patients who had hyperthyroidism, all were older and appeared to have been diagnosed a while back. Since there weren't that many patients, Sam looked at each of their labs, and they all had what would be expected: high T4 and T3, low TSH. Two of them had ultimately been diagnosed with Graves' disease, an autoimmune disorder where the patient's own body attacks the thyroid gland, and the other with thyroiditis, which had resolved on its own.

But something else caught her eye—the number of patients with *hypo*thyroidism in the report seemed quite high. She quickly looked up the prevalence in the US, which was around ten percent, and in this small clinic, the rate was nearly double what she'd expected. She clicked on a few of the patient records, and their labs made sense: *low* T4 and T3, with elevated TSH. They'd all been prescribed Synthroid, and subsequent bloodwork had shown a normalization of their levels. Maybe the pharmacist could give her some insight to see if these numbers really matched up, if they made sense.

She packed up her things and got on the road. She'd stop by the pharmacy before heading to the brewpub in Timmons where James had told her to meet him.

It was a short drive, and fifteen minutes later, she turned into the parking lot of a small strip mall, with the Dry Wells Pharmacy on one end, a liquor store on the other end, and Knotty by Nature, Sally's hair salon, in between.

Sam checked her watch. If her conversation with the pharmacist didn't take very long, maybe there was enough time to squeeze in a haircut, since she'd had to cancel her appointment in Austin last week. She was certainly overdue.

As Sam stepped into the quaint pharmacy, the air was rich with the scent of candles mingling with a dash of nostalgia. The space was snug yet neatly arranged, its shelves showcasing a harmonious blend of tradition and innovation, from age-old remedies to the latest pharmaceuticals. Behind the counter stood an older gentleman, his presence exuding a warmth that was instantly comforting.

"Can I do something for you?" he inquired with a friendly nod.

"Good afternoon," Sam said, making her way to the counter. "My name is Samantha Jenkins, and I have a bit of an unusual request."

The pharmacist's eyes lit up with recognition. "It's Dr. Jenkins, right? I've come across your name on prescriptions more than a few times." He reached over the counter with a welcoming hand. "Howard Shaw's the name. Pleasure's all mine."

"It's mine, as well," Sam said, taking his hand and shaking it. "I was wondering if you might help me with something."

"Of course," Howard replied, leaning forward and resting his elbows on the counter. "What's on your mind?"

Sam hesitated, searching for the right words. "Have you noticed any strange patterns lately? For instance, a specific medication being dispensed more than usual?"

Howard paused, his gaze introspective, before responding, "Well, nothing unusual on my radar." He then squinted a bit, concern edging into his voice. "You're not talking about opioids, are you? Because I run a tight ship here. Heard some talk about Timmons having issues, but we're clean."

Sam held up her hands. "No, no. I'm not talking about opioids. But what about Synthroid?"

"Synthroid?" Howard echoed, scratching his head in thought. "That's unusual, but not unheard of. Every now and then, you might catch wind of a case or two of misuse. What's got you digging into this?"

"I noticed that there seem to be a lot of patients with hypothyroidism in Dr. Carlisle's practice. Nearly double the national prevalence."

Howard's expression shifted to one of mild surprise.

"Well, we do dispense a good bit of levothyroxine, but it's pretty much what I'd expect around here. You know, with the demographic leaning towards the elderly, particularly women, thyroid issues are more common."

"That makes sense." Sam nodded, taking in the information. "But what about younger patients? Have you noticed any unusual patterns or prescriptions for thyroid medications from younger individuals?"

Howard paused, giving the question its due consideration. "Can't say I have, but then again, I haven't been keeping a close watch on that. Let me get my son to dive into our electronic records. He's pretty sharp with all that tech stuff," Howard offered, with a hint of pride in his voice.

"That would be incredibly helpful, Howard, thank you." Sam smiled gratefully. "And, just out of curiosity, are there any controls in place for monitoring these types of meds? You know, to prevent misuse or diversion?"

"It's not something that's tracked, not like the Schedule II's," the pharmacist assured her. "But in a small town like ours, things stand out if they don't look right. Give me a couple of days, and I'll circle back with what we find."

23

When she walked out of the pharmacy, Sam's attention was caught by a familiar figure through the window of the adjacent hair salon. Sally, with panache, spun a woman around in the elevated chair at her station as she held up a mirror. Noticing Sam through the window, Sally paused, waved enthusiastically, and then motioned for her to come inside.

Sam checked her watch. She still had an hour before she was to meet James. Stepping into the salon, she was immediately enveloped in the intimate warmth of Sally's boutique space, which housed just three stations. The air was fragrant with an array of hair products, mingling with the gentle murmur of conversations between the stylists and their clients.

"Dr. Jenkins! Perfect timing. I was just finishing up here. You need a haircut, don't you?"

Sam couldn't help but laugh, touching the ends of her hair self-consciously. "You caught me. I was going to get it cut last weekend, and then this weekend . . . But, my plans keep changing."

"Say no more. I've got an opening as soon as I'm finished with Mrs. Hargreaves." Sally gestured towards a comfortable chair by the front door. "Let's get those ends taken care of."

While waiting for Sally to finish with Mrs. Hargreaves, Sam's gaze wandered to the meticulously arranged array of hair products on the shelves by the front door. The shelves, bathed in the soft glow of the salon's ambient lighting, offered a dizzying display of choices available in the realm of hair care. Bottles of shampoo and conditioner stood in neat rows, their labels boasting benefits from volumizing to smoothing, for every hair type under the sun. Beside them, an assortment of serums, oils, and leave-in conditioners promised to tame frizz, enhance shine, or protect against heat damage.

Sam found herself bewildered by the offerings. The world of hair care had apparently evolved far beyond her usual routine, and she couldn't help but feel a bit out of her depth. The variety was overwhelming, a stark contrast to the simplicity she preferred in her own life. Yet, there was something fascinating about the promise each bottle held, a potential for reinvention and care that was both alluring and slightly intimidating.

Soon enough, it was Sam's turn. As she took her seat, Sally draped the cape over her with a flourish. "Bonnie mentioned you're staying with us another week," Sally said.

Sam, amused yet slightly taken aback by how quickly her plans had spread, replied, "News sure travels fast around here, doesn't it? I'm starting to realize that Dry Wells might outdo the internet in spreading gossip."

They both shared a laugh, then Sally shifted the conversation toward the task at hand. "Alright, how are we doing this? Keeping the length or feeling adventurous today?" she asked.

"Just a trim, I think. Could you clean up the ends and maybe add some long layers?"

Nodding in approval, Sally extended her arm toward the back of the salon. "Let's start with a wash to make the cut smoother."

As Sam followed Sally to the sinks nestled at the back, the salon's ambiance, filled with the soothing sounds of music and the distant hum of dryers, enveloped her in a cocoon of calm. Settling into the plush chair, Sam tilted her head back into the basin, letting out a contented sigh as warm water cascaded over her scalp.

Sally expertly massaged shampoo into Sam's hair, its lavender and chamomile scent enveloping her in a promise of relaxation. The fragrance intensified as she worked up a lather, easing Sam's tension with each gentle, circular motion across her scalp. This unexpected serenity offered Sam a peaceful break from her bustling clinic life. Following the shampoo, Sally applied a conditioner infused with rosemary, enhancing the experience with its invigorating aroma. After the final rinse, Sam's hair felt refreshed and rejuvenated.

Guiding Sam back to her chair, Sally began the haircut, deftly snipping away the split ends. While she worked her magic, she chattered on about various people that Sam should meet, if she were to stay permanently. But then, at one point, she leaned in slightly, lowering her voice to a confidential murmur. "You know, living next to Luann has put me in a tough spot more than once. I've had to call the sheriff's department a few times because of the arguing and loud noises coming from her place. It's heartbreaking, really." She paused, her scissors momentarily stilling as she caught Sam's eye in the mirror. "Isaac's temper . . . I've seen bits of it, and it scares me. I just wish there was more I could do to help her."

Sam met Sally's gaze in the reflection. "So do I." She turned her head to look up at Sally directly. "And thank you for taking her to the hospital the other day. She was really resistant, but I think having you there helped change her mind."

Sally put her hand on Sam's shoulder, giving her a light squeeze. "It was the least I could do. Like I said, I wish I could do more."

They both sighed, sharing a silent moment. Then Sally asked, "Can I call you if I notice anything?"

Sam nodded. "Absolutely."

"It's good to have an ally," Sally said, giving Sam's reflection an appreciative look, before shifting the chair to continue her work on the sides of Sam's hair.

A few minutes later, Sally was done. With the final snip, she spun Sam around to face the mirror. The transformation wasn't dramatic, but the cleanup made a world of difference. Sam's hair now framed her face with purpose, her appearance now revitalized.

After finishing the blow dry, Sally offered, "Would you like to try some styling products to keep your hair looking this great? I can give you a special discount."

"Sure," Sam agreed, not out of necessity, but to offer Sally additional support.

As Sally picked out a few items for Sam near the front door, she said, "You know, some months I actually make more money from selling products than providing styling services."

"Is that so?" Sam said.

Sally nodded. "Seems incredible, but it's true." She went over to the cash register, and as she was ringing up the sale, she said, "It seems Olivia has started selling her

ZenithVita products. I noticed the new display at the clinic the other day." Leaning in, she shared more privately, "Dr. Carlisle was always against it. He was very traditional, insisted the clinic should only focus on healthcare."

Sam nodded as she paid, silently agreeing with the late Dr. Carlisle's sentiment.

After a brief drive, Sam reached the brewpub on the edge of Timmons, where the setting sun cast elongated shadows across the parking lot. As she pushed open the heavy, iron and glass door, the vibrant buzz of conversation and the aroma of malt and hops welcomed her. With its eclectic selection of craft beers and a cozy vibe, the pub was clearly a favored hangout.

She spotted James at a table near the back, close to several fermentation tanks. He was seated with two others, all engrossed in their open laptops. As she neared, James caught sight of her, offered a welcoming smile, shut his laptop, and slid it aside.

"Hey, Sam!" James got up to hug her, then stepped back, taking her in. "Did you get a haircut? It looks great."

"It's just a trim, but you always seem to notice the tiniest of details."

"I do, don't I?" he said with a smug grin. "Plus, you're carrying the scent of upscale hair products, which totally isn't your style." As he resettled into his seat, he gestured towards his laptop. "Thanks for giving me some time to work on my article. It's coming along, but," he paused, casting a discreet look around the pub before lowering his voice, "Troy has stumbled onto something interesting."

Before Sam could ask for more details, James introduced the two people sitting opposite him. "Sam, meet

Troy Babbage and Elena Forde. Troy's from Dallas, and Elena's from Houston."

Troy extended his hand with an amiable nod. "Nice to meet you, Sam. I'm from Las Colinas, actually, but no one knows Las Colinas, and everyone knows Dallas."

Elena, with a warm smile, added, "Just Houston for me. It's pretty much swallowed up everything around it."

Sam shook Troy's hand and returned Elena's smile as she sat down at the table's last vacant chair. "Pleasure to meet both of you."

James leaned in, his voice tinged with excitement. "Troy's been following one of the FBI agents who testified at the trial—an Agent Harper."

Sam felt a jolt at the mention of Agent Harper's name, but she managed to mask her reaction with a polite nod.

Troy picked up the thread, his eyes alight with the thrill of the chase. "Yeah, I think he's onto something new, not just the case he's here to testify for. I saw him at one of the businesses here in Timmons, and it looked like they'd just performed a raid."

"Really?" Elena said. "How do you know?"

"They were carrying all kinds of evidence boxes out and taking them away," Troy replied.

"Huh," Sam said, as casually as she could. "Where did you see this?"

Troy pulled out a notepad and flipped it open. "Someplace called 'East Tex Diagnostics.'"

Sam's thoughts were in overdrive. Kelly's account of mysterious men in suits, the lab's closure, and Agent Harper's involvement all clicked together, hinting at a more complex investigation than Sam had imagined. She listened closely to Troy and Elena's theories about Mason's interest in the lab, maintaining a neutral face. James chimed in, occasionally casting curious glances at Sam, as if sensing her inner turmoil.

As the conversation flowed around her, Sam pondered her next move. The link between Mason's probe and her experiences in Dry Wells remained murky. Yet, she couldn't shake the feeling that the threads of these disparate elements might be intertwined.

24

Sam spent Sunday afternoon with James again, both seeking a reprieve from the relentless demands of their jobs. They opted for an escape to the quaint charm of Lufkin, a short drive away, where a vintage movie theater promised a dive into nostalgia. Despite the less-than-stellar acoustics, the grandeur of the theater's old-world architecture provided a welcome distraction, its ornate moldings, velvet curtains framing the stage, and flickering lights from antique chandeliers a reminder of a bygone era.

As they exited, with the fading sunlight casting a soft glow over their faces, James seemed to notice Sam's distant demeanor.

"You've been pretty quiet," he observed, focusing his attention on her as they walked. "Especially last night, when we were talking about that FBI agent's activities. It's almost like you know him or something."

Sam's chuckle came out a bit too hastily, her attempt to lighten the mood almost too eager. "Not really," she said, hoping to end the topic there.

But James, ever the perceptive one, caught the slip. "Not really? Sounds like there's a story there."

"No, there's no story. I happened to meet him because Miranda was in town, and they know each other."

"That's right, Miranda did testify, didn't she?" James recalled, nodding slowly. He was also acquainted with Miranda, having met her around the same time Sam had. Miranda had become a valuable resource for some of his articles.

He kept his eyes on Sam, as if trying to decipher a hidden message. The faint, skeptical arch of his brow spoke volumes, leaving a trail of doubt hanging between them.

She shifted her gaze to evade his. Despite having confided in James before, she found herself reluctant now. Maybe it was the way he'd interacted with his fellow reporters, their relentless pursuit of the next big story making her uneasy. She couldn't shake the fear that her confidences might not stay with him. In the competitive world of journalism, she knew that new friendships often formed over exchanged information, but such exchanges could lead to premature conclusions, and hastily drawn conclusions could easily spiral into disaster.

As they returned to Dry Wells, their conversation naturally evolved, taking on the easy, familiar tone of old friends. They ended up at the diner, since Sam had raved about the pies, and James couldn't resist. When they entered, Cindy greeted them, her warmth as inviting as ever.

They settled into a booth, each ordering a slice of apple pie along with coffee.

Cindy playfully teased, "Are you two an item?" as she poured coffee into their cups.

"We're just friends," Sam replied, exchanging a glance

with James, both dismissing the question with a practiced ease.

Undeterred by their denial, Cindy beamed at them. "Well, I'm just glad you're sticking around a bit longer, Dr. Jenkins. Maybe you'll decide to stay for good one day," she said, her eyes twinkling with hope.

After Cindy's light-hearted comment, the mood at the table shifted subtly. Sam toyed with the edge of her napkin, feeling the magnitude of her decision looming over her like a towering shadow. As she and James discussed her options again, it became evident that he was trying to be supportive, offering advice without bias. However, Sam could sense his underlying concern that she might not find true contentment in such a small, secluded town.

After they'd finished their pies, while James was away in the restroom, Cindy came over. Leaning in and lowering her voice, she asked, "Any updates on Sarah's labs?"

A twinge of guilt stirred within Sam. Mia's results had come in, but Sam hadn't seen if Sarah's were available. There hadn't been any alerts in the system, though, so she shook her head. "Not yet, but I promise to look into it." She studied Cindy's face, noticing a touch of weariness behind her genial façade. "How's she doing?"

"The same." Cindy's shoulders dropped slightly. "I wish we could get to the bottom of it."

"We will," Sam said.

With that, Cindy's eyes sparkled with unwavering belief as she smiled at Sam. "Thank you." She then straightened up, her demeanor shifting seamlessly into her usual cheerfulness, before she moved on to the next table.

Sam inhaled deeply as she watched her walk away, questioning whether she'd made too many promises she might not be able to keep.

Once James returned to the table, he said, "Since you

have tomorrow off, why don't you come to the courthouse with me? See what all the hubbub is about."

"Sure, why not?"

WITH CINDY still on her mind, Sam logged in to the EHR after she got back to her motel, to see if Sarah's labs had come in. However, she found their status still marked as pending.

Feeling unsettled, Sam prepared for bed, her mind racing with the unresolved issues of the patients under her care. The challenge of maintaining professional detachment loomed large; the very dilemma that often led to burnout among healthcare professionals. It was a fine line between caring deeply and becoming too emotionally involved. Yet, to Sam, the essence of being human was to care, even at the risk of caring too much.

THE NEXT MORNING, Sam found the Timmons town square bustling with energy, the fragrance of pine and dew-soaked grass mingling in the air with a palpable sense of expectation. Camera crews from across the state had established their presence around the courthouse, marking out their territories with an array of equipment. Cables sprawled across the pavement while microphones stood ready to catch every utterance. The reporters, attired in sharp suits and elegant dresses, were a vision of professionalism, their hair and makeup flawlessly styled.

The influx of reporters lent an unusual frenzy to the town square. Spectators jostled for room, eager to catch a glimpse of the journalists and their gear, significantly elevating the noise level beyond its typical hum.

Sam paused beside an elderly man who shook his head at the pandemonium. "Never seen Timmons this stirred up before," he muttered.

"Must be tough," Sam remarked, her gaze sweeping over the sea of faces, a wave of compassion swelling within her. She could only imagine how disruptive it must be to have all these outsiders descending on their town, bringing with them their big city chaos.

She weaved her way through the crowd and found James waiting for her outside the courthouse. "Hey, Sam," he said, flashing a smile. "You got here just in time."

They merged with the swarm flowing into the building, gradually forming lines for security. The throng pulled them through at a steady pace, and soon they crossed the threshold. With James navigating, they efficiently made their way to the courtroom and managed to slip inside.

After securing a spot on a bench towards the back, they noticed Troy and Elena a few rows ahead. Elena, catching sight of James, offered a friendly wave. The room buzzed with activity, packed with reporters and spectators alike, all jostling for the best view of the proceedings.

Moments later the jury filed in, followed by the marshal escorting the defendant. Sam craned her neck to catch a glimpse of him, but all she could see was the back of his head. She'd seen his mugshot in news articles online, and there was something familiar about him. She thought perhaps she'd crossed paths with him in med school or residency, at one of the many facilities where she'd rotated. However, based on his training and work history, it seemed unlikely that they'd met before.

The judge finally entered and brought the court to order. The prosecution then continued to lay out their case. To Sam's surprise, their first witness was Agent Harper. Sam listened intently as they interviewed him, but his testimony was pretty droll. It appeared that the only reason why Agent Harper was involved was strictly because of the location of the crime—at the VA hospital, which was federal property. The prosecution tried to expand their questioning, by asking Agent Harper about other cases with defendants similar to the one on trial, but the defense kept objecting, and the prosecution eventually ended their inquiry. The defense had no questions for cross-examination, so the judge excused Agent Harper from the witness stand.

As he walked down the aisle to exit the courtroom, Sam caught his eye, and he gave her a slight nod. Maybe Miranda was right. Maybe Sam should just ask Agent Harper why he'd been at Dr. Carlisle's clinic.

She glanced at James, and fortunately, he hadn't noticed her brief exchange with Harper. He was scribbling in his notebook, as he'd done throughout the testimony, being careful to keep his movements discreet as the judge had banned laptops in the courtroom.

The judge then called a short recess, and as the courtroom began to empty, Sam spotted Bonnie sitting near the front with her cantankerous mother. Bonnie seemed to be completely engrossed in something her mother was saying.

James was still scribbling, so Sam stood up to go say hello, but before she could make her way against the flow of people, Bonnie looked over her shoulder and saw Sam. A look of horror crossed Bonnie's face, and she quickly dashed off through a side door of the courtroom.

Sam stood there, confused and bewildered. Why would Bonnie react that way?

She returned to her seat next to James, who'd stopped

scribbling and was now flipping through his notebook as he reviewed what he'd written.

"That's strange," Sam said as she sat down.

James looked up, his brow furrowed. "What is?" he asked.

"I saw the nurse practitioner I work with, up front," Sam said, pointing towards the spot where Bonnie had been. "She was sitting next to her mother—the older lady up there."

James looked up from his notebook to see where Sam was pointing. "Oh, that's the defendant's mother."

25

Freezing momentarily before she could speak again, Sam asked, "Are you sure?" She hoped it wasn't true.

"Pretty sure," James replied as he continued flipping through his notebook. "At least, that's what Elena told me."

By this time, Troy and Elena had approached, having opted to stay in the courtroom during the brief, fifteen-minute recess.

"I guess they're done with Agent Harper, so he can continue working on whatever case he's involved with," Troy said. "Too bad I need to be here; otherwise, I'd try to follow him."

"Maybe you should ask Sam," James suggested. "She knows him."

Elena and Troy gaped at Sam.

"Why didn't you say anything the other night?" Elena asked.

Raising a hand, Sam clarified, "I don't really know him. He just knows a friend of mine."

James closed his notebook and chimed in. "Sam *says* she met him last week because one of the other witnesses

—Miranda Curran—knows him from this investigation. Sam and Miranda are friends."

"You know her too," Sam said.

"You do?" Troy frowned. "You two are just full of surprises."

James shrugged. "Miranda's an investigator for the Travis County Medical Examiner. Of course I know her." Then he asked Elena, "Sam's curious about how you recognized the woman up there as the defendant's mother." He gestured at Mrs. Wright. "Remember, this morning, you pointed her out before we came in?"

As he was talking, Sam nudged him, and he gave her a puzzled look. She just pursed her lips.

Elena glanced over her shoulder, then turned back to the group. "She just looks like the woman I saw in a photo of the defendant with his mom. But really, I'm not certain. Why do you ask?"

Briefly locking eyes with Sam, James perceived her unvoiced appeal. "We were just wondering."

THE NEXT DAY at the clinic, Sam's thoughts lingered on the previous day's court proceedings. She'd attempted to speak with Bonnie at the trial, but she'd skillfully avoided Sam, eventually leaving for lunch with her mother without returning afterwards. Sam had hoped to catch her before the day's routines kicked in, but Olivia informed her that Bonnie would be coming in late.

Instead, Sam geared herself up for the patients on the packed schedule, including an appointment with Mia Fontaine that promised to be challenging. As she tried to focus on her tasks, however, Bonnie's elusive behavior at the courthouse was never far from her mind.

Upon Bonnie's arrival, Sam offered a welcoming wave, only for Bonnie to avert her gaze and hurry into an exam room with a patient, leaving Sam's questions unanswered.

After Sam saw a few more patients, she got sidetracked taking care of a man with a small laceration on his hand from a box cutter. Since his was an urgent case, some of her scheduled patients had to be pushed back. Olivia had Bonnie help out by seeing a few who'd originally been assigned to see Sam, and by the time Sam finished sewing her last stitch, they were almost back on track.

As Sam's eyes glanced at the name of her next patient, her body tensed, tangling her gut into a tight, queasy knot. She paused momentarily, drawing a lungful of courage-infused air, and nudged open the door to the confines of the exam room.

Perched on the sterile table was Mia Fontaine, her knuckles white against the contrasting darkness of her denim lap, her fingers twisted into a desperate knot. Her gaze, flickering with the same spooked uncertainty Sam remembered from her last visit, was a mirror reflecting her own apprehension.

Natalie Fontaine was standing nearby, tapping her foot impatiently. "Finally," she said as Sam walked in. "We've been waiting for twenty minutes."

Sam plastered on a smile. "I apologize," she said, hoping her tone conveyed sincerity. "I had an emergency with another patient."

Natalie huffed, clearly unimpressed. "Well, can we get started?"

Sam nodded, pulling up Mia's chart on the computer. She started to go over the lab results with them, trying to focus on the clinical details instead of Natalie's overbearing presence.

But it wasn't long before Natalie began to get antsy.

"What does all of this mean?" she cut in. "And what are you going to do about it?"

"To help us figure out the root cause of her condition, we probably need to do more tests."

"More blood tests?" Natalie asked.

Sam leaned forward, her voice soft but firm. "We need to start with an imaging study to understand Mia's condition better. It's called a radioactive iodine uptake test. It sounds more intimidating than it is, but it's crucial for us to find out what's going on with Mia's thyroid."

Natalie's brow furrowed, a mix of worry and confusion in her eyes. "Radiation? That sounds serious. Is it safe?"

Sam nodded, understanding the concern. "Absolutely, it's a very low dose, similar to what we might be exposed to during a few hours of natural background radiation, something we all experience daily. It's a valuable tool for us to see if Mia's thyroid is working too hard, too little, or just right."

"Is that something you can do here?"

Sam shook her head. "It requires specialized equipment. There's an imaging center over in Timmons that offers this type of test."

Natalie's expression tightened, her brows knitting together in a clear sign of annoyance. "Great, one more thing we'll have to do."

Sam took another deep breath, reminding herself to stay calm. She decided not to mention the fact that the study happens in several stages over twenty-four hours. But, there was something else she needed to do first. "Before we order that test, though, I'd like to talk to Mia alone," she said, looking at the teen. "Is that okay with you?"

Mia glanced from Sam to her mother, a moment of hesitation visible in her expression. Then, placid agreement was evident on the teen's face as she offered a soft nod.

Natalie, on the other hand, scowled. "Why do you need to talk to her alone?" she demanded. "I have a right to know what's going on with my daughter."

Sam's jaw tightened before she consciously relaxed it. "Of course, Mrs. Fontaine," she said, "but sometimes, teens feel more at ease talking about their symptoms and concerns without a parent present. It's just a matter of making sure Mia feels comfortable." She didn't dare mention that she still needed to be sure ordering this test was the right thing to do, since there was one explanation that Sam had been wondering about, and only Mia could provide the answer.

Natalie glared at Sam, but after a few moments, seeing that Sam wasn't going to back down, she eventually acquiesced with a grumbled, "Fine." As she left the room, she shot Mia a sharp look.

Once the door closed behind Natalie, the room seemed to breathe a sigh of relief. The space felt more intimate, a private cocoon where Mia could voice her thoughts without fear of judgment.

Turning her attention back to Mia, Sam asked, "How have you been feeling since our last visit?"

The girl hesitated, her eyes darting to the door. "Not great," she finally said in a small voice. "I still feel anxious. And now I'm all jittery."

"Listen," Sam said, perching herself on the edge of the table next to Mia, "I'm here to help you, okay?"

Mia's shoulders slumped forward, her eyes now glued to the floor.

"Have you been feeling pressure to lose weight?" Sam asked, softening her voice.

Mia's lower lip wavered. "Yes," she whispered. "I just want to be skinny, like all the other girls at school."

Sam offered a nod of understanding. "Have you been taking anything?"

The teen paused again before finally admitting, "Yes."

"Can you tell me more?"

Mia shrugged. "I don't know what it is," she said.

"How did you get it?"

"From a friend. He just told me it would help me lose weight."

Sam nodded. "What do the pills look like?"

"They're just little, white."

Sam understood the sensitivity of Mia's circumstances intimately. They found themselves at a pivotal moment, needing to navigate between Mia's desire for privacy and Natalie's responsibilities as her mother. In explaining to Mia the importance of Natalie being informed about her health, given Mia's minor status, Sam could see the apprehension in Mia's eyes.

"I know this isn't easy," Sam said. "But I want to help you, and I need to make sure that your mom is involved in your care. So I really must tell her."

Mia bit her lip, her eyes downcast. "I know," she whispered. "I just don't want her to be mad at me."

Sam placed a reassuring hand on Mia's shoulder. "I understand that you're worried," she said. "But I promise you, I will handle this delicately. We can talk to her together, or if you prefer, I can speak to her first and then bring you in. Whatever you're comfortable with."

Mia's eyes flicked up to meet Sam's, and for a moment, Sam saw the trust and vulnerability in her gaze. "Could you talk to her?" Mia said, her voice small. "But please, don't make her too mad at me."

Sam nodded, her heart breaking for this young girl who was shouldering so much.

When Sam opened the door, Natalie stood right outside the exam room, like she'd been trying to listen in on their conversation.

"What's going on?" she demanded. "What are you telling my daughter?"

Sam held up a hand as she closed the door behind her, keenly aware of the other patients and staff in the hallway. "Let's discuss this in private."

She gently guided Natalie toward Dr. Carlisle's office and refrained from saying anything further, despite Natalie's attempts to ask questions.

Once they were alone, with Sam feeling a little more authoritative behind Dr. Carlisle's desk, she said, "It seems she's been taking something to lose weight."

Natalie's face turned red with anger, her hands clenched at her sides. "What? Why would she do that? What's she taking?" The words tumbled out, edged with disbelief and frustration.

"She doesn't know what it is, but it's probably what's affecting her thyroid levels," Sam explained.

Natalie's eyes narrowed. "Are you accusing Mia of taking drugs?" she asked, her voice rising.

Sam held up her hands. "No, no, I'm not accusing anyone of anything," she said quickly. "I'm just trying to figure out what's going on with Mia. It's possible that she didn't even realize what she was taking."

"How could she do that?"

"Mrs. Fontaine, I know how alarming this must sound. But we need to understand what she's going through and make sure we address it properly."

Natalie stood and paced the small space of the office, her earlier posture of indignation softening with each step, the fury in her eyes dissolving into a pool of worry. "I just . . . I don't understand. I thought I was doing everything right for her," she whispered, more to herself than to Sam.

Seeing an opening, Sam spoke gently, "It's clear how much you care about Mia's success and well-being. But sometimes, children face pressures we might not fully see or understand. It doesn't reflect on your parenting—it shows how challenging it is for kids to navigate their world today." Even as she said this, Sam still felt that Natalie's own ambitions may have contributed to the situation.

Natalie stopped pacing, her gaze settling on the framed picture of Dr. Carlisle's family on the desk. Her voice cracked as she turned back to Sam, the hard edges of her demeanor eroded by a tide of realization and fear. "I've been pushing her, haven't I? Always on her about her grades, her activities . . . I thought I was helping her be her best."

Sam nodded, offering a sympathetic smile. "It's a fine line. Parents push because they want the best for their kids, but sometimes, it's about stepping back and asking what they need. Right now, Mia needs your support to navigate through this."

As Sam spoke, Natalie's face, once a mask of defiance and control, softened, vulnerability seeping through the cracks of her composed exterior. Tears, unbidden, welled up in her eyes, the floodgates of her defenses yielding under the force of insight and fear. "I just want my daughter to be happy and healthy. I didn't mean to . . . I didn't see."

"It's okay," Sam reassured her. "The good news is, we're here now, and we can work together to support Mia. Let's focus on understanding her needs and how we can help her feel better."

As they walked back into the exam room to face Mia

together, Natalie's approach had softened. Her earlier anger was replaced by a resolve to listen, to understand, and most importantly, to support her daughter through this challenge. Mia looked up, a flicker of hope in her eyes as she saw the change in her mother.

Natalie embraced her daughter in a way that Sam didn't think was possible after the first time they'd met. Then they turned to Sam, ready to listen.

Sam explained that she needed to examine the pills Mia had been taking to determine whether they were indeed levothyroxine or another form of synthetic thyroid hormone, as well as the dosage Mia had been on. This information was crucial for devising a plan, if she needed to taper Mia off. Given Mia's description of the medication as a white pill, Sam suspected the dosage wasn't very high, but she had to be sure.

"Does she still need that radioactive test?" Natalie asked.

"No, not if the pills are what we think they are. That would explain everything."

As mother and daughter left the room and walked down the hallway to the front office, Sam could hear Natalie say, "It's because I was pushing you to try out for the cheer team, isn't it?"

Maybe there is hope for their relationship after all, Sam thought.

She now wondered where Mia's friend had gotten those pills, but Mia refused to give up her friend's name because she didn't want to get him in trouble. She'd have to look into it more later—the next patient poked his head out of an exam room door to ask how much longer he had to wait. It seemed like Sam would always be running behind.

26

As the clock inched closer to noon, Sam's attention increasingly wavered during visits, often leading her to ask patients to repeat themselves as her mind drifted.

Her focus was fractured. On one front, she was troubled by the mystery of how Mia had gotten her hands on the pills she'd been taking. On the other, she was consumed by Bonnie's connection to the ongoing trial, a puzzle that deepened with each of Bonnie's calculated attempts to avoid her. Whenever she saw Bonnie, who would quickly change course or slip into a patient room at the sight of Sam, it only fueled her curiosity, which was beginning to transform into irritation.

Why was Bonnie so intent on avoiding any conversation with her? What was she hiding? Sam's frustration grew with every evasion, her professional concern intertwined with a personal drive to uncover the truth behind Bonnie's elusive behavior.

Determined to resolve this and put an end to the game of cat-and-mouse, Sam took decisive action after seeing her final patient of the morning. She tracked down Bonnie and found her in the break room. There, Bonnie sat alone, quietly eating a homemade salad, seemingly engrossed in her thoughts.

Sam inhaled deeply, the scent of brewed coffee and disinfectant mingling in the air, as she stepped into the break room. "Got a minute?"

Bonnie looked up, surprise flickering across her face before she masked it with a polite nod. "Sure," she said, though her voice wavered, betraying her reluctance.

"Sorry to interrupt your lunch," Sam said, easing into the seat next to Bonnie. She paused and scanned Bonnie's face, searching for a clue, any indication of how to delicately approach the pressing question on her mind. Bracing for what was to come, she leaned forward slightly, the words slipping out in a rush of boldness fueled by necessity. "I saw you at the trial yesterday . . . Is Dr. Morton your brother?" Her eyes searched Bonnie's, looking for the truth that lay hidden behind them.

Bonnie's gaze dropped to her hands, trembling like leaves in a light breeze. "Yes," she whispered.

Sam's tone lightened, seeking understanding rather than expressing shock. "Why didn't you tell me?" Her eyes met Bonnie's with a look of genuine curiosity. It wasn't so much a question of accusation but an invitation for Bonnie to share her perspective.

Bonnie exhaled a weary sigh, a sound heavy with unspoken sorrow and the weight of secrets too burdensome to bear alone. "I didn't want you to treat me differently," she admitted, her voice low, as if the words were difficult to push past her lips.

As she spoke, her eyes glazed over, locking onto a vision only she could see. "I wanted to keep it separate from work with you. I mean . . . everyone else in this small town knows—you can't really keep any secrets here. But at least with you . . . you're new here, and you didn't know all the history, all the details."

The pieces finally fell into place for Sam, as the clues and hints from the past two weeks came together. Initially, she'd thought people were treating Bonnie delicately because of the challenges of managing her mother's dementia. However, she now understood that these interactions were connected to an entirely different matter.

Bonnie shook her head, a small, almost imperceptible movement that conveyed her turmoil and indecision. "I knew you'd find out eventually, and I kept trying to find the right way to tell you, especially since we really want you to stay. But, I just . . . I didn't know how." Her voice faded, the last words barely audible as she reached for a tissue, her movements slow and hesitant.

"I understand," Sam murmured, her voice warm and devoid of any judgment. "The weight you've been carrying . . . I can't even begin to imagine." She waited a moment, giving Bonnie's revelation the space it deserved, before gently probing further. "Being there yesterday, at the trial, how was that for you?"

Bonnie paused, biting her bottom lip. "I just . . . I needed to be there," she eventually confessed, each word echoing the depth of her personal turmoil. "He is my brother, after all, and my mother insisted I go, especially since I had the day off." As she spoke, a vulnerable sniff broke through. She reached for another tissue, delicately dabbing her nose. "It's so hard," she continued, her voice trembling slightly, "because even after everything that's happened, she still puts him on a pedestal."

Each utterance she made was taut, as if ready to break free, yet restrained by a dense web of reluctance.

Sam's fingers twitched with the urge to reach out, to gently unravel the knots of Bonnie's story, seeking the clarity hidden within. Yet, she remained still, acutely aware of the delicate dance of their growing connection. Her gaze lingered on Bonnie, catching the faint glimmer of newly formed tears in her eyes, a silent signal of her inner turmoil. Sam knew all too well what it was like to have a parent whose expectations crushed you instead of lifting you up.

The space between them was charged with an unspoken understanding, a boundary drawn not just by professionalism but by a budding trust, compelling Sam to tread lightly, respecting the fragile bridge they were building.

"I'm so sorry," Sam offered softly, her voice carrying a warmth meant to comfort.

A shadow of a smile, brief but genuine, flickered across Bonnie's face as she acknowledged Sam's concern with a subdued nod. "Thank you, Dr. Jenkins," she murmured. "I really appreciate it."

Leaving the break room, Sam caught a flicker of clarity in the space between her and Bonnie, a slight easing of the tension. However, Bonnie's hesitations, the careful choice of words, and the occasional silence that stretched a bit too long painted a picture of untold stories. Annoyance simmered within Sam, a realization dawning on her: Bonnie's eagerness for her to stay in Dry Wells had been shadowed by the omission of crucial details. As she walked away, Sam's mind churned with unanswered questions about Bonnie and the tightly knit fabric of this community that seemed to have selectively filtered what she should know.

It was a silent reminder to Sam that, despite the moment of connection, Bonnie was still guarding parts of her story closely—leaving Sam enveloped in a mist of uncertainty yet filled with a resolve to be there when Bonnie was ready to share more. In the end, Sam clung to her steadfast belief, refusing to taint the innocent with a culprit's brush—a belief that not all who stand with the guilty are guilty themselves.

27

In the quiet moments between patients that afternoon, Sam found herself reflecting on the revealing conversation with Bonnie, feeling its impact amidst the clinic's bustling activity. Each interaction with her patients served as a lighthouse, illuminating her path and reminding her of her purpose amidst the unfolding mysteries of Dry Wells. The difference between the tangible clarity of her medical responsibilities and the intangible complexities of personal connections and hidden truths within the community was stark.

During a brief lull, Sam seized a few minutes of solitude in the hallway, standing at the computer to strategize for the rest of the week. She deliberated over her next moves to assist Mia and contemplated actions to support Luann, to make sure she was safe, before Sam's departure.

Suddenly, Cindy burst through the door to the front office with a force that echoed down the quiet hallway, her grip on Sarah's arm just tight enough to convey urgency without causing harm. Sarah stumbled slightly behind her mother, a shadow of reluctance in her steps. As Sam's eyes met theirs, she couldn't help but notice the fear etched into Cindy's features—her brows knitted together, eyes wide and darting, as if scanning for threats. Sarah's face was a canvas of confusion and fright, her lips pressed into a thin line, the color drained from her cheeks, making her look ghostly under the fluorescent lights.

"Is everything okay?" Sam asked, moving closer to the pair.

Cindy acted swiftly, retrieving a clear baggie filled with pills from her purse and extending it toward Sam. "I found these in Sarah's bathroom," she said. "I don't know what they are, but they've got me really scared."

Sam gestured with her arm, guiding Cindy and Sarah to Dr. Carlisle's office for more privacy. Just as she was closing the door, Olivia appeared in the hallway, curious about the unfolding situation. "Don't worry, I've got this," Sam assured her, before shutting the door.

After sitting down at the desk, with Cindy and Sarah positioned in the chairs opposite her, Sam took the baggie and began examining the pills inside. Containing about thirty, she pinched the bag with her fingers, isolating one in a corner for a clearer view through the plastic. It was a white, capsule-shaped tablet, slightly narrower than her thumbnail, marked with an "M" on one side. On the reverse side, there was an "L" and a "5", separated by a score mark to facilitate splitting the pill in half. As she focused on the tablet, a sudden wave of guilt washed over Sam. It was the same guilt that had struck her in the diner the other night when Cindy had inquired about Sarah's labs. Despite her intentions, Sam had let it slip through the cracks amidst the maelstrom of the last couple of days. "I'm so sorry, Cindy. You asked about Sarah's labs, and I've neglected to follow through. Let me pull them up now."

"Do you think it will help? What do the labs have to do with the pills?" Cindy asked anxiously.

"It might," Sam said as she started typing on the keyboard.

While waiting for Sam to access the lab results, both mother and daughter fidgeted nervously, shifting in their seats. With a few clicks, Sam brought up the data on her screen. The results revealed that Sarah's lab patterns mirrored Mia's: elevated levels of T4 and T3, along with a high TSH.

Cindy must have noticed a change in Sam's expression, because she said, "What? What is it?"

"Hang on just a second, while I check on something else." Sam then pulled up a pill identifier website. She picked up the baggie again, studying the pill she'd isolated to make sure she entered the details for the search into the computer correctly. Imprint, color, shape. Clicking "Search," the results came up instantaneously. Levothyroxine sodium 50 mcg. The generic version of Synthroid.

When Sam looked up, Cindy was watching her expectantly, while Sarah focused on her lap as she picked at her fingernails.

"What's going on?" Cindy asked.

"These pills are levothyroxine," Sam began, "which is a synthetic thyroid hormone. And Sarah's lab results suggest she's been taking this medication." She paused, allowing Cindy a moment to absorb the information, aware of the sensitive request she was about to make. "I understand you have many questions, but could I have a word with Sarah in private for a moment?"

Confusion and disappointment intertwined in Cindy's eyes as she glanced between Sarah, who kept her gaze lowered, and Sam. She nodded and then stood up. "Sure, Doctor. I trust you. You know what's best."

"No, it's okay," Sarah said, turning her head to look up at her mom. "You can stay."

Sam observed the tumult of emotions on Cindy's face, where worry and fierce protectiveness swirled together. Her furrowed brows and tense frown seemed at odds with the soft, steadfast light in her eyes—a beacon of motherly love offering safety amidst chaos. Then, gradually, the edge of concern softened, as the tender affection started to become prominent. Sarah's words had acted as a key, a password that allowed her mother to step back into her life, bridging the distance that had formed between them.

As Cindy took her seat again, Sam found herself reflecting on the contrast between the relationship of this mother-daughter duo and the one she had encountered earlier in the day. She turned to Sarah, taking a brief pause to center herself, keenly aware of the delicate situation, shaping her lips into an encouraging smile, offering silent reassurance. Drawing a steady breath, she asked in a voice that mixed firmness with kindness, "Could you tell me where you got these pills from?"

For a long moment, Sarah remained silent, her gaze flitting between the worn carpet and the concerned faces before her. The air seemed to thicken with anticipation, each second stretching longer than the last. A tremble coursed through her hands, clasped tightly in her lap as if holding onto the words that threatened to spill. Her eyes then lingered on her mother's anxious face, seeking reassurance in the familiar lines of worry etched there. The tears brimming in her eyes betrayed the turmoil churning inside her—a battle between the fear of consequences and the burden of her secret. Finally, with a voice frayed at the edges by emotion, she whispered, "I'm sorry, I can't."

Cindy turned to her daughter, her eyes filled with a mix

of hope and urgency. "Please, Sarah, you have to tell us. We just want to help you."

"That's right, we're here to help," Sam added, keeping her voice level. "Not to judge. But we need to know what's going on so we can figure out the best way to take care of you."

For a moment, Sarah seemed to retreat further into herself, her shoulders hunched as if bracing against an invisible storm. As she looked down at her lap again, her fingers continued to twist her shirt nervously. "I don't want to get anyone in trouble."

"I know you're reluctant to tell us," Sam said, "but it's important for us to know because if others are taking these pills, we need to help them as well."

Sarah seemed to collapse inward, her once restless movements ceasing as a heavy silence fell over her, the burden of her secret anchoring her to the spot. Sam could barely make out the young girl's face, partially obscured by the untamed tendrils of her hair falling forward. Yet, beneath this veil, she could almost envision the gears spinning in Sarah's mind, tirelessly working through the alternatives before her.

"It was . . ." she began, her voice fragile and laced with shame. She paused, swallowing hard, as if the words were physical objects she had to force out. "I got them from . . . from someone at school."

Cindy adjusted her chair, turning her whole body towards Sarah, her eyes filled with a mix of concern and unwavering love. With a gentle but firm grasp, she took Sarah's hands in her own, blending urgency with the warmth of a mother's touch. Her voice, soft yet insistent, carried the weight of her worry and the depth of her care. "Who?" she asked, leaning in closer to bridge not just the physical distance between them but the chasm of fear and uncertainty. "Like Dr. Jenkins said, we need to know . . . so we can help them too."

Sarah hesitated, her silence stretched on, a tangible manifestation of her internal struggle. Her eyes darted away, seeking refuge in any corner of the room that didn't demand answers or bear witness to her vulnerability. The pressure of the question seemed to clamp down on her, squeezing the air from her lungs, as she wrestled with the fear of betraying a confidence against the gravity of her current situation. Finally, after what felt like an eternity, her voice emerged—barely louder than a breath, laced with the heavy burden of reluctance. "Mia. I got them from Mia."

This confirmed Sam's suspicions. However, she couldn't disclose that she had seen Mia earlier that day for a similar issue. Mia hadn't revealed her source for the pills, assuming they were the same as those on the desk in front of her. Sam had to navigate this situation carefully to avoid breaching patient confidentiality.

"Can you tell me where Mia got them from?" she asked.

Sarah shook her head. "She just said they would help me lose weight."

Sam nodded. "Do you know if anyone else has been taking these pills?" she asked.

Sarah shook her head once more, her eyes wide with fear. "I don't know," she admitted, her voice trembling. "I just wanted to fit in, you know? All the girls at school are so thin, and I wanted to be like them."

Sam leaned forward, resting her arms flat on the desk, attempting to strike a balance between connecting with the teen and emphasizing the gravity of her actions."I understand how you feel," she said gently. "But taking medication without a doctor's supervision . . . it can be dangerous, especially if you don't know what you're taking . . . or how much."

Sarah nodded, her lower lip trembling as the tears that had pooled in her eyes finally breached the barriers, tracing paths down her cheeks. "I know," she said, her voice cracking. "I'm sorry."

"It's alright," Sam reassured, pulling a tissue out of the box on the desk and offering it to the teen. "I'm not here to judge you. I just want to help you get better. But I need you to be honest with me. Are you taking anything else that I should know about?"

Sarah shook her head as she dabbed her eyes. "No, just those pills," she said.

As Sam studied the baggie of pills, a series of chilling thoughts crossed her mind. *Where did Mia get these? Were any other kids taking them? And how deep does this go?*

She tried asking Sarah one more time, "Are you sure you don't know where Mia got these from? Any rumors? Anything you've heard from the other kids at school?"

Sarah's face crumpled. "I'm sorry, but I really don't know," she sobbed. "All I know is that Mia said they were safe."

Cindy asked, "Are you sure you don't know anything else? What about the other girls in theater?" Her voice was gentle, but insistent.

Relaxing a little, apparently from her mom's calming demeanor, Sarah shook her head again. "No. She just acted super secretive, said I couldn't talk to anybody about it."

As Cindy attempted to coax more information from Sarah regarding where Mia might have obtained the pills, Sam's mind continued to race with possibilities. Since these pills required a prescription, someone had to be providing them. But who?

She hadn't heard back from the pharmacist yet. Maybe he would find something to go on. She'd have to give him a call.

And Sam could discuss this with Bonnie, but after what had happened the day before, along with how Bonnie had avoided her this morning, she found herself harboring some reservations.

As she thought through possible plans for what she could do next, Cindy's voice brought her back to the situation in front of her.

"I could call Natalie," Cindy said. "Mia's mother. Maybe she knows something." Then she rolled her eyes. "If she'll even talk to me . . . She's always treated me like I'm beneath her."

Cindy's mention of Natalie stirred memories of the encounter earlier that day, along with Sam's shared sentiment, yet she concealed her reaction behind a veil of professionalism. After a moment, she said, "That's okay. I have a couple of ideas for how I might find out who's behind this." She picked up the plastic baggie with the pills. "In the meantime, I need to keep these."

28

After Cindy and Sarah left, Sam saw two more patients before retreating back into Dr. Carlisle's office to work on her notes. The setting sun cast long shadows across the floor, bathing the room in a warm, yet somber light. Leaning back, she sighed deeply, feeling the clinic's walls reflect her sense of duty amid the day's revelations and confessions. The baggie of pills represented the mystery she was determined to unravel: who supplied Mia with these meds, and why? Feeling the urgency of the situation, yet recognizing she couldn't solve this alone, Sam contemplated her next move. She'd start with the pharmacist.

She looked up the number for the pharmacy on the computer and punched it into the pad on the desk phone. After a few rings, the line picked up. "Dry Wells Pharmacy. Howard speaking. How can I help you?" She was a little surprised he answered the phone himself.

"Hi, Howard. This is Samantha Jenkins. I stopped by the other day."

"Of course, Dr. Jenkins. I remember," Howard said.

"I've been meaning to call you. My son ran those reports you asked about. We scoured those prescriptions, finer than a comb through cotton. But everything looks as regular as clockwork. No strange spikes in numbers or anything unusual with the dosages. Care to share more details about what you're lookin' for? Maybe there's another way I can assist you." Howard's tone was a blend of curiosity and concern.

Keeping the conversation broad, she informed him about the abnormal thyroid function tests, mentioning their ties to Synthroid use, along with her goal to track down the source of the pills.

"That's a real noodle scratcher," Howard mused after listening. "From what we've seen, our Synthroid's been going out steady to the regular crowd. We're mighty careful about keeping prescriptions on the up and up. But you know, with the internet nowadays, along with all those mail order outfits, folks have ways of getting things that don't always involve us."

"You're right about that," Sam conceded, feeling a bit disheartened but not surprised. "Any thoughts on what my next steps should be?"

Howard didn't hesitate. "I reckon you might want to check in with the other pharmacies around here, see if they've seen anything out of the ordinary. Might also be worth having a chat with the Sheriff. He could have insights into things we don't."

"Those are some good ideas." Sam mulled over the information he'd given her. This was ballooning into a bigger investigation than she'd expected. How could she, as a single individual, without any real authority, get to the bottom of it? "Well, thank you for looking into it for me."

"Anytime," Howard said.

Shortly after she hung up, the door to the office

creaked open, and Olivia's head poked through the gap. "I've locked up the front door, Dr. Jenkins. The last patient just left."

"Thanks, Olivia," Sam said, her voice reflecting her exhaustion more than she realized. "I've got a few more things to finish, then I'll take off. Are you leaving now? I could lock up like I did the other day—you know, go through the break room again."

"That's okay. I have some things I need to do up front." Olivia lingered a moment more, then asked, "Have you given any more thought to my offer?"

Sam sighed, her fingers absently tracing the edge of the desk. "I'm sorry, but I'm still thinking about it. It's a big decision, and I want to make sure it's the right one." Then she remembered her conversation with Renee. "However, I have a friend who's board certified in family medicine, and she told me she'd love to practice in a town like Dry Wells. Do you want me to connect you with her?"

Olivia considered this for a moment. "Perhaps, but, really, I think you're the perfect person for us." She patted the doorframe. "Anyway, take your time, Doctor. I just want you to know how grateful I am that you stayed for another week. And that everyone really appreciates you here." With a small smile, she disappeared.

Alone again, Sam reflected on the suggestions Howard had offered. She dug Sheriff Perkins's card out of her bag and dialed his number. She drummed her fingers nervously on the desk as the phone rang.

"Perkins," the sheriff answered, his voice gravelly and warm.

"Hi, Sheriff. It's Samantha Jenkins."

"Dr. Jenkins, what an unexpected surprise. How can I help you?"

"I was wondering if you could assist me with something."

"Is this about the individual we were discussing the last time we met?" Sheriff Perkins asked, concern evident in his voice.

"What?" Sam furrowed her brow, momentarily taken aback. "Wait—has anything happened? Is she alright?"

The sheriff paused before answering, his tone guarded. "I stopped by to check on her after our last conversation. I heard she's had a rough time lately, and I wanted to make sure she was okay."

"When was this?" Sam asked. He was right—a lot had happened with Luann in the past week. And it certainly was true, that nothing stayed secret long in this small town. Yet, she couldn't shake the feeling of being an outsider, still looking in.

"I went by a couple days ago," Sheriff Perkins said. "I heard she'd been ill."

Sam hesitated before answering, wary of revealing too much. But, having not received any updates about Luann since visiting her house, curiosity got the better of her. "How was she?"

"Reserved, as usual, but she seemed okay."

Sam nodded to herself, her heart aching for her. She'd have to stop by this evening to see how Luann was doing, but for now, she faced another pressing issue. "I'm glad you checked on her, but that's not why I called. I, uh . . . I have some pills that a couple of teenage girls at the high school have been taking to lose weight. I'd like to get them analyzed, and I'm not sure if there's a crime that needs to be reported—at least, not at this stage." Even though she was fairly certain that these pills were synthetic thyroid hormone, she needed to be sure.

"I'm sorry, Dr. Jenkins, we just don't have the resources

for something like that. But tell me more about the situation. Who's involved?"

Sam hesitated, her loyalty to her patients wrestling with the need for the truth. "I'm not sure I can give you all the details right now. I don't want to point fingers when I don't know the whole story yet."

She could hear the tension in the sheriff's voice as he replied, "You know I'll do what I can, but you're asking me about a possible crime. I need something to go on."

"I understand. I have an idea, though," Sam said, as she remembered who Sheriff Perkins had called when he needed help to investigate the case leading to the trial going on in Timmons. "I'll let you know when I have more information."

The sheriff didn't sound completely satisfied, but he accepted her response. "Alright, Doctor. Keep me in the loop."

After she hung up the desk phone, she pulled out her cell and dialed Miranda's number. Her friend's expertise as a forensic nurse and medical examiner investigator was the lifeline she needed. But the call went directly to voicemail.

"Hey, Miranda," Sam began, her voice steady despite the uncertainty churning in her gut. "It's Sam. I need your help with something. Give me a call back when you can."

Sam slid her phone into her pocket and scooped up her things, with the baggie of pills and its mysteries tucked inside her bag. The clinic's halls were hushed and dim, an aura of stillness pervading the air as she made her way to the front office, her thoughts clouded by the unknown. She hadn't made any progress on her charting, but after speaking with the sheriff, she was compelled to drop by Luann's house.

She waved goodbye to Olivia as she walked through the waiting room and then stepped outside. The scent of the evening air, tinged with the aroma of damp earth and moss, greeted her. The clinic door slowly swung shut behind her, the click of the latch echoing in the quiet evening.

As the sun dipped below the horizon, Sam drove toward Luann's house. When she turned down a side street, she thought she saw Sheriff Perkins's cruiser on the cross street behind her in the rearview mirror. If he'd been so close, why hadn't he said so on the call?

She shrugged to herself. Maybe it wasn't him. Maybe it was one of the deputies.

She gripped her steering wheel, focusing on her current mission: to check on Luann.

29

In the fading daylight, Sam's car rumbled along the gravel streets, shadows stretching long and dark. She pulled into the driveway of the Clark residence, cut the engine, and took a deep breath, steeling herself for the confrontation that might follow. Chipped white paint clung to the house's sides, weathered by time. The flowerbed's wilted plants and brown leaves whispered stories of neglect.

She stepped out of her car, and instantly, the front door flew open. Isaac stood there, with a scowl deep and unwelcoming, tension radiating from his towering presence. His tall, broad-shouldered frame cast an imposing shadow over the small yard as he approached Sam, his stride full of purpose. He stopped at the edge of the carport, the disassembled stacks of parts behind him like the flanks of an army.

"What do you want?" His voice was a growl, dripping with hostility.

"I'm just here to check on Luann," Sam replied, her voice calm and steady despite the tension coiling within her. "It's been a few days since I've seen her, and I wanted to make sure she's alright."

Isaac crossed his arms, his eyes narrowing as he studied Sam. "Luann isn't here right now. She's gone to her mother's house."

Sam's spirits lifted. At least Luann wasn't here, with this man—for now.

"Take care of your own business, Doc," he spat. He turned on his heel and strode back into the house, slamming the door behind him.

The sound pierced the quiet evening air like a bullet's report. Standing alone in the driveway, a wave of frustration washed over her, isolating and intense. Isaac's disdain, a cold slap to her concern.

She would just text Luann and find out how she was doing directly.

As she reached for her phone, it began to vibrate, the screen lighting up with Miranda's name. The call from her friend sparked a mix of relief and keen anticipation. Maybe she'd get the insights she desperately needed.

"Thanks for calling back so quickly," Sam said as she slid back into the driver's seat of her car. "I've got a situation here, and I could really use your help."

"Sure," Miranda said. "What's going on?"

"I've come across some pills I need tested. Any idea how I can get that done?"

Miranda began to list off several options, and as Sam listened to her response, she couldn't help but cast one last glance at Luann's house.

"Wait a second," Miranda said. "Why do you need to have these pills tested? Where did you get them from?"

Sam switched the phone's audio to speaker so she could keep talking while she backed out of the Clark's driveway. "The mother of one of my patients brought them in after she'd found them in her daughter's bathroom. Apparently she'd gotten them from a friend because she'd been trying to lose weight."

"Are there any markings on the pills? Have you used one of the pill identifier websites to look up what they are?"

"I did," Sam said. "It looks like they're levothyroxine, and the girl's labs suggest factitious hyperthyroidism." Normally, Sam wouldn't have shared that much information about one of her patients, but she knew Miranda was trustworthy. Plus, she had no way of knowing who Sam was talking about. They were just two professionals discussing cases, like a curbside consult.

"Huh," Miranda said. "So why do you need to have them tested then? It sounds like you have pretty good evidence for what they are."

"Because she's my patient, and I want to make sure that I'm treating her appropriately, to see if I need to taper her off or not." Sam said. "But you're right, it is pretty clear what's going on."

"Have you reported this? Do you know who gave them to her?"

"I called the sheriff to ask the same question I asked you about testing, but he said the county doesn't have the resources. Then I realized I don't even know what to report. The girls are the victims."

"There's more than one?"

"Yeah, two of my patients—I think, anyway. I only have the pills from one, but she said she got them from the other. And that girl isn't saying who gave her the pills. So, if there is a crime, if there's a guilty party, it's really the person selling these pills."

"You're right about that."

"So, what should I do?"

"Well, I have some ideas—" Miranda began, then stopped. "But are you sure you want to be investigating this?"

"I want to help these girls, and I'll bet they're not the only ones involved."

"Maybe you could talk to the school nurse," Miranda suggested, "as one professional to another. I'm sure they see lots of things going on in the student population."

"That's a good idea," Sam said as she turned into her motel parking lot.

James was there, leaning against the hood of his car, a solitary figure under the flickering motel lights. She'd forgotten their dinner plans.

"I've gotta go," Sam said. "I'm back at my motel and James is waiting for me."

"How's the trial going?" Miranda asked. "Have you heard anything new?"

"Since I had the day off, I sat in the courtroom yesterday. And I saw Agent Harper on the stand. But not much else happened."

James knocked on Sam's window, looking mildly impatient, tapping his watchless wrist.

"Anyway, James is getting antsy. I'll find out if anything interesting happened today."

"Well, tell him I said, 'hi,' and fill me in on the details for the trial—and the pills—when you get a chance."

"I will."

30

Under the rising moon's watchful eye, Sam and James made their way into the diner, its exterior awash in a serene lunar light that seeped inside, casting a soft, ethereal illumination across the checkered floor and the red vinyl booths. Sam breathed a sigh of relief when she saw that Cindy wasn't working that night; she wasn't quite ready to answer all of Cindy's questions. At least, not yet.

They slid into a booth near the window, and the conversation soon turned to the trial in Timmons. He admitted, "The testimony can be a bit dry, and sometimes it's hard for me to focus on exactly what's going on."

As Sam empathized with him over the tedious nature of court proceedings, her thoughts drifted back to Bonnie and her brother. She trusted James more than anyone, yet she had reservations about sharing the day's revelations with him. Her hesitation wasn't due to a lack of trust in him, but rather a concern about his overzealous colleagues. After she'd subtly nudged him in the courtroom the previous day during their conversation with Elena about the defendant's—and Bonnie's—mother, he seemed to understand that he should not press Sam on the issue. Once they finished their slices of pie—the very reason James had traveled to Dry Wells to have dinner with Sam—he dropped her off at her motel before returning to his hotel in Timmons.

Even though she was physically and emotionally exhausted, Sam opened her laptop, determined to finish up a couple of charts. Then she remembered, she'd wanted to see how Luann was doing. She quickly texted Luann, saying she'd stopped by to check on her and that Isaac mentioned she was staying with her mom.

Luann responded within a few minutes that she was indeed at her mother's house, and that she was doing well. She thanked Sam and said she'd see her for an appointment the next day.

Feeling reassured, and with a rerun of *Law and Order* playing in the background, Sam finished her notes, then scrolled through the clinic's records again. Why were so many of Dr. Carlisle's patients diagnosed with hypothyroidism?

She filtered for the condition and noticed Sally's name pop up the list. Not too surprising, although Sally was on the younger side for those who were usually afflicted. Of course, Sam wouldn't talk to Sally about it, if they were to see each other again. She wouldn't want Sally to know she'd been snooping around in her medical record.

The show finished, and having not found any new answers in her search, Sam closed her laptop and got ready for bed. She'd tackle this problem with a fresh approach after a good night's rest.

~

The next morning, Sam looked out the window of Dr. Carlisle's office at the fog enveloping the clinic as she held the phone to her ear. She glanced at the clock and sighed; it was already shaping up to be another busy day. Despite this, she'd decided to take a few minutes to continue pursuing the source of those pills. Finally, the high school receptionist transferred her call.

"Nurse's office, this is Linda Becker speaking," a frazzled voice answered.

"Hi, Nurse Becker, this is Dr. Samantha Jenkins from the Dry Wells clinic."

"Oh, yes, I've heard about you. Rumor has it that you might be taking over Dr. Carlisle's practice. Is that true?"

"Well, uh . . . I'm considering it. But the reason I'm calling is because I have a few questions about a medication that may be circulating around the school."

"If you've got questions about opioids," Linda said, "the sheriff has a task force with one of his deputies and a K-9 unit dropping by the school for regular visits. They started the program last year, and it seems to have curtailed some of the issues we'd been having."

"Actually, my question isn't about opioids," Sam said. "It's about something else. Have you noticed anything out of the ordinary? Any kids exhibiting unusual symptoms?"

"I have been dealing with all sorts of problems lately—mainly a lot of somatic complaints since school started." Linda paused a moment, then said, "You know, there is one thing—I called Dr. Carlisle to discuss it before he passed away, but we never had the chance to talk."

Sam's interest piqued. "What did you want to discuss with Dr. Carlisle?"

Before Linda could answer, a commotion erupted in the background. "Hold on," she said, her voice becoming muffled as it sounded like she'd covered up the handset while she spoke to someone else. A moment later she came back clearly on the line. "A student just came in, says he vomited."

Sam's concern deepened, but before she could press further, Kelly appeared at the door. "Dr. Jenkins, one of your patients who just arrived has another appointment soon. They need to see you immediately."

Sam sighed. She'd have to wait to probe further into this situation. "Can I stop by later to talk with you?"

"It's usually quiet during the lunch periods—could you stop by then?"

Sam quickly scanned her afternoon schedule. It didn't look too crazy, with only one patient scheduled immediately after lunch, and then Luann's visit a little later in the day. "Okay, I can do that."

After she hung up, she continued seeing patients until she had only one more appointment for the morning, shortly before noon. At that point, she and Bonnie happened to be in the hallway at the same time, so Sam took the opportunity to check in with her.

"I have to go to the high school to talk to the nurse during lunch. It shouldn't take too long, but if I'm not back in time, could you cover for me? I see only one patient on the schedule at one o'clock."

Bonnie, clearly preoccupied with her own concerns, tacitly agreed. "Yeah, that should be fine."

Olivia, who happened to be watching the exchange, approached Sam with a hopeful look in her eyes. "I'm glad you're taking the initiative to meet the nurse at the high school. Maybe it's a sign that you'll stay?"

Sam offered a noncommittal smile, her thoughts too tangled to give Olivia a clear answer, before she stepped into the next exam room.

UPON ARRIVING at the high school, Sam noticed the approaching cold front on the horizon, signaling the forecasted rain. She considered bringing her umbrella inside but ultimately decided against it, confident there was sufficient time before the onset of the downpour.

As she approached the building, her eyes settled on the locked double doors, their metal frames slightly weathered with time. Above the entrance, the school's name was etched in bold letters, a proud declaration of its identity: Dry Wells High School. The surrounding brick façade was aged but well-maintained, with ivy creeping up the walls, softening the building's stern appearance. To one side, a flagpole stood tall, with the American and Texas flags fluttering gently in the breeze.

A sign to the right of the doors, above a small metal box mounted on the wall, instructed visitors to use the intercom to speak with the front office. The amount of security unnerved her, a reminder of how much had changed since her own high school days.

She pressed the well-worn button, and after a moment, a tinny voice came through the grill covering the speaker. "Can I help you?"

Sam leaned over to speak into the intercom. "Hi, I'm Dr. Samantha Jenkins. I have an appointment with Linda Becker, the school nurse."

After a brief pause, the doors buzzed, and Sam was granted entry. She signed in at the front office, received a visitor's name tag, and was directed down the hall to the nurse's office.

She entered the small room, the walls adorned with posters illustrating proper hand-washing techniques and the dangers of drug abuse. A counter stretched along one wall, covered with medical supplies and paperwork organized in bins and trays, while a student lay on one of the cushioned exam tables. A skeleton wearing a cowboy hat, with a stethoscope hanging around its neck, stood in one corner, a silent witness to the countless students who had sought care in this office.

The nurse, a middle-aged woman with short, wavy hair streaked with gray, typed on a computer, which was partially hidden behind a small privacy screen in another corner next to a tall, gray filing cabinet. She looked up and greeted Sam with a smile. "Dr. Jenkins, welcome. Do you mind waiting a moment while I get this student situated for dismissal?"

Sam nodded, understanding the need to prioritize the student's care. The bell rang, signaling the end of the class period, and the student, looking a bit woozy, slowly got up. Linda asked her gently, "Are you sure you don't want me to call your mom?"

The student took a deep breath, then said, "Mom can't take off work no more. I'll be okay." After a few moments, she seemed a little steadier on her feet. Linda finally nodded and allowed the girl to leave.

Once they were alone, Linda turned to Sam. "I suppose you want to know what I had called Dr. Carlisle about."

"Yes, that would be great."

"Have a seat." Linda motioned for Sam to sit in one of the chairs against the wall next to the desk. After Linda took her own seat, she said, "Last spring, there were quite a few kids who'd come in, feeling a bit nauseous, with their heart rates elevated, and many were quite agitated. So I called Dr. Carlisle and left a message about it. I just wanted to get his opinion, to see what might be going on. It could have been some bug going around, or maybe nerves right before finals, but I'd seen maybe . . . five or six girls—always girls—over the course of several weeks. The pattern was strange, and just didn't . . . feel right. You know what I mean?"

Sam nodded. "I do. Sounds like clinical intuition."

"Yes, I suppose so."

"But you never got the chance to talk to Dr. Carlisle?"

"No. The day after I left the message, I found out he'd died." Linda hung her head. "He was such a nice man. Always available to answer any questions I had, and always willing to see any kids I sent over. He even came here on a couple of occasions, to help figure out if we needed to send someone to the ER in Timmons."

"Wow," Sam said. "I wish I'd known him."

Linda rotated her chair to face Sam, braving a smile to cut through her grief. "So now you're here. And, obviously, you're interested in what's going on. What did you want to ask me about?"

"I've seen a couple of teenage girls with similar symptoms, and one of the moms brought in pills she'd found in her daughter's bathroom. I think it's levothyroxine."

Linda's eyes lit up. "Yes, that all makes sense now. At first, I'd wondered if maybe it could be related to the chemicals they use to treat lumber out at the mills. But in the back of my mind, I was thinking this could be hyperthyroidism—I have hypothyroidism myself and take Synthroid. "

Sam remembered seeing Linda's name in the EHR when she'd done her search the night before. "I had the same concerns about chemical exposure," she said, "but the lab results for these girls seem to be consistent with factitious hyperthyroidism. And now that I have some of the pills they've been passing around, and the markings match those for levothyroxine, I'm pretty sure that's the cause."

Linda looked thoughtful for a moment. "I remember reading about cases over the years where people abuse Synthroid to get more energy or to lose weight. I suppose that's what these girls are doing."

Sam nodded. "Yes, I suppose so."

"And I bet you're hoping I might be able to help you figure out who's been giving these pills to the girls?"

Sam smiled. "You've read my mind," she said. "It sounds like there's a boy at the center of it all, but the girl who got the pills from him is reluctant to give up his name."

Linda asked for the girls' names, and Sam hesitated momentarily before sharing the information. They were both healthcare professionals, after all, and the girls' safety was at stake. Linda confirmed that she had seen both girls on occasion. She promised to look into the matter and get back to Sam.

"I'm sorry I don't have anything solid to share with you," Linda said. "But I'll keep an eye out and let you know if anything comes up."

Sam expressed her gratitude, and despite not gaining any new information, she sensed a flicker of progress in her investigation. Stepping outside, she was relieved to discover the front had not yet arrived, making her earlier decision to leave the umbrella behind a wise one.

A smile played on her lips as she entered her car, invigorated by the anticipation of answers on the horizon. The pursuit of truth, with its twists and turns, appealed to her more than she would admit. Now, with another ally by her side, she felt a subtle thrill of being one step closer to unraveling this mystery.

31

Later that afternoon, Luann arrived for her follow-up appointment. As Sam entered the exam room, Luann blinked slowly, the dark crescents beneath her eyes telling stories of sleepless nights. She seemed to shrink into her oversized sweater, as if seeking refuge from the world. A knot of worry tightened in Sam's stomach at the sight of her distress, deepening her apprehension.

"How have you been holding up?" Sam's voice was gentle, wrapping around the question like a warm blanket, inviting Luann into a space of care and concern.

Luann paused, her fingers twisting the bottom of her sweater in a small, nervous motion. "I've been doing alright," she replied, avoiding Sam's gaze as she spoke. "Just trying to move forward, I guess."

"Well, I'm glad you're here," Sam said, her tone warm and reassuring. "Anything you want to talk about before I take a look at your records from the hospital visit?"

Not looking up, Luann shook her head.

As Sam reviewed the records, she noted that the obstetricians had performed a D&C, short for dilation and curettage. This procedure clears the uterus after a miscarriage to ensure no retained tissue could become infected. Luann hadn't mentioned this during Sam's visit, likely because she was too distressed to recall everything from that night.

Sam paused, allowing the grief of revisiting Luann's hospital visit to settle. She knew that behind the clinical terms lay a world of pain and healing, a journey Luann had to navigate almost entirely alone. "Please, take a moment, Luann," she said softly, offering a compassionate smile. "We can take this one step at a time."

Luann's response was subtle, almost imperceptible—a small nod that barely disturbed the air between them. This gesture, slight yet powerful, served as a mute witness to a maelstrom of pain and resilience that words could hardly capture. In her quietude lay a depth of feeling, an acknowledgment of shared understanding and the complexities of her inner struggle.

After a thoughtful silence, Sam asked, "Are you still staying with your mom?"

"Yes," Luann replied, her gaze fixed on her hands in her lap. "I needed some time away from Isaac. Mom's been really supportive,"

The room filled with a quiet comprehension as Sam processed Luann's words.

"Have you told Isaac about the miscarriage?" Sam asked, watching Luann's expression closely.

Luann hesitated, then answered, "I did. He was upset, but he'll be okay. We just need a little time apart."

Sam nodded, accepting Luann's response for the moment, and proceeded with the physical examination. As Luann lay on the table, Sam rolled up her sweater to expose her abdomen. While Sam carefully palpated, her gaze occasionally lifted to study Luann's face. It wasn't just the shadows under Luann's eyes that caught Sam's attention; a faint discoloration beneath her left eye hinted at something more. This wasn't merely a sign of fatigue—Luann's foundation barely hid the telltale sign of a black eye.

"Luann," Sam murmured, "what happened to your eye?"

Turning her head toward the wall, Luann squeezed her eyes shut, and remained still. Sam reached out, clasping Luann's hands in her own, silently channeling all the strength she could summon into her patient.

Finally, Luann spoke. With a trembling voice, a reluctant confession escaped her lips: "Isaac . . . he punched me." She grimaced, swallowing hard, as she turned back to face Sam. "But he was just upset about losing the baby. It's not like him." Her words tumbled out, a fragile attempt to reconcile the inconceivable.

A sense of dread settled on Sam, heavier than any textbook or medical journal could encapsulate. This wasn't just about physical injuries that could be documented, treated, and healed. It was about the scars left on the psyche, the kind that festers in the absence of light, compassion, and understanding.

As she helped Luann sit up, Sam asked, "Have you thought about reporting him?" She tried to keep her voice steady despite the turmoil swirling within her. "No one should have to endure that kind of treatment." The statement felt both necessary and inadequate, a feeble beacon in the storm that now raged silently before her.

With a shake of her head, Luann's demeanor betrayed an inner dissonance, visible in her subdued posture. It was as if she was wrestling with an invisible opponent, torn between loyalty and fear. The shift in her expression, the way her voice wavered, spoke volumes to

Sam. "I don't want to get him in trouble. It was just a one-time thing."

Luann slumped, as though her words exhausted her further, trying to convince herself, just as much as she was trying to reassure Sam. The fear of reprisal and Luann's longing for a semblance of safety and normalcy were evident, even if unspoken.

During all of this, Sam had subconsciously clenched her fists, not fully recognizing it until the bite of her nails digging into her palms alerted her. A profound sense of duty enveloped her, underscoring the critical nature, the vital importance of how she chose to speak her next words.

For a long moment, the room was engulfed in silence, a palpable tension settling over them like a thick fog. Sam watched as Luann averted her gaze, her eyes glimmering with the sheen of unshed tears, revealing the battle waging within her. It was a dance of silence, where the words unsaid reverberated louder than those spoken, a painful reminder of the chasm between what should be done and what could be done.

I must provide support without pushing too hard. How can I guide her towards help in a way that empowers her? There was a thin line she walked in these conversations, remembering Sheriff Perkins's words, how difficult it was to charge offenders without the cooperation of their victims.

"Are you sure you feel safe at your mom's place?"

"Of course, I feel safe there," Luann replied, her voice firm. Now she looked directly at Sam. "Why wouldn't I?"

Sam paused a beat, then asked, "How long do you plan on staying with her?"

"As long as it takes for Isaac to cool down," Luann answered, offering a weak smile.

Sam let out her breath, the tension of her professional boundaries stretching her like never before. In the delicate balance between professional obligation and personal empathy, she stood at the threshold, her heart guiding her through the murky waters of human anguish. Each step felt like walking a tightrope between two worlds. *How can I respect her autonomy and ensure her safety?* she pondered, her mind racing through possible interventions that wouldn't overstep her bounds.

In the end, she realized that being available was the most she could offer. At least, for now.

"If you need anything, Luann, please don't hesitate to call me. I'm here for you," she said, infusing her words with as much warmth and assurance as she could muster.

Yet, beneath her composed exterior, a torrent of frustration and helplessness swirled. She was trained to heal, to intervene, but the complexities of human emotion and legality often left her feeling handcuffed.

"Thank you, Dr. Jenkins," Luann murmured, her features softening with sincere appreciation. "It means a lot to me."

After Luann departed from the clinic, Sam withdrew to the tranquility of Dr. Carlisle's office, her thoughts laden with anxiety. She was numb, not able to process anything, really, as she typed notes about Luann's case into the EHR, noticing once again the terminology Dr. Carlisle had used for Luann's previous miscarriage. Emotionally exhausted, with her mind jumbled, Sam mechanically echoed the same words he had written, "spontaneous abortion," though it felt clinical and cold.

32

As Sam stepped out of Dr. Carlisle's office, she blinked against the clinic's fluorescent lights. Their blinding glare made the stark white hallway seem like a swirling blizzard of light, briefly disorienting her. After Luann's visit, she'd been tucked away in the office, darkened by the thunderstorm outside, having spent a few minutes searching for resources for domestic violence victims. Unfortunately, most of the resources she found were based in larger cities, far from Dry Wells. She needed to find another way to help Luann. But for now, it was time to see more patients.

However, as she prepared to enter the exam room for her next appointment, Olivia hurried over, her face marked by a look of concern.

"Dr. Jenkins, the nurse from the high school is on line three," she said, glancing at the phone on the wall next to the computer in the hallway. "She'd like to speak with you. Said it's important."

"Thank you, Olivia," Sam said, ignoring the phone on the wall. "I'll take the call in the other room."

After Sam returned to the office, Olivia lingered near the door expectantly. She gave Olivia a polite smile as she closed the door.

She reached for the phone on the desk and pressed the blinking button to answer line three.

"This is Dr. Jenkins."

"Hi, Doctor," Linda's voice crackled over the line. "I'm glad I caught you. Well, Mia still won't reveal who gave her the pills, but I talked to some of the other girls, and they mentioned a boy who might be involved. His name is Brian Hudson."

The name sounded familiar, and Sam searched her mind for how she knew it, but it was eluding her at the moment.

"I'm not sure how that helps you," Linda continued. "But I just wanted to share that piece of information, in case we need to get the authorities involved."

"Could you share more details?" Sam asked. "What exactly did the girls mention about this boy?"

Linda hesitated for a moment, then said, "Apparently he's been hanging around with a group of kids who've been experimenting with different drugs. Not necessarily the usual street drugs, but different substances that they think might give them an edge in school, bulk up for competition, or, as you'd mentioned, to lose weight. So, they think he might be the one supplying the pills, but they're not certain."

As Sam processed the information, a growing sense of unease began to seep into her thoughts. "Thanks for getting back to me so quickly, Linda. I appreciate your help," she said. "I'll keep looking into this as well and let you know if I find anything."

Sam hung up the phone and sat back in her chair, thinking through what to do next. She decided to ask

Cindy about the boy when she went to the diner for dinner that evening. Maybe Sarah knew him. It seemed like a natural opportunity to gather information.

Armed with her plan, Sam opened the door to Dr. Carlisle's office, only to find Olivia still in the hallway. The office manager was feigning nonchalance, but it was clear she had been trying to eavesdrop on Sam's conversation with the nurse.

Sam raised an eyebrow, but chose not to comment on Olivia's behavior. Instead, she simply said, "Thank you for letting me know about the call."

A scarlet wave of embarrassment swept over Olivia's cheeks, betraying her appearance of indifference. "Of course, Dr. Jenkins," she replied, her voice wavering slightly. She quickly turned and walked back to the front office, her heels clicking against the linoleum floor.

Sam sighed, a mix of frustration and curiosity trailing Olivia as she vanished through the door. She couldn't shake the feeling that there was more to the office manager turned widow than met the eye.

33

As Sam bid farewell to her last patient, the clinic's wall clock ticked rhythmically, marking the end of her long day. She gathered her things out of Dr. Carlisle's office, her mind still racing with thoughts of the troubling events in Dry Wells and her desire to uncover the truth. She stepped out of the office, and caught sight of Bonnie and Olivia chatting as they went through the door to the front of the clinic.

She stayed back a moment, not really wanting to interact with either of them. Given the recent revelations, she felt drained, lacking reserves for the sympathy Bonnie needed or the energy to fend off Olivia. She could escape through the door in the break room, but that seemed silly. Instead, she steeled herself, digging deep to put on the face she'd need with these two.

But when she walked through the door and entered the waiting room, she could see Bonnie and Olivia continuing to chat inside Olivia's office. Sam took the opportunity to slip out of the clinic, offering a casual wave and a "See you tomorrow!" without waiting for a response.

Once outside, she hurried to her car. The storm had passed, so it had stopped raining for now, but there were more clouds looming in the distance. Slipping into the driver's seat, she started the engine and drove to the diner, being careful not to spin her wheels on the slick asphalt.

Pulling into the diner's parking lot, she hoped that a conversation with Cindy might reveal whether Sarah knew the boy in question. The diner's neon sign buzzed softly, casting a warm glow over the cracked pavement as Sam pushed through the door. The comforting scents of frying onions and freshly brewed coffee enveloped her, mingling with the faint, familiar aroma of grease. The room hummed with the quiet chatter of patrons and the sound of forks clinking against plates. Having been in town for more than a couple of weeks now, she received nods of recognition from many as they saw her.

Sam scanned the room, her eyes flitting from table to table, hoping to find Cindy. Instead, she spotted Sheriff Ken Perkins and Agent Mason Harper sitting together, deep in conversation. In some ways, Sam was relieved; with everyone around, this wasn't the right environment to ask Cindy about the boy.

Sam hesitated near the entrance, her fingers curling around the strap of her purse, unsure of what to do next. The waitress, who had been there previously during Cindy's absence, approached her with a cheerful expression. "Want a booth or a table?"

Sheriff Perkins glanced up and noticed Sam, his warm eyes crinkling with a smile. "Dr. Jenkins! Come join us," he called, his voice friendly and inviting as he motioned to the seat beside him at their table. Agent Harper remained stoic, his gaze assessing Sam as she approached, his square jaw set, eyes shielded.

Sam hesitated for a moment before she sat down next

to Sheriff Perkins, across from Agent Harper, feeling a bit out of place. The waitress hovered nearby, her pen poised and ready to take Sam's order. "I'll have a cheeseburger and fries, please," Sam said, handing the laminated menu back to the waitress. So much for watching what she ate. She needed comfort food. As the waitress walked away, Sam turned her attention to the two men.

"How's your day been, Dr. Jenkins?" Sheriff Perkins asked, genuinely interested.

"It's been busy, as usual," Sam replied with a weak smile. Then she locked eyes with him. "Actually, Sheriff, I wanted to mention something. I had a patient this afternoon who seemed to be in some trouble. She's the one we've kind of talked about before . . ." She glanced sidelong at Agent Harper. Even though he was also a law enforcement agent, she didn't want to divulge too much in front of him.

The sheriff gave her a knowing look with a brief nod.

The image of Luann's black eye, poorly covered by makeup, flashed in Sam's mind, along with how Luann had finally admitted Isaac had hit her while still trying to downplay the incident.

Sam yearned to disclose everything to the sheriff, yet all she could manage was, "She's taken refuge at her mother's house after something happened." She looked back and forth between the two men, the sheriff's brow furrowed, the agent with a curious look. "Anyway, I just thought you should know."

Sheriff Perkins' expression grew serious, his eyes clouding with concern. "Thank you for sharing that, Dr. Jenkins. It's important to watch this situation. Do you think she's in immediate danger?"

Sam shook her head. "I'm not sure, but she seems

scared. I couldn't convince her to file a report or talk to someone who might help her."

Sheriff Perkins nodded, his jaw clenched. "I appreciate you telling me. We'll look into it and make sure she's safe."

"Thanks, Sheriff. But, I'm just wondering . . . is there anything else we can do?" Sam asked.

Before Sheriff Perkins could answer, his phone rang, its shrill tone cutting through the din of the diner. "Excuse me," he said, stepping away from the table to answer the call, his forehead creasing as he listened intently.

Sam and Agent Harper sat in awkward silence, the tension between them palpable. Sam's thoughts raced, wondering if there was some excuse she could use to leave. But just as curiosity was getting the better of her, hoping to learn more about the agent's investigation at the clinic, the waitress came back with their meals. She set down a club sandwich in front of Agent Harper, and cheeseburgers with piles of fries in front of Sam and Sheriff Perkins's empty seat.

"Can I getcha anything else?"

They shook their heads.

Sheriff Perkins returned to the table, his expression grave. "I have to go." To the waitress he asked, "Can you box this up for me?"

"Sure thing." She picked up his plate and returned to the kitchen.

As he pulled a twenty out of his wallet and set it on the table, he said, "I've got to respond to an incident, but it was a pleasure catching up with you, Agent Harper. And I'll be sure to check on our mutual friend, Dr. Jenkins."

Sam and Agent Harper both nodded.

Sheriff Perkins hurried out of the diner, stopping only to grab his cheeseburger from the waitress, leaving Sam alone with the enigmatic agent. She nervously picked at the edge of the table, the metal cool beneath her fingertips as she debated whether she should just leave or attempt to engage him in conversation.

Sam's heart raced as she considered what to say to Agent Harper. But just as she was about to speak, he beat her to it. "So, Dr. Jenkins, have you noticed anything unusual at the clinic lately?" he asked, his eyes piercing into hers.

"What do you mean?" She picked at her cheeseburger, trying to delay answering his question. Of course there was plenty unusual going on—from Luann's situation, which at least Sheriff Perkins now knew about, to the teenaged girls taking thyroid hormone to lose weight—but she had to measure how much she should share. She glanced up at him, watching as he took a bite of his sandwich, his eyes never leaving hers.

After he swallowed, he said, "Oh, I don't know. Just anything unusual."

Sam wasn't sure she wanted to say anything about her own investigation just yet. "Well, we do encounter a variety of medical issues. It's a diverse community, after all."

Agent Harper nodded, then said, "How are things going at the clinic, considering the circumstances with Dr. Carlisle?"

Sam was thrown off by the change in subject. "Fine, I guess." She shook her head. "It's pretty awful what happened to him."

"Indeed, it is." Then he returned to his initial line of questioning. "Are you sure you haven't encountered any issues with your patients? Haven't seen anything out of the ordinary?"

Sam thought for a moment, wondering how to respond. "There have been a few cases that stand out, but I'm sure you understand that I can't go into detail."

"Of course," he replied, leaning back in his chair. "Patient confidentiality is crucial. However, if there's anything that you believe might warrant further investigation, I would appreciate hearing about it."

Sam bit her lip, considering where to take the conversation. She still wanted to know why he'd been at the clinic the week before. "What exactly are you investigating, Agent Harper?"

He hesitated, then said, "I can't divulge too much, but it involves insurance fraud."

"Medicare?" she asked.

"As a matter of fact, yes, Medicare is involved."

Was Olivia involved with insurance fraud? Or was it related to her cousin and East Tex Diagnostics? Based on what Troy had said, that's where Agent Harper's investigation was centered, since they'd shut the lab down and had boxed up evidence. Maybe Agent Harper had just been speaking to Olivia because of her cousin, nothing more.

Agent Harper appeared lost in thought, seemingly assembling the pieces of a puzzle. Meanwhile, Sam seized the moment to nibble on a few fries, her thoughts swirling with strategies on how to inquire about testing the pills Cindy had provided, all while revealing as little as possible.

Finally, she ventured to ask, "Agent Harper, if someone were to come across a suspicious substance, possibly related to your investigation, how would they go about getting it tested?"

He looked at her, his eyes narrowing slightly. "I suppose they could contact their local law enforcement or bring it to the FBI's attention, and we would handle it from there. Why do you ask?"

"Oh, I was just curious," Sam said. "It's always interesting to learn about how these investigations go." She smiled. "I mean, look at how many TV shows there are about the FBI."

Agent Harper nodded. "Well, those shows make things seem much more glamorous than they really are." Then he turned serious and suddenly asked, "Have you seen any unusual lab results at the clinic?"

The question left Sam momentarily disoriented, as if the ground had shifted beneath her feet, her mind scrambling to process the unexpected turn in the conversation. Were the factitious hyperthyroidism cases she'd encountered related to his investigation? And had Miranda shared their conversation about the teenagers with him?

Feeling cornered, Sam finally said, "Well, I have seen a few atypical things, but I can't really go into specifics."

With an air of understanding, Agent Harper pulled out a business card with his contact information. "Give me a call if—no, *when* you figure it out," he said confidently.

Sam raised an eyebrow. "How do you know I'll figure it out?"

For the first time, a smile spread across Agent Harper's face. "I just know you will."

34

Sitting across from Agent Harper in the bustling diner, surrounded by the hum of conversation and the clatter of dishes, a wave of apprehension washed over Sam. She picked at the crispy fries next to the steaming cheeseburger on her plate, but her appetite had vanished. The tightness in her chest wasn't just from the greasy food; it was the gnawing worry that Miranda might have revealed too much about her investigation into the pills.

"Did Miranda mention anything about me to you?" she asked, trying to sound casual as she wiped her hands on a napkin.

The FBI agent paused, his coffee cup halfway to his lips, and gave her a long, assessing look that made her skin prickle. "Yes, she did," he finally said, setting his cup down with deliberate slowness. "She spoke highly of your deductive skills. Said you cracked several murder cases back in Austin before coming here."

Sam let out a breath she didn't realize she'd been holding, relief unfurling within her, grateful for Miranda's discretion. She knew she'd need to involve law enforcement at some point, but she didn't want to do more harm than good, didn't want to make accusations without solid confirmation.

His questions must be related to his own investigation. She wondered how she could elicit more information from him, knowing he'd likely clam up if she asked directly. So she decided to keep things light. "Miranda can be a little too enthusiastic sometimes," she said with a small, forced laugh.

Agent Harper smiled, though it didn't quite reach his eyes. "She seems to have a lot of faith in you, Dr. Jenkins. That speaks volumes."

Just then, the waitress approached their table, her expression constricted with concern. "You're Dr. Jenkins, right?"

Sam nodded, a sense of foreboding creeping over her.

"You have a phone call," the waitress said, motioning to the wall-mounted phone over the counter.

"Excuse me," Sam told Agent Harper, rising from the table. As she walked to the counter, her pulse quickened, a tight knot forming in her stomach. The other patrons' eyes on her felt heavier with each step, amplifying her sense of unease. Picking up the receiver, she gripped the phone tighter than intended, the cold plastic pressing against her ear. "Hello?"

"Dr. Jenkins, it's Sheriff Perkins," the voice on the other end said, his tone somber.

A sudden chill ran down Sam's spine, her heart thudding louder in her chest. "What's wrong, Sheriff?" she asked, her voice barely above a whisper, betraying the dread that was rapidly coiling inside her.

"I have some bad news, grave news, about one of your patients," his words fell like stones, heavy with a sorrow yet unspoken. "But I'd rather discuss it with you in person. Can you meet me?"

Her grip on the phone became a lifeline, knuckles bleaching white as if trying to wring hope from the receiver itself. Her heart was racing now, a frantic drumbeat echoing her spiraling thoughts. "Yes, of course. Where?"

He gave her an address, and she quickly scribbled it down on an order pad lying on the counter. "I'll be there as soon as I can," she promised, her hand shaking slightly as she hung up the phone.

As she returned to the table, the FBI agent watched her with curiosity. She forced a smile, trying to hide her anxiety. "I have to go," she said, pulling out her wallet and leaving some cash on the table for her meal. "I enjoyed speaking with you, Agent Harper."

"Likewise," he replied, his expression inscrutable. "Take care, Dr. Jenkins. And don't hesitate to contact me if you need any assistance."

Sam nodded, a silent goodbye, and fled the diner, her mind a battlefield between fear and fortitude. She couldn't shake the feeling that something terrible was unfolding. As she climbed into her car and put the address into the maps app on her phone, her brain swarmed with uncertainties.

The moment she started the engine, the world outside seemed to shift. The diner's warm glow faded into the rearview mirror as she merged onto the road, the night enveloping her in its cool embrace. The streets were nearly deserted, with only an occasional car passing by, its headlights cutting through the darkness like a solitary beacon.

Sam's mind buzzed as she drove, the silence of the car amplifying her agitation. The sheriff's grave tone replayed in her mind, each word a weighty echo of the dread building within her.

It must be Luann. What could have happened to her?

The drive seemed to stretch on, time warping as her thoughts tangled. The scenery outside transitioned from the well-lit streets of the town center to the quieter, tree-lined roads of residential areas. Streetlights flickered overhead, casting long shadows that danced across the road.

A faint drizzle peppered the windshield as Sam parked her car near the address Sheriff Perkins had given her. The quiet, tree-lined street was just a few blocks from Bonnie's house, where she had enjoyed a warm, home-cooked dinner only a couple of weeks before. The unsettling scene that greeted her stood in stark contrast to her pleasant memory: the sheriff's cruiser, along with a couple of deputies' cars, their red and blue lights flashing, surrounded a modest ranch-style home, with yellow crime scene tape fluttering in the breeze.

The scent of damp earth filled Sam's nostrils and cold raindrops pelted her face as she walked through the crowd gathered on the street. As she attempted to approach the house, a young deputy with a crew cut stepped in front of her, blocking her path. "I'm sorry, ma'am. This is a crime scene. No one is allowed in."

"I'm Dr. Samantha Jenkins," she replied, keeping her voice steady. "Sheriff Perkins asked me to come."

The deputy hesitated, his eyes darting between Sam and the house. "I'm not sure I can—"

Before he could finish, Sheriff Perkins appeared, striding towards them with a purposeful gait. "It's all right," he said. "I asked Dr. Jenkins to come here."

The deputy stepped aside with a nod.

"Let's talk over here," the sheriff said, guiding her to the side of the house, away from the prying eyes of the neighbors who had ventured out in the rain to observe the commotion.

In the dim light, the strain was evident on the sheriff's face. He inhaled deeply and revealed, "This house belongs to Luann's mother." His words struck Sam like a punch to the gut, causing her heart to sink. "I have some terrible news," he continued, his voice heavy. "Luann and her mother are no longer with us."

Sam's hand flew to her mouth, her eyes filling with tears. "What happened?" she managed to choke out. A torrent of thoughts and emotions surged through her, the sharp sting of self-reproach pricking at her conscience. *I noticed the signs*, she berated herself internally, recalling the black eye, the tension in Luann's voice, the way she flinched at sudden movements. *I should have done something.*

The sheriff sighed, running a hand over his damp hair. "The emergency call I received at the diner came from Luann's neighbor. Luann had been staying at her mother's house but returned to her place with Isaac to retrieve some items. Isaac began yelling at her, and the neighbor witnessed Luann running out of the house with Isaac in pursuit," he paused, his voice cracking. "Luann managed to get into her car and drive away. Almost immediately afterward, Isaac, carrying his shotgun, got into his truck and followed her. Concerned for Luann's safety, the neighbor called us."

Sam clenched her hands into fists as she listened to Sheriff Perkins. He described visiting the neighbor for information, only to be interrupted by a dispatch call regarding an incident at the mother's house. "By the time we arrived," he said, his voice filled with regret, "it was too late. Luann and her mother were already dead."

"Have you arrested Isaac?" Sam asked, anger welling within her.

The sheriff shook his head, a mix of frustration and determination evident on his weary features. "He fled before we arrived," he admitted, the lines around his eyes deepening. "We've already notified the State Troopers to assist in the search. We'll find him, Dr. Jenkins, that's a promise."

With a steely resolve, she narrowed her eyes and squared her jaw, her entire being focused on the sheriff. "What can I do? How can I help?"

"I need you to provide a statement regarding what you noticed during Luann's visits to the clinic. I assume she's the individual you've been referring to in all of our discussions."

Sam nodded.

"And this evening, when you mentioned her, you appeared to possess some insights. Especially since you looked relieved that Luann was staying here." He glanced at the house over his shoulder.

Guilt rushed over Sam as she dropped her shoulders. "Just a few hours ago, Luann was talking to me at the clinic, and that's when I noticed the black eye."

"She had a black eye?"

"Yes, poorly covered up with makeup, but it was still visible. I managed to get her to admit that Isaac had punched her. I urged her to report it, but she insisted it was a one-time occurrence, not as serious as it appeared," Sam said, hanging her head low. "Clearly, I was wrong. I should have insisted she stay at the clinic. I should have contacted you immediately. But she assured me she was safe here," she gestured towards the house, tears blurring her vision. "And now both she and her mother are dead."

Sheriff Perkins hesitated for a moment, then placed a hand on her shoulder. "It's not your fault. I told you I'd been called to their place many times. But each time, Luann just wouldn't give us a statement," he lamented, shaking his head. "And the couple of times it was obvious she'd been injured, she would always say she tripped or was clumsy or gave some other excuse." He dropped his hand by his side. "If *you* are guilty, then *I* am just as guilty for not trying harder, for not doing more to prevent this tragedy."

One of the deputies came up hesitantly, and when Sheriff Perkins noticed him, he motioned him over. "They need you inside, Sheriff."

He nodded. To Sam, he asked, "So, would you be willing to give a statement?"

"Of course," Sam answered.

"Okay, then. It looks like we'll be a while, but I'll reach out to you. Just be careful and stay alert. Keep an eye out for anything unusual and let me know."

Sam nodded, swallowing hard. "I will. Thank you, Sheriff."

The sheriff's boots crunched on the damp gravel as he turned to go into the house with the deputy, leaving Sam alone, her heart pounding in her chest. The chilly night air prickled her skin, but it couldn't penetrate the numbness that enveloped her. She stood there, rooted to the spot, her mind reeling from the horrifying revelation. The drizzle that had been falling earlier had stopped, leaving the world around her eerily still, as if it too was mourning the terrible loss. Sam's gaze remained fixed on the darkened windows of the house, the scene of such violence and pain hidden behind those walls. A tangled knot of astonishment, anger, and grief twisted in her gut.

For now, she stood frozen, the world around her a blur as the full, crushing weight of tragedy threatened to pull her under, the silence around her a heavy cloak woven with threads of shock and sorrow.

35

The night air, thick with agony, hung around Sam as she took her first steps away from the somber reality of the crime scene. The echoes of Sheriff Perkins's words lingered in her mind, a haunting melody of regret and unresolved questions. The chill of the evening did little to cool the turmoil that seethed within her, a maelstrom of anguish for Luann and her mother, fury at Isaac, and self-reproach that clung to her like a second skin. As she navigated through the crowd that had gathered, drawn by the flashing lights and the grim spectacle of tragedy, each step felt like wading through a fog of disbelief and despair.

Neighbors whispered among themselves, their faces etched with concern and morbid curiosity. It was in this sea of tense murmurs and shadowed expressions that Sam found herself adrift, a lone island of knowledge in the midst of speculation and fear.

As she continued to process the events of the evening, her name sliced through the murmurings, pulling her back to the present.

"Dr. Jenkins! Dr. Jenkins!"

Turning, Sam saw Olivia emerging from the crowd, her face a mirror of the distress and confusion that gripped them all. The older woman reached out to Sam, seeking answers in a world that had suddenly become unrecognizable.

"What's going on?" Olivia asked, her lips quivering. She glanced at the house next door, her face shadowed with worry. "My parents heard gunshots and called the police. Is everything okay?"

Sam knew it was up to law enforcement to give out information, but she could see the panic in Olivia's eyes. She swallowed hard, struggling with her decision.

"I think it's best if we let the sheriff handle any announcements," Sam muttered.

Olivia's gaze darted back to the scene of the crime, her expression darkening. "Did Isaac do something?" she asked, now glancing at the others around them as if seeking confirmation.

Sally stepped forward, her complexion ashen, her hands twisting together in agitation. She scanned Sam's face anxiously, searching for a glimmer of hope as she leaned in, her words barely escaping in a breathy murmur. "Is Luann okay? I called the sheriff because I heard shouting earlier and I was worried about her."

Olivia seconded Sally's sentiment, her voice splintering under the strain. "Yes, is Luann alright? Please, Dr. Jenkins, tell us she's okay."

Sam's heart ached, torn between the urge to share what she knew and restraint, knowing that it wasn't her place to reveal such information. "I really can't say," she replied, avoiding their gaze. "Please, let's wait for the sheriff's statement."

Desperate, Olivia persisted. "But I saw the sheriff

talking to you. You must know something!" Her eyes pleaded with Sam for answers.

Sam remained firm, her own eyes filling with tears. "I'm sorry, I just can't say anything right now."

Just then, a man who'd been speaking with a deputy standing nearby came over and joined the group. "There's going to be a press conference soon," he informed them. "They'll tell us more then."

Sam felt a sliver of relief. She wouldn't have to be the one to break the horrible news to Olivia and Sally, or the fact that Isaac was still at large.

With the announcement, the crowd began to chatter, sharing conjecture and rumors. Amidst the throng of onlookers, Sam spotted James. He made his way over to her, his face filled with intrigue and concern. "Sam, are you alright?"

She swallowed hard, overwhelmed by the enormity of the calamity. "No, James. I'm not. I couldn't save her."

"Who couldn't you save?" he asked, perplexed.

"One of my patients," she whispered, then burst into tears.

James put his arm around her, guiding her away from the crowd. He tipped his head toward the crime scene. "Were they one of the victims?"

Sam nodded, her resolve crumbling as she fell into James's embrace. His hands, warm and familiar, pressed gently against her back—a silent promise of unwavering support that only an old friend could offer. In that moment, enveloped in the safety of his hold, Sam felt a surge of gratitude wash over her. Here, in a town where faces were still unfamiliar and connections shallow, James was her anchor, a cherished link to a past that felt both distant and desperately needed.

After a moment, she pulled back, wiping away the tears from her eyes. "Wait. What are you doing here?"

James glanced over his shoulder, down the street. Several vans bearing the insignia of news stations around the state were parked along the curb. "Some of the local reporters heard the radio calls about a shooting, so we came over from Timmons."

"Guess this beats sitting in a courtroom," Sam said, trying to muster a light tone despite the heavy atmosphere.

He shrugged. "Since court adjourned for the day, and nothing was going to happen tonight, we figured we'd check out what was going on."

"This is probably more than you bargained for."

"It's a two-for-one for a lot of us," James said with some levity, then his voice became sober. "I'm just sorry you had a connection to one of the victims."

Olivia drifted from the crowd to join them, curiosity clearly written across her face. She extended her hand to James. "I'm Olivia Carlisle. And you are . . . ?"

"James Lewis," he said, shaking her hand.

Her gaze flitted between them, a puzzle clearly forming in her mind. "How do you two know each other? Especially here, of all places, and under such dire circumstances?"

Sam and James exchanged a look, a silent communication passing between them that spoke of years of friendship. Sam's voice carried a blend of nostalgia and sorrow, "We've been through thick and thin since our high school days in Austin. You know, the kind of friends who know all your secrets—the good, the bad, and everything in between."

James nodded in agreement, his tone adding depth to their shared past. "And I've been in Timmons covering a trial for the *Austin Tribune*. Thought it was just another day at work until it led me here, to this . . ." His voice trailed off.

Olivia nodded in understanding, then she started to ask, "Are you two—"

But she was cut off by a deputy's voice announcing the beginning of the press conference. He was standing by the Sheriff in front of a a set of microphones.

"Sorry, I need to focus on this," James said, as he began weaving his way closer to the heart of the action. Glancing back at Olivia, he added, "Nice to meet you," before turning his attention fully towards the unfolding police press conference.

"What a nice young man," Olivia said. "Are you two dating?"

Sam shook her head. "No, we're just friends."

She couldn't believe, amongst the awfulness that had just happened, that Olivia was still pressing for gossip. Or maybe Sam should give Olivia a break. They were all in shock right now, and Olivia was just trying to be friendly.

At the hastily organized press conference, the first piece of information shared was the tragic news that Luann and her mother, Doris Fanning, had been killed that evening in a domestic altercation, a revelation that cast a somber mood over the crowd. Law enforcement officials, with Sheriff Ken Perkins at the forefront, then provided a detailed account of the events leading up to the urgent manhunt for Isaac Clark, underscoring the gravity of the situation and the concerted efforts underway to apprehend the suspect. The conference culminated in Sheriff Perkins addressing the assembled reporters with a serious demeanor, highlighting the dedication of his team. "We're doing everything in our power to locate Isaac Clark and bring him to justice. We urge the public to remain vigilant and report any suspicious activity."

As the press conference came to a close, Sheriff Perkins approached Sam. "Dr. Jenkins, could you come by my office to make a statement tomorrow? We need to gather all the information we can on Isaac and Luann, especially since you were one of the last people to see either of them. It will help build our case once we apprehend him."

Sam nodded, still processing the tragic loss. "Of course, Sheriff. I'll be there."

James, sensing Sam's unease, suggested they stick together for safety while Isaac was still at large. He volunteered to stay with her in her motel room, and she accepted.

THE NEXT DAY at the clinic, the atmosphere was heavy with sorrow. Sam and Bonnie attended to their patients while Olivia kept mostly to herself, lost in her thoughts. Many appointments had been canceled, as the residents of Dry Wells were reluctant to leave their homes with a killer on the loose.

Later in the day, Bonnie's son Trevor and his friend Brian arrived at the clinic after school. Bonnie had asked them to come straight to the clinic, as she was worried about their safety during the manhunt. Hearing Brian's name triggered a realization, as if a switch flipped in Sam's mind.

Brian. Sally's son.

Sally's last name was Hudson.

Brian Hudson.

He was the same boy the high school nurse had

mentioned in connection with the mysterious pills. The pieces were starting to fit together, and Sam felt a growing suspicion that her perceptions of the people in this community had been misguided once more.

Sally and Bonnie were good friends, just like their sons. Did their relationship go deeper?

Previously, Sam had grappled with whether or not she should discuss these cases with Bonnie. However, her trust in Bonnie had been undermined by Bonnie's attempts to conceal her family's connection to the murder trial in Timmons. Now, with her son's friend appearing linked to these cases, Sam couldn't help but wonder—could Bonnie be involved?

Sam needed to talk to Bonnie, but the clinic was now bustling with patients, leaving her little opportunity for a private conversation. It seemed like once school had let out, everyone had decided to come to the clinic.

Finally, toward the end of the workday, Sam spotted Bonnie heading to the break room by herself. Taking a deep breath, she followed her in, determined to get to the bottom of the matter.

However, upon entering, Sam found Trevor and Brian seated at the table, engrossed in their phones. She hesitated, feeling uncertain about discussing a delicate topic in front of the boys, even though she suspected Brian might be involved. Bonnie, oblivious to Sam's internal conflict, approached the teens.

"How are you boys doing?" Bonnie asked.

The boys mumbled a half-hearted "fine" in response, their attention still glued to their screens.

Bonnie faced Sam, her forehead creased in concern. "This manhunt has me on edge," she confessed. "But at least I know these boys are safe."

Sam's gaze shifted to Trevor and Brian, their youthful

innocence sharply contrasting with the shadow enveloping Dry Wells. Bonnie placed a comforting hand on her son's shoulder, and in that moment, Sam couldn't bring herself to ask her about the pills, to confront her. What if she was wrong? She couldn't shake the feeling that Bonnie genuinely cared for the well-being of her son and the people around her.

Sam gave Bonnie a weak smile. "It's a difficult time for everyone. We're all worried."

It was time to reach out for help, from someone who would know what to do, how to sort through all the facts. Sam had a meeting set up with Sheriff Perkins to give him her statement right after she finished up at the clinic for the day. And during that meeting, she would discuss her suspicions with him.

36

The night's embrace was a cold one as Sam stepped out of the clinic and made her way to her car. Her footsteps echoed on the pavement, a solitary beat against the backdrop of an autumn evening that whispered of change and decay. As she drove away from Dry Wells, the car's interior became a sanctuary of sorts, a place where the chaos of her thoughts could unravel in the silence that enveloped her. During the journey to the Timmons County Sheriff's Office, Sam wrestled with the torrent of information and suspicion that had amassed in her mind. How should she articulate her concerns to Sheriff Perkins?

The trees along the roadway stood as sentinels, evergreens mixed with deciduous, their leaves a blaze of oranges, reds, and yellows, a vivid display of the season's beauty, even as they heralded its demise. This juxtaposition of life and death, of grace and decay, reflected the turmoil within Sam.

Upon arriving at the Sheriff's Office, she parked her car and steeled herself for what lay ahead. The block was brimming with activity amidst the encroaching darkness, with television crews camped out around the perimeter, waiting for updates, their lights a harsh reminder of the manhunt that had cast a shadow over the area.

She entered the building, the weight of the door mirroring the heaviness in her heart. The atmosphere inside was tense, a palpable undercurrent of urgency and angst permeating the air. Officers moved with a purpose, their faces etched with the strain of the ongoing search for Isaac, a man now synonymous with tragedy and threat.

Sam was quickly escorted to Sheriff Perkins's office, where he was busy poring over paperwork. He looked up with a welcoming gesture, exhaustion evident in his warm eyes.

Breaking with formalities, Sam asked, "Any news on Isaac?"

"We're still looking," the sheriff's reply came, laden with a shared concern that seemed to fill the room, leaving little space for anything else. "Have a seat, Dr. Jenkins. Let's get started with your statement."

She settled into the chair, the wood cold and hard beneath her. Before they could begin, the deputy, who had stopped her at the crime scene, stood at the door, his hand gripping the frame as if unsure whether to enter or retreat. "Sorry, I'll come back later," he muttered.

Sheriff Perkins looked up, a gentle authority in his gesture. "No, that's okay, Wade." He tipped his head toward Sam. "We haven't started yet. What have you got for me?"

With a reluctant shuffle, the deputy stepped into the room, his gaze flitting towards Sam before settling on the floor. The fluorescent light glanced off his badge, revealing his last name as Hermsdorf. Shadows clung to the edges of his eyes, hinting at the sleepless night spent in the hunt for Isaac.

"Whatever you've got to say," the sheriff said, "you can say it in front of Dr. Jenkins."

Deputy Hermsdorf nodded, then began his report. "Word is, Isaac was known to have a Remington 870. He likely emptied the mag tube, first with two blasts through the door, and then by putting two rounds into each victim's chest."

With a hint of nervousness in his eyes, he darted another glance towards Sam, as if he doubted her capacity to absorb such grave details. In response, Sam simply held his gaze with an unwavering steadiness, wondering if the youthful deputy could withstand the visceral realities she'd encountered during her residency in the emergency department.

"Any word on his whereabouts?" the sheriff asked.

"We're still working down the list of relatives—still need to talk to one of his uncles and his brood."

Once the sheriff relayed a set of instructions and the deputy obediently sauntered off to complete them, he promptly turned his attention to the matter at hand. He briefed Sam on the specifics of the information she could furnish in her statement that would prove beneficial to their investigation. Then, positioning himself at the keyboard, he focused on her as if he were a courtroom stenographer, rather than on the computer screen.

But before she commenced her statement, concern regarding professional duties pricked at her. "Sheriff," she began hesitantly, "how much can I disclose about Luann? I mean, considering the constraints of patient confidentiality and all . . ."

The sheriff leaned back in his chair and sighed. "My understanding is that confidentiality doesn't apply if someone has the potential to be harmed, but in this case, use your best judgment. After all, you did tell me about this before, just not with all the details. And you know that I had already suspected Luann was a victim of domestic violence, but my hands were tied since she was reluctant to give any statements."

His hands fell from the keyboard to his lap as his shoulders slumped slightly. "I have to admit," he said, "I've been feeling guilty about not doing more to help Luann. I should've acted on my suspicions earlier, but I just didn't have enough evidence." The corners of his mouth twitched downward as he opened and closed his fists.

Meeting the sheriff's gaze, Sam felt the heavy burden of his regret, a silent echo of her own. "I feel the same way, Sheriff. We both wanted to help her, but we were limited by our professional roles."

The sheriff ran a hand over his graying head, his face mired with misery. "Yeah, sometimes it feels like we're powerless in these situations." He sucked in a deep breath. "But we've gotta keep trying to do what we can, right?"

Sam nodded, tears gathering in her eyes. "You're right, Sheriff," she said. "We might not be able to save everyone, but we can still strive to make a difference."

They shared a somber moment, fully grasping the seriousness of the situation. However, aware that there was still work to be completed, Sam sat up, as did the sheriff, and she proceeded to give her statement. She detailed Luann's visits to the clinic and described Isaac's controlling behavior.

As she recounted her interactions with the couple, her voice trembled with emotion. "During Luann's first visit, Isaac answered all the questions for her and wouldn't let her speak, but then he changed when—"

Sam hesitated again, remembering an article she'd read that patient confidentiality didn't always end with the patient's death. But Isaac had seemed friendlier once Sam gave them the news of Luann's pregnancy.

The sheriff stopped typing and gave her an inquisitive look.

The pregnancy and the miscarriage weren't necessarily directly related to the domestic abuse issue. Sam decided to hold this information back for now. It seemed too personal.

"Is something wrong?" the sheriff asked.

Sam shook her head. "No, it's nothing."

She continued relaying the details of her interactions with the doomed couple, focusing on Isaac's standoffish behavior and the last time she'd seen Luann, just the day before.

The sheriff recalled, "That's when you mentioned her, back at the diner with Agent Harper. You had just witnessed signs of Isaac's abuse, and Luann had confessed to you that he'd hit her."

"That's right," Sam said. "At that point, I thought she'd be okay, since she'd gotten away from him and was staying with her mother." She shook her head. "But for some reason, she went back home."

"It seems like she wanted to pick up a few things," the sheriff said, "but then Isaac followed her to her mother's house, and . . . well . . . we know the rest."

He turned back to his computer, clicked a few times with his mouse, and the printer in the corner behind him whirred to life. After a few moments, he pulled the freshly printed statement from the tray, placed it on the desk in front of Sam, and presented her with a pen.

"Please read over this and let me know if you want to make any changes. If everything looks good, just sign at the bottom."

Sam nodded as she began scanning the document.

Everything was just as she'd told the sheriff, so she signed and dated it.

"Thank you, Dr. Jenkins," the sheriff said. "That's all I need from you."

For a moment, Sam hesitated, debating whether it was the appropriate time to broach another subject, especially amidst the ongoing manhunt. Yet, realizing the urgency to trace the origin of the pills, particularly with the potential of more individuals being affected, she decided to proceed.

"Sheriff," she said, "there's something else I need to talk to you about. Remember when I mentioned the pill issue earlier?"

Sheriff Perkins leaned back in his chair, his interest piqued. "Yes, I do. What have you found out?"

Sam began to detail the instances of factitious hyperthyroidism she'd discovered among the high school girls. As she spoke of the pills Cindy had brought to her, she pulled the baggie out of her purse and placed it on the sheriff's desk.

"I should probably give these to you," she said.

The sheriff nodded as he inspected the bag. "Have you identified them?"

"Yes," she said. "The markings are consistent with levothyroxine, a synthetic thyroid hormone."

"Is this what you were referring to when you called me about having some pills analyzed?"

Sam nodded.

"And what happened next?"

She continued her story, explaining how the pills led to her discussions with the high school nurse and ultimately drew a line connecting the circumstances from Mia to Bonnie. All the while, she'd omitted the names of the individuals involved, with one exception: Bonnie.

Sheriff Perkins had been listening, nodding along

throughout Sam's account, until that moment. His eyebrow arched skywards, a clear manifestation of his disbelief. The room fell silent, but despite his evident skepticism, he leaned in, eager to understand the puzzling details of the case laid before him.

"That's some fine detective work, Doctor, but there's no way Bonnie's involved. I just know."

"How can you be so sure?" Sam asked.

Sheriff Perkins paused, his face flushing slightly. "I know her well enough, that's all. You should talk to her . . . and maybe give Agent Harper a call, too."

37

The sheriff's unwavering certainty, coupled with his mention of Agent Harper, was perplexing. The FBI agent's probing questions from the previous evening only deepened Sam's intrigue about the teenagers' situation. She wondered if there was a link between his visit to the clinic, his investigation at the laboratory owned by Olivia's cousin, and the pills.

Sheriff Perkins checked his watch before standing up. "C'mon. I need to see Bonnie about something anyway, so why don't we both go over there?"

"But what about the manhunt for Isaac?"

"Honestly, it's the State Troopers' operation now. Wade and the others will keep me informed."

After making his way through the throng of reporters bombarding him with questions outside, the sheriff managed to get to his SUV and set off for Dry Wells, with Sam trailing behind in her car. As they drove to Bonnie's house, the clouds parted, unveiling a full moon, prompting Sam to ponder the upcoming conversation and its potential outcomes. She anticipated the sheriff would spearhead the questioning once they arrived.

Parking in Bonnie's driveway, Sam inhaled deeply, seeking to calm her nerves, unsure of what lay ahead. She exited her car, passed through the gate of the white picket fence, and met the sheriff on the front stoop.

As Bonnie opened the door, her face lit up with a warm, welcoming smile upon seeing Sheriff Perkins. Yet, as her gaze shifted to Sam, who stood slightly behind him, her smile wavered, becoming more reserved and cautious. "Sheriff Perkins! It's good to see you. Please, come in." Then she added, "And you too, Dr. Jenkins."

Ushering them into the living room, she said, "Have a seat. Make yourselves comfortable."

But before they could get settled, Bonnie's mother appeared in the doorway. Her eyes narrowed when she saw Sheriff Perkins, and she snapped, "You can't be here!"

Bonnie quickly moved to her mother's side, gently placing a hand on her arm. "It's okay, Ma. Sheriff Perkins is a friend."

Mrs. Wright scowled. "Well, I don't like it. He's not *my* friend. He shouldn't be here."

With a sigh, Bonnie turned back to her guests. "I apologize for my mother's behavior. She's not quite herself these days."

"It's alright, Bonnie," the sheriff said. "We appreciate you letting us in. We won't take up too much of your time."

Sam smiled reassuringly, aiming to dissolve the tension. "We just have a few questions, and then we'll leave," she said. She surmised that Mrs. Wright's hostility towards the sheriff was likely rooted in the murder trial involving Bonnie's brother. It was natural for a mother to defend her child, and in Mrs. Wright's eyes, the sheriff probably symbolized the entirety of law enforcement and the perceived threats posed to her family.

After glaring at the sheriff for a moment more, the old woman huffed in response and retreated down the hallway.

"I'm really sorry about that," Bonnie said, her cheeks flushing. "My mother is just having a tough time lately."

Sheriff Perkins waved away her apology, smiling kindly. "Don't worry about it. I understand."

After everyone had taken their seats—Bonnie on the couch, flanked by Sam and the sheriff in chairs on either side—Bonnie turned to the sheriff, her eyes wide with concern. "I've been hearing all sorts of rumors," she said. "Do you have any updates on Isaac's whereabouts?"

"We're still looking for him," he said. "But I promise, we're doing everything we can to find him."

Bonnie continued, her voice trembling, "The whole town is on edge. It's just so . . . horrible."

"Yes, it's been a real shock to all of us," he agreed. "But we're here on a a different matter." He then turned to Sam, nodding encouragingly, and said, "I'll let Dr. Jenkins take over. She's the one who's been investigating it."

Sam was taken aback by his request for her to lead the discussion. Pausing to gather her thoughts with a deep breath, she proceeded to share the details she had gathered. She explained her suspected diagnosis of factitious hyperthyroidism in the teens and recounted how Cindy had brought her the pills.

As Sam spoke, Bonnie's eyes widened in disbelief.

"It's not like you can just buy Synthroid off the street," Bonnie said. "Where did they get it?"

"Well, I talked to the school nurse," Sam said, then stopped, reluctant to go further.

Bonnie nodded. "I remember you went to see her the

other day. So this is what it was about." She lifted her eyebrows. "Did you learn anything?"

Sam bunched her lips together, not sure if this was a good idea. Maybe they should talk to Sally first, to get permission to speak with Brian. He was the key individual, the lead she'd received. Additionally, she was reluctant to make any accusations without further information, particularly because she still harbored doubts about Bonnie's involvement, despite her apparent surprise.

"I did," she said. "She gave me the name of a boy." She paused again.

Finally, Sheriff Perkins said, "Dr. Jenkins, I understand this is a tough decision, but we need to know who the boy is. You wouldn't reveal his name to me before, but it could help us solve the case and put an end to this."

Sam hesitated yet again, the decision's gravity pressing heavily upon her. She scanned their faces, searching for reassurance or perhaps a sign to direct her choice. Drawing in a deep breath, she was about to reveal the name when the sound of boys' voices from another room interrupted her.

Trevor and Brian emerged from a bedroom along the hallway, their laughter fading as they entered the living room. Upon spotting the sheriff, Trevor greeted him with a wave, while Brian stopped in his tracks. The atmosphere in the room tensed, with Sam's gaze shifting back and forth between the young man and the sheriff, as if the air itself was suspended in anticipation.

Trevor, oblivious to his friend's anxiety, asked. "Any news on the manhunt?"

"No, not yet, son," Sheriff Perkins said, then glanced at Sam. "We're here for another reason. You heard anything about the girls at school using weight loss pills?"

Trevor shook his head, seemingly nonplussed by the

question. Brian, however, remained motionless, his eyes wide and hands clenched at his sides, resembling a mouse ensnared by a snake's stare.

Noticing Brian's heightened alertness, the sheriff invited both boys to take a seat. "We'd just like to ask a few questions," he began, casting a quick glance at Sam before refocusing on the boys. "Our concern is for the girls, and we're eager to find out if there's any way we can assist. We simply need some information."

"Okay," Trevor said, going over to the couch and plopping down comfortably next to his mom. "Ask away."

But Brian remained by the hallway, as if keeping his distance would somehow protect him.

"Hey, man," Trevor said. "What's up? It's just the sheriff. We don't know anything, right? But it doesn't hurt to help if we can."

Brian continued to keep his statuesque stance, his breath shallow, his eyes darting around the room, looking as if the gears in his mind were working through various scenarios.

Sheriff Perkins stood, holding out his hands in a nonthreatening gesture, and slowly approached Brian. "Please, have a seat. We just want to talk."

Brian, his posture stiff and eyes wide, managed a weak nod but remained silent, his discomfort palpable in the charged atmosphere. With gentle guidance from the sheriff, he shuffled to the couch, joining Trevor who continued to look confused as he scooted closer to his mom to make room.

Sheriff Perkins returned to his chair, speaking with a tone that, while soft, hinted at an underlying firmness. "We're just trying to piece together some information to learn more about this situation. Anything you can share with us, even if it seems small or unimportant, could really make a difference." He paused, allowing his words to resonate, while carefully watching Brian's reactions.

Moments later, Brian broke down. Tears welled up in his eyes as he began to confess. "I did it . . . I gave Mia those pills," he stammered, his voice cracking under the strain of his admission. "I just wanted her to like me. I didn't mean for it to go this far." He took a deep, shaky breath before continuing, "I overheard Mom talking about the pills at her salon. She said they helped her clients lose weight and gave them energy. I didn't think they were dangerous." His eyes darted around the room, seeking any semblance of understanding.

Bonnie's face grew pale, her hand instinctively covering her mouth. "Brian, I never thought you'd do something like this," she whispered, her voice laced with a mixture of bewilderment and betrayal. The once welcoming living room now felt as though its walls were constricting, no longer warm and cozy.

Sheriff Perkins leaned forward, his face etched with concern. "Tell us everything, Brian."

Brian wiped his tear-streaked face with the back of his hand. "Like I said, I just wanted Mia to like me," he explained, his voice heavy with remorse. "She was always going on about how her mom wanted her to lose weight, how her mom thought that was why she didn't make the cheer squad. So I gave her the pills, to help her, to make her like me. I thought it was harmless. I had no idea it would lead to . . . to this." He gestured weakly at the room, the unspoken consequences of his actions hanging heavily in the air.

Sam and Bonnie exchanged a glance before they began to question Brian more closely about the origin of the pills. He shifted uncomfortably in his seat, the moonlight from the window casting shadows across his anxious face.

“I really don’t know where they came from,” he insisted, his voice tinged with desperation. “Mom always had them in the salon. I just assumed they were safe.”

Bonnie shook her head, disappointment evident in her eyes. “I had no idea,” she murmured, more to herself than to the others in the room.

Their conversation was interrupted by the sudden ringing of Sheriff Perkins’s phone. He answered it, his brow furrowing as he listened intently to the voice on the other end. He stood as he disconnected the call. “There’s a lead on Isaac. I’ve gotta go.”

38

Following Brian's confession and Sheriff Perkins's swift departure, the boys retreated to Trevor's room, casting an uneasy silence behind them. In the living room, Bonnie and Sam sat, their quiet contemplation filling the space left by the day's tumultuous events.

"I just can't imagine Sally's involved in something like this," Bonnie said, hugging one of the pillows on the couch. "There has to be another reason. Maybe Brian misunderstood something he overheard."

Sam listened intently, her gaze fixed on Bonnie. "You think it's a misunderstanding?" She wasn't sure this was actually the case, but she held back her judgment for now.

"It's possible," Bonnie replied, turning to face Sam. "Sally has hypothyroidism, you know. Those pills Brian found could just be her medication. Maybe he took them, thinking they were something else."

The theory hung between them, a slender thread of hope in a tangled web of confusion. Just then, Sam's phone buzzed with a message from James, breaking the tension momentarily. "Saw you at the Sheriff's Office earlier. Everything okay?" the text read. She ignored it for now, slipping her phone back into her pocket.

Before Sam could contemplate her next move, Bonnie's voice brought her back to the present as she switched topics. "I really hope that lead Sheriff Perkins has on Isaac turns out to be solid. We need to catch him."

"I hope so too," Sam said.

As they were talking, Bonnie's mother shuffled back into the room, her eyes narrowed. "Is that *boy* gone?" she asked. Sam assumed she was referring to Sheriff Perkins.

"Yes, Ma, he's gone," Bonnie replied, her voice strained.

Her mother scowled. "It's bad enough that *boy* arrested your brother, but it's disgusting that you're cavorting with the likes of him and shaming the family."

As soon as the words left her mother's mouth, Bonnie's posture stiffened, a visible bristle at the harsh criticism. Tension rippled through Bonnie, a silent battle of defiance and hurt playing out before Sam's eyes. "I can date whoever I want, Ma," Bonnie retorted, her voice carrying a mix of anger and determination.

The dots connected rapidly in Sam's mind, providing her with a moment of clarity: the subtle displays of familiarity between Sheriff Perkins and Bonnie earlier in the evening, along with his certainty in her innocence.

Sam's thoughts drifted to her upbringing in Austin, where progressive values were commonplace, realizing she had overlooked how, in this secluded part of east Texas, surrounded by dense woods, tolerance wasn't as easily embraced.

Mrs. Wright's scowl deepened, the disapproval in her eyes unmistakable. "Your father would be rolling over in his grave if he knew." The words hung heavy in the air, charged with unsaid implications. With a dismissive huff, she turned and left the room, leaving a palpable stillness in her wake.

Watching the exchange, a surge of compassion for Bonnie swept over Sam. She understood the complexity of navigating parental expectations, a feeling all too familiar from her own experiences. It was clear that Bonnie was caught in a struggle between her desires and her family's prejudices.

Bonnie exhaled a weary sigh, a mix of frustration and resignation. "I'm so sorry," she murmured.

"No need to apologize," Sam said.

She felt a deep urge to remain with Bonnie, to offer solace, to demonstrate through her presence that, in her, Bonnie had a steadfast ally amidst the storm of family conflict. Gently placing her hand atop Bonnie's, Sam offered a squeeze filled with empathy, a silent show of support. However, as much as her heart ached to ease Bonnie's burden, a pressing reality tugged at the edges of her resolve. The mystery of the pills loomed large, a puzzle that demanded her undivided attention.

Despite her desire to stay ensconced in the warmth of comforting Bonnie, Sam saw her efforts would be a drop in the ocean of complex family dynamics that had Bonnie caught in its currents. And Bonnie, with her loyalties and love divided, was perhaps too enmeshed in the situation, too ready to find excuses for Sally, to be of substantial help in unraveling the secret behind the pills.

With a sense of regret, Sam recognized she had to step away and pursue the mystery of the pills, leaving Bonnie to handle her family issues on her own. Driven by a duty to protect, she knew she needed to investigate further, even beyond Sally's influence, to uncover the unsettling truth.

So, she found herself apologizing to Bonnie before asking how late Sally's salon would be open.

"She's usually open until nine." Bonnie gave Sam a weak smile. "And *you* don't need to apologize. This is nothing new. I'll be fine." Now, she patted Sam's hand. "You're a good doctor. You just want to do what's right for these girls."

As Sam left, James texted her again, since she hadn't responded the first time. Instead of sending a message, she called him and told him that she was tied up with something.

"What?" James asked. "Does it have anything to do with the double murder?"

"No."

"Then what is it?"

"Look," Sam said, "I need to talk to someone, but I can meet you afterward, then I'll fill you in."

"Hmm. Is it the FBI agent?"

Sam rolled her eyes. James was relentless.

"No," she said with a sigh. "I'm looking into something else, and I need to verify some information."

"Sounds exciting. Can I come along?"

She was about to say "no," but then she reconsidered.

Maybe James could help her. He'd been helpful in questioning people before, much like having Sheriff Perkins at Bonnie's house had proven beneficial. Moreover, with the manhunt ongoing, she felt safer having someone with her. So, she relented, giving James the address of the hair salon. During the drive, Sam briefed James over speakerphone on her reasons for wanting to speak with Sally.

They arrived as dusk settled, the salon bathed in a soft glow, nestled between the pharmacy and the liquor store. Inside, Sally was silhouetted against the inside lights, finishing up with a client in the otherwise deserted space. It seemed Sally was working alone this evening, and Sam wondered if she worried about her safety with Isaac on the loose.

Seeing the shelves of styling products by the door as they entered, Sam recalled how, during her previous visit, Sally had mentioned she often made more money selling products than services. Sam wondered if some of her extra income was actually from the pills she was selling.

Once the customer left, Sally flashed a warm smile at Sam and James, her eyes sparkling with genuine friendliness. "Good to see you again, Dr. Jenkins. Who is this you've brought with you?"

Sam introduced Sally and James to each other, and they exchanged pleasantries. Then Sally asked James, "Do you need a haircut? I can fit you in right now if you'd like."

Sam shook her head. "Actually, Sally, we're here for a different reason. We've got some questions about some pills a couple of high school girls were taking to lose weight."

Sally frowned, her expression wavering between confusion and a hint of recognition.

James nodded in agreement, his eyes scanning around the salon. "Yeah, we thought you might know something about it, given your connections with a lot of the local ladies."

Sam was a little annoyed at James's conjecture—after Sam had explained what she knew about the situation to him on the phone, he immediately jumped to the conclusion that Sally basically had a drug ring running out of her salon.

Sally gripped the back of the styling chair next to her, her face hardening, her eyes narrowing. The friendly atmosphere evaporated. Maybe having James come along wasn't such a good idea. Seems she'd forgotten how he could sometimes push a little too far, which is exactly what he did next.

"You wouldn't happen to know anything about some magic weight loss pills floating around town, would you?" he said. "We're just dying to know more about this miracle cure."

Sam shot James a warning look, knowing that his sarcasm was unlikely to be productive. She quickly stepped in to smooth things over. "What James is trying to say is that we're investigating a situation affecting some of the girls in the community. We're not here to accuse you of anything, but we'd appreciate any information you might have."

"What? There are girls taking these pills?" Sally sat down in the styling chair and slumped her shoulders. "How did they get them?"

Sam hesitated, remembering her promise to Brian that she wouldn't mention him. At least not for now. She figured in time, mother and son would have to reckon with each of their decisions.

Instead, Sam deflected. "I just know that they've been taking them, because I've seen a couple of cases where girls have been using synthetic thyroid hormone to lose weight."

"But they shouldn't have gotten the pills," Sally said, shaking her head. "Maybe they got them from their mothers."

With that statement, Sam realized that maybe James had been on to something. She took a seat in the adjacent styling chair, and reached over to Sally, taking her hand.

"We're not here to accuse you of anything. We're just trying to get to the bottom of this, to keep more girls from making the same mistake. If you know anything that could help us, please share it. We're here to listen, not to judge."

Sally hesitated, her eyes darting between Sam and

James, clearly weighing her options. Finally, with a resigned exhale, she said, "Okay, I may know something about the pills, but I never thought they'd hurt anyone. I swear."

Sam nodded, encouraging her to continue. "Thank you for being honest, Sally." She waited a moment, then asked, "Can you tell us where you got the pills?"

James stepped closer to the women, his tone more serious as he interjected. "You know, we've heard some interesting things about Dr. Carlisle lately. Rumor has it he might have had some connections with the FBI or DEA. Quite intriguing, don't you think?"

Sam glared at him, a complex mix of emotions tumbling inside her. Alarm stirred with annoyance at his hasty conclusions, along with confusion and curiosity bubbling up regarding his source of information. She found herself struggling to sift the facts from the swirling chaos of speculation.

Where did these notions come from? Had Troy uncovered more about Agent Harper's investigation?

In return, James offered Sam a noncommittal shrug.

But Sally's eyes widened at the mention of Dr. Carlisle, and, fortunately, she hadn't paid much attention beyond that. Gripping the arm rests of her chair, she said, "Dr. Carlisle diagnosed me with hypothyroidism a few years ago, and he prescribed Synthroid for me. It was supposed to help with my thyroid, but I noticed some other changes too."

Sam nodded, urging her to continue. "What kind of changes?"

"Well, I started losing weight and feeling more energetic," Sally explained. "I didn't think much of it at first, but then I mentioned it to Olivia during one of my appointments at the clinic. She seemed really interested in the effects of the medication, and not long after that, she started giving me extra pills."

James raised an eyebrow. "Extra pills?"

"Yes, she told me I could share them with my friends, and that there was an opportunity for us," Sally said, her gaze fixed on Sam, imploring her to grasp the full context. "You know, some of the ladies at church had been wondering how they could lose weight. Olivia suggested that, since my salon is practically a gathering spot for almost everyone in town, I was perfectly placed to help them out." She paused, taking a deep breath as if bracing herself to reveal more, her shoulders tensing slightly.

Sally's eyes briefly darted away, then back to Sam, her expression growing troubled. "But she was adamant about keeping it a secret, especially from Bonnie or Dr. Carlisle." She let out a small, nervous laugh, shaking her head as if still trying to piece together the puzzle herself. "She claimed they were too traditional, too closed off to the potential of medicines like these. It sounded . . . odd to me."

Her voice softened, tinged with a hint of relief, as though unburdening a heavy load. "Honestly, it struck me as strange, but the idea that it could cause any harm? That never entered my mind."

A gasp escaped Sally's lips as a sudden realization dawned on her. "Olivia . . . Luann said her mother told her that Olivia was staying at her parents' house after a big fight with Dr. Carlisle. What if . . . what if it was because he found out about this?"

A jolt coursed through Sam's body, her heart hammering against her ribs as she considered the implications.

Then Sally looked up at the clock on the wall and

jumped out of her chair. She tipped her head toward the door. "You need to leave. Now."

"Why?" Sam asked, confused by Sally's sudden urgency.

Before anyone could move, the door opened, and Olivia entered.

39

Sam's gaze flitted between Olivia and Sally, the air between them charged with a tension both silent and formidable. James stood beside her, his presence calm yet alert, embodying a quiet vigilance.

Olivia's bright smile failed to dispel the pervasive sense of unease. As the door shut behind her, her tote bag began to slide off her shoulder. Reacting quickly and with seamless grace, she shifted it from her right shoulder to her left. Her right hand then fell to rest on top of her purse, her fingers idly caressing the leather surface.

Sally, in stark contrast, was a portrait of barely contained distress. Her feet shuffled restlessly, and she steadfastly refused to meet Olivia's gaze, her attention fixed on the floor as if it held the answers she desperately sought. She clenched the back of the styling chair in front of her, her knuckles white against the black vinyl.

"Dr. Jenkins, what a pleasant surprise," Olivia said, her smooth voice laced with an edge, betraying her welcoming words. She then turned her focus to James, her professional mask slipping into place as easily as if she were at the clinic. "And it's James, right? You *must* be the reason she's been taking her sweet time making a decision about staying in Dry Wells permanently."

Sam frowned, a little annoyed that Olivia obviously wasn't accepting her answer about their relationship from the night before. But Olivia's statement wasn't just curious. It was a veiled jab, an attempt to unsettle.

James tried to slice through the strain with a quip, chiming in, "Oh, we're just friends. But I'm starting to look a bit shaggy." He gave his head a quick shake, displaying his scarcely long hair. "Just here for a haircut, nothing more." His laugh, meant to lighten the room, flickered weakly against the tense undercurrents.

"He's right," Sam jumped in, perhaps too eagerly.

Olivia's gaze intensified, honing in on Sally. In response, Sally appeared to diminish even more, her evasion extending beyond mere eye contact to avoiding the confrontation altogether.

James casually ran a hand through his hair. "Yep, been a couple of months since my last cut. I'm definitely due."

"So I recommended Sally. She's the best," Sam said, trying to bridge the chasm of discomfort with the inconsequential.

"Well, she certainly is the best," Olivia conceded, her voice like silk but fringed with something sharper. "Before you get started on James, I have something for you, Sally." She nodded towards the back office as she continued to hold the younger woman with her eyes, laden with an unspoken ultimatum. "Shall we?"

Sally's response was a deep, steadying breath. Her posture was stiff, like a soldier bracing for battle. She cast a nervous glance towards Sam and James, then followed Olivia into the office, the door closing with a soft, ominous click that seemed to echo throughout the room.

Left behind, Sam and James exchanged troubled glances. "What do we do now?" James whispered, leaning in closer. The concern in his voice mirrored Sam's own feelings of helplessness and determination to unravel the mystery that now encompassed Olivia.

"I don't know," she admitted, her voice barely above a breath. "We need to prove Olivia's involvement with the pills. But how?" The question hung between them, a challenge that seemed as insurmountable as it was urgent.

James rubbed his chin thoughtfully, his eyes scanning the salon as if searching for inspiration. "Maybe we can find some evidence in her office at the clinic, or maybe Sally has something."

The clinic. "The FBI's already been to the clinic. *This* has to be why," Sam whispered.

"So they haven't just been snooping around the lab in Timmons?" James asked.

"As it turns out, Olivia's cousin runs the lab." Sam snapped her fingers. "I bet they've got some sort of Medicare scam going on, even more reason for the FBI to be investigating. The auditors would be looking for labs to prove these patients have hypothyroidism in order to pay for the drugs."

James started toward the front door. "Let's go, then. If the FBI is already investigating, then we should just leave."

"But that would be suspicious, wouldn't it? If we just left when we told her you wanted to get your haircut." Sam glanced back at the office. "And what about Sally? There's something not right. What if Olivia hurts her?"

Through the large front window, several cars drove past, their headlights slicing through the darkness of the fall evening. Another car turned into the parking lot, pulling in front of the pharmacy, which was now closed.

That's strange, Sam thought, as she moved closer to the window to get a better look.

"I think she'll be fine," James said.

"But Olivia seemed rather on edge, don't you think?" She saw a figure, vaguely familiar, emerge from the car.

"Yes, but—"

The door to the back office swung open, cutting off James mid-sentence. Olivia and Sally emerged, the latter's eyes red-rimmed but her stance defiant. Olivia, ever the picture of composure, and now only carrying her purse, smiled thinly at James as she walked past him. "It was great meeting you. Perhaps we'll see more of each other, especially if Dr. Jenkins decides to stay here."

It was Sally, however, who fractured the thin veneer of serenity. Stepping forward just outside the office door, her voice quivering, yet underscored by a newfound strength, she said, "It's all over, Olivia. They know everything."

Olivia halted, her pretense slipping momentarily, her confusion quickly giving way to a chilling realization. "Know what, exactly?" she asked, her tone deceptively calm.

"That you've been using me to peddle your pills," Sally confessed, her eyes welling with tears, but her voice gaining volume. "To women all over town, endangering their lives for profit."

Olivia's surprise morphed into cold calculation, her face becoming a mask of conniving control. "Well, well," she said, her voice low and sinister. She took a step closer to Sam. "It seems I underestimated you, Dr. Jenkins. With your wayward career path, I thought you'd jump at the chance to run a practice, no questions asked." She shook her head sadly. "Then, I would have been able to continue operations as usual."

As Olivia spoke, Sam stepped backward, bumping into

the reception desk. She peeked over her shoulder and, through the stocked shelves in front of the window, spotted a figure in the dark outside the salon. *Is that Agent Harper? What is he doing here?*

Sam turned back to Olivia just as her hand, with unsettling elegance, delved into her purse. Time seemed to slow down as Olivia's hand emerged, her fingers clenched firmly around the grip of a small handgun. She drew the weapon smoothly, a movement that demonstrated a disturbing ease and familiarity. The air, thick with dread, contracted around Sam, each breath a struggle as she braced for the inevitable.

As Olivia raised the gun, its cold metal glinting ominously, she aimed with devastating precision, sending a shiver down Sam's spine.

Her mind raced, thoughts fragmented by fear and an urgent need to act.

She had to do something.

Her eyes darted around, searching for something, anything, that could be used to thwart Olivia's deadly intent.

Behind Olivia, James seemed rooted to the spot, his body tensed for action yet momentarily paralyzed by the gravity of the situation. It was a mere heartbeat, a split second in which decisions were made and fates could be altered.

Agent Harper's presence, initially unnoticed by Olivia, now drew her attention as he opened the door to the salon. Sam kept her focus narrowed to Olivia's extended arm, the barrel of the gun, and the imminent threat it posed. But she was too far away.

Sam's decision crystallized in that instant. With no thought for her own safety, she propelled herself toward the agent, driven by a mix of adrenaline and sheer willpower.

Her movement was a blur, a rush of determined energy. She collided with Agent Harper just as the gun fired, the sound a sharp crack that split the air.

They tumbled to the ground in a heap, narrowly avoiding the bullet that thudded into the wall where Harper had stood moments before.

Behind Olivia, James's hesitation shattered. With a roar of effort, he launched himself at her. His tackle was a study in controlled fury, a physical manifestation of the fear and anger that had built up in the silence of the standoff. He hit Olivia with the force of a human battering ram, sending them both crashing to the ground. The gun flew from Olivia's grasp, skidding across the floor, coming to a stop tantalizingly close to Sam.

Ragged gasps tore through her as she pushed herself up, her eyes locked on the gun. With a swift motion, guided by instinct rather than thought, she kicked the weapon out of reach, her actions fueled by the chaotic symphony of fear, relief, and the pounding of her heart.

James pinned Olivia beneath him, his hands clamping down on her wrists with an iron grip. The struggle was desperate, a wild clash of wills, but his determination was unyielding. Olivia writhed under his hold, her defiance as fierce as her actions were futile.

Sam stood over them, her chest heaving, her mind reeling from the rapid shift from tranquility to terror and back again. "You killed your husband over this, didn't you?" she managed to say, her voice a mix of accusation and disbelief. The question hung in the air, a bridge between the chaos of the moment and the search for truth that had led them here.

Olivia's response, even in defeat, was laced with the same cold defiance that had marked her actions. "No," she growled, her eyes burning with a complex mix of emotions. "I didn't kill him. Yes, he was angry, he threatened to expose everything, but his death wasn't my doing." Her struggle stopped abruptly as she added, "I swear, I wasn't there. I . . . I wish I had been. If anything, I should have died too."

40

Sam and James stood together amidst the disarray of Sally's salon, their pulse rates beginning to settle. She took a moment to absorb the chaos, the remnants of their skirmish with Olivia painting a vivid picture of desperation and determination mixed together. The sharp tang of spilled hair products mingled with the mustiness of fear, clinging to the air long after the mayhem had subsided. The metallic click of handcuffs securing Olivia played a stark contrast to Agent Harper's steady recitation of Miranda rights. As Sam's gaze flitted across the salon, unanswered questions lingered in her mind.

"Why was Harper already on the scene?" she murmured, more to herself than to James.

Sheriff Perkins entered the salon with a stride that was calm yet determined, his uniform subtly betraying signs of his earlier activities, including a crust of mud on his boots. The urgency of his steps, combined with traces of the outside world clinging to his attire, served as a quiet reminder of the broader reality that lay beyond the salon's current turmoil.

After speaking with the sheriff, Agent Harper walked over to thank Sam for her quick thinking and James for subduing Olivia. Sam seized the opportunity to ask the question that had been bothering her.

"Why were you here, Agent Harper?" she asked. "Were you following Olivia?"

He paused, his eyes momentarily flickering to the sheriff before returning to Sam. "I can't discuss ongoing investigations, but your timing was . . . fortunate."

James's eyebrows knitted together in a visible sign of his frustration. "Can't you just give us a clue?"

"You'll learn more in due time," Harper conceded, a ghost of a smile not quite reaching his eyes. "But let's just say I already knew about what happened in that back office." With that, he turned and walked away.

With Harper's words hanging in the air, Sam furrowed her brows in thought. She turned to look at James, seeking a shared sense of understanding, only to find him already observing her, a silent question in his eyes. Their mutual confusion was palpable, an unspoken dialogue of bewilderment.

In that moment of shared perplexity, Sam's attention drifted across the room, where she noticed Sally engaged in a subdued yet intense conversation with another FBI agent. Their heads were close together, speaking in whispers too low for anyone else to hear. Sam's curiosity spiked as she tried to decipher clues from what she observed.

James, catching the direction of her gaze, turned to follow it. The sight of Sally with the agent seemed to act as a catalyst, igniting a thought within him. He looked back at Sam, a light of realization dawning in his eyes that hadn't been there a moment before. "That explains the quick FBI turnout," he muttered almost to himself, as if putting the last piece of a puzzle into place.

"What explains it?" Sam asked, eager to grasp the thread of insight James seemed to have caught.

"Sally was acting as an informant," he replied.

Sam raised her eyebrows as her gaze returned to Sally. The fog of confusion lifted, unveiling her clandestine assignment, and with it, a newfound respect for her covert courage.

Sheriff Perkins made his way over to them, shaking his head in disbelief. "Normally, this is a sleepy little town, like I told you before. But these past few days . . ." He looked at the friends directly, and said, "Tell me what you know."

Sam and James looked at each other for a moment, before she took the lead in explaining what had happened, bringing the sheriff up to speed. She started from the point when she'd last seen him at Bonnie's house, where they'd learned about Sally's involvement in the pill operation from her son. Then the two friends alternated in their narrative, painting a vivid picture of the harrowing events that had unfolded within the walls of the hair salon. It was Sam who delivered the concluding details, her voice steady but marked by disbelief. "After learning how angry Dr. Carlisle was with Olivia, I couldn't help but suspect she had a hand in his untimely death. But she seemed pretty adamant that she wasn't involved."

The sheriff considered her words. "She may or may not be telling the truth. I'll have to question her more. But for now, you've helped us bring this crisis to a close."

"So, did you know about the pills?" Sam asked.

The sheriff's eyes twinkled with a mix of amusement and secrecy as he leaned in, "Now, you know, I can't discuss—"

"An ongoing investigation," James and Sam both finished his sentence in unison, a wry smile passing between them. "We know."

Noticing the mud on the sheriff's boots, Sam then remembered the manhunt. "What about Isaac? That is an ongoing investigation you *can* talk about, at least a little, right? Since the public's safety is at stake."

The sheriff nodded, his demeanor shifting to one of guarded optimism. "Yes, I can say that we may have located Isaac. He appears to be holed up on his uncle's farm. And now I need to get back to that situation." With a tip of his hat, Perkins excused himself, leaving the friends to process the day's revelations.

Once Sheriff Perkins left, Agent Harper, along with a couple of other FBI agents, made their way over to Sam and James. Sam took a deep breath, readying herself for the onslaught of questions she anticipated. Following brief introductions, the agents divided them, escorting each to separate areas of the salon for questioning.

Assigned to a corner with Agent Rankin, Sam detailed the day's events, culminating in the confrontation in the salon. As she relayed her experiences, she found herself analyzing her reactions during the crisis, noting the stark contrast between her instinctual actions in the heat of the moment and her reflective state now, in the aftermath.

Agent Rankin meticulously reviewed Sam's account, ensuring clarity and completeness. He concluded the session by collecting her contact details, along with the name of her motel in Dry Wells. James, having finished his interview, waited nearby. Meanwhile, Sally was still undergoing in-depth questioning at the back of the salon.

After a final word of thanks, Agent Rankin informed Sam that she was free to leave and mentioned that he or another agent might contact her if they had any follow-up questions. He then returned to his team, and Sam joined James. Both felt a sense of relief and a hint of closure.

When they stepped outside, Sam allowed the evening

air to envelop her, its coolness caressing her skin like a balm against the day's chaos that seemed to cling to her. A breeze picked up, almost as if drifting through her, gently encouraging a revelation of vulnerability that had been hidden away for too long. Her shoulders, which had been braced against the day's relentless demands, finally sagged, releasing the weight of a thousand worries with a single, exhausted exhale.

James glanced at Sam, his smile reflecting a shared fatigue. Their stomachs growled in unison, and they both laughed.

"How about we get something to eat?" he suggested.

She nodded in agreement. "Sounds perfect." Together, they left the hair salon and the mayhem behind them, looking forward to a well-deserved meal and a sense of normalcy.

41

They opted to return to the brewpub on the outskirts of Timmons, the very place where they'd met with James's fellow reporters the previous weekend. Seeking a bit more anonymity and a respite from the hustle and bustle of Dry Wells, they found the brewpub to be an ideal spot. Upon entering, they were greeted by the amber glow of hanging lights casting cozy shadows and the rich scent of grains and hops emanating from the nearby tanks, contrasting with the cool evening air outside. The low hum of conversation and the slightly rowdy crowd suggested that for many, the weekend had begun early on this Thursday night.

Navigating through the crowd, they finally spotted an empty booth. When they sank into its worn, vinyl seats, their weariness overtook them. Sam yawned and rubbed her eyes, while James leaned back heavily against the booth.

A college-aged waitress, her tattoos peeking out from under the sleeves of her flannel shirt, approached and placed a couple of glasses of water on the table. With a friendly smile, she launched into a detailed explanation of the daily specials, and then took their orders. Considering everything that had happened, it was definitely a cheeseburger and beer night for Sam, and James felt the same. As they waited for their food, a comfortable silence settled between them—the kind unique to friends who have weathered many storms together.

Suddenly, a burst of laughter erupted from a large group at a nearby table, drawing Sam and James's attention. Both smiled in response to the shared amusement, even though they hadn't heard the joke.

"Remember that trip down to Port A senior year?" Sam said. "And that seagull incident?"

"How could I forget?" James chuckled. "We were all eating those massive sandwiches, and Claire decided to feed one tiny piece to a seagull. Next thing we knew, a whole flock descended on us. Emily's shriek could have shattered glass!"

Their laughter mingled with the background noise of the pub, a momentary escape to a time of carefree youth and innocence.

The waitress came with their beers, and as she set them down on the table in front of each of them, she said, "Did you hear about what went down at that hair salon in Dry Wells?"

Sam and James shared a knowing look, then he said, "No, what happened?"

The waitress leaned closer, lowering her voice. "I heard there was a huge drug bust, some kind of heroin ring."

Sam kept mum while James feigned surprise and said, "Really?"

"Yeah," the waitress continued, her eyes wide. "And it turns out, the FBI sent in an undercover agent to take it all down. They've been tracking the ring's operations for months."

As the waitress shared what she'd heard, Sam fought to keep her expression neutral, but a small, incredulous smile betrayed her amusement.

A man from the lively table called over to the waitress, and before she left to take care of him, she said, "Crazy, right? Anyway, I'll have your food out in a bit."

Once she was out of earshot, Sam said, "Can you believe the stories people come up with?" She shook her head slightly. "I mean, there's a sliver of truth in there . . ."

With a light-hearted grin, James commented, "It's amazing how fast news spreads, and how it gets twisted along the way." He paused, his expression turning thoughtful. "So how did Olivia get those pills?"

"I'm not entirely sure, but something she said stuck with me—that once I took over the practice, it would be business as usual."

"What does that mean?" he asked.

"She must have been using Dr. Carlisle's prescribing authority to write prescriptions for Synthroid under his name. And when he died, her supply must have become more difficult to secure. That's why she wanted me to stay—she thought I wouldn't notice her scheme. She planned to use my prescribing authority without my knowledge."

James's eyes narrowed, digesting this. "But what about the nurse practitioner? Couldn't Olivia just use her name?"

Shaking her head, Sam explained, "That would be too risky for Olivia. Bonnie's being supervised by a doctor here in Timmons right now. Part of that supervision involves reviewing notes and prescriptions and all that. It'd be too easy to get caught." She paused, her fingers absently tracing the rim of her beer glass. "But most doctors hardly ever review their own prescriptions after they've written them. I know I certainly don't, but after this, maybe I should."

Their food arrived, with the aroma of cheeseburgers and fries making Sam's mouth water. She hadn't realized how hungry she was. As they prepared to indulge in this small comfort, the waitress lingered a moment longer than necessary.

"On top of what happened at the hair salon, have you heard about the commotion over at the Clark family farm?" she asked, her tone casual yet tinged with excitement. "My cousin in the sheriff's department says the State Troopers have someone cornered there—that guy who killed his wife and her mother. It's been a major standoff."

"Really?" James prompted. "Has there been any update on that situation? Last we heard, things were still unfolding."

The waitress shrugged, her expression reflecting the mix of concern and fascination that gripped everyone. "That's the latest from about an hour ago. Everyone's on pins and needles, waiting to see how it all plays out. But rumor has it, they're going in soon." She laughed as she shook her head. "With all that's happened lately, I think we've had enough excitement for the next decade."

As the waitress moved on to other customers, Sam and James began eating, their thoughts consumed by the news. Between bites, they discussed the possible outcomes of the standoff. The conversation gave Sam a chill as she recalled her interactions with Isaac, how demeaning and controlling he was.

"You okay?" he asked. "You seem on edge all of the sudden."

She shook her head to clear it. "I was just remembering how awful Isaac was, the times I talked to him." She let out a slow, measured breath, her gaze momentarily fixing on a spot on the table. "That, and I guess I'm a bit rattled after what happened at the salon tonight."

James gave her a sympathetic look, his eyes softening. "It's completely understandable."

They finished eating, paid their bill, and then headed outside to their cars. The lively chatter and clinking glasses of the pub faded behind them, replaced by the stillness of the night. The cool air brushed against Sam's face, as if carrying an unspoken warning. She paused, a sense of unease settling over her as the reality of returning to her motel alone struck her.

James, noticing her hesitation, offered a reassuring smile. "You'll be okay," he said, his voice carrying a hopeful note. "Remember what Sheriff Perkins and that waitress inside told us? It will all be over soon."

They said their goodbyes, with James heading to his hotel to ensure a good night's rest. With closing arguments scheduled first thing in the morning, he wanted to arrive early to secure a good seat in the courtroom.

Driving back to her motel, the roads seemed more desolate than usual, the shadows stretching longer under the flickering streetlights. Sam's thoughts churned, replaying the events of the day and the rumors swirling around. The brief respite at the brewpub now seemed like a distant memory.

The motel's parking lot was dotted with vehicles, the moon's beams reflecting off their windshields, their owners having turned in for the evening. Sam eased her car into a space in front of her room and cut the engine, its purring coming to a stop. After a final check of her surroundings, she reached for the door handle. A sudden shiver raced up her spine as her shoes touched the pavement, prompting her to pull her jacket tighter. She told herself it was just the cool night air, but deep down, she couldn't shake the nagging feeling that something was off.

The surrounding stillness magnified her feeling of exposure. She stopped, heart accelerating, as she surveyed the moonlit parking lot. What was once familiar now appeared threatening. The wind picked up, whispering through the trees, casting unsettling movements in the corner of her vision. For a moment, she stood paralyzed, a knot of apprehension tightening in her gut.

"Enough!" Sam chastised herself. "It's because of all that's happened," she told herself firmly, trying to inject reason into her spiraling thoughts. "Everything is fine." She drew in a deep breath, willing herself to dismiss the eerie feelings.

Even so, as she approached her motel room door, she fumbled in her purse for the key, her fingers finally closing around the cool metal. Her heart thumped as she slid the key into the lock, her hands shaking from a mix of adrenaline and fear. With a gentle push, the door creaked open, revealing the dimly lit interior of her motel room. But before she could step inside, a sudden movement caught her eye, sending a jolt of terror through her.

Sam froze again, her heart now pounding in her chest. She scanned the black contours that stretched across the parking lot.

The darkness seemed to swallow potential threats, and she couldn't make out anything clearly. Her breath caught in her throat as her eyes adjusted, and then she saw something—or someone—move.

Then, without warning, the night's silence shattered. The booming sound of a shotgun blast erupted, the noise so loud it felt as if the air itself had split apart.

Sam flinched, thrown off balance, falling to the ground.

She slowly lifted her head from the concrete. She could now see a figure, advancing out of the night's inky veil, armed with a shotgun.

It was Isaac.

Her blood ran cold.

Before she could get up, another blast rang out, this time shattering the windshield of a nearby SUV.

With adrenaline coursing through her veins, Sam lunged through the doorway, her heart pounding in her ears. She slammed the door shut with a resounding bang. Just as she clicked the lock into place, a deafening blast exploded from the other side, sending a shower of wood fragments flying through the air, leaving a stellate pattern in the door.

The acrid smell of gunpowder seeped into the room. She gasped for breath, the taste of fear sharp and metallic on her tongue. Her hands and face stung where small bits of shrapnel had glanced off her skin.

Reeling from the near-miss, Sam's mind raced. The stark contrast between the calm moments ago and the current chaos was jarring. She realized with terrifying clarity that her life hung in the balance, dependent on her next actions. Desperation fueled her movements with frantic energy as she scrambled for anything that might slow Isaac down.

She spotted the bulky television on the dresser. With a surge of determination, she grabbed it and hurled it toward the door. It crashed to the ground, a small obstacle in Isaac's path but buying her precious seconds.

Another blast echoed, this time obliterating the makeshift barricade along with the rest of the door.

She was cornered.

With nowhere else to go, she sprinted into the bathroom, slamming the door shut. She ducked behind the vanity as yet another blast sprayed the bathroom door.

Sam's ears rang as she frantically searched for a way out. The full moon's rays were the only light coming through the tiny transom window. It was too small and wouldn't provide an escape route. She had to confront her attacker.

Her eyes darted around, searching for a weapon, anything. Her gaze landed on the shower curtain rod. A flicker of hope sparked within her. The metal glinted in the moonlight, an unexpected ally in this nightmare.

She reached up and tugged at the shower curtain, her fingers grasping the fabric firmly. As she yanked, the tension rod, previously wedged tightly between the bathroom walls, released suddenly. The rod and curtain collapsed onto the floor with a muffled thud. She grabbed one end of the rod and pulled it closer, the curtain rings clinking together as they slid off the other end.

Through the mangled door came a crunch-crunch from the shotgun.

With her improvised weapon in hand, she crouched down behind the vanity again, waiting for the blast.

But instead of a blast, through the ringing in her ears, she heard Isaac yell, "Come out here, bitch, so you can pay for what you did. For giving my Luann an abortion."

"What?" Sam said, confused. "I didn't give her an abortion! She had a miscar—"

Another blast blew the rest of the door away, fully revealing Isaac.

Sam cowered down, trying to stay small, waiting.

Waiting for the inevitable.

But it didn't come.

She peeked around the vanity.

Isaac stood just outside the bathroom, calmly loading

more shells into his shotgun, like a hunter, confident his prey wouldn't pose a threat.

Sam seized her chance.

Fueled by fear, she sprang into action. Leaping up, she charged at Isaac with a wild, desperate determination, the makeshift battering ram clutched tightly in her hands. In one swift motion, she thrust the rod into his chest, catching him off guard and knocking him backward onto the floor.

Sam vaulted over his fallen form, her breaths coming in ragged gasps as she tried to flee. But in her haste, she tripped, her feet tangling beneath her.

As she looked back in horror, Isaac lunged for her, his fingers wrapping around her ankle. Panic flooded her senses as she kicked furiously, her heart racing. Finally, her foot broke free, and she scrambled out the motel door, only to trip once more over a parking block.

Gasping for breath, she stole a quick glance behind her as she pushed herself up off the pavement.

Isaac stood menacingly in the doorway as he raised his shotgun and aimed at her.

But before he could pull the trigger, he suddenly collapsed, disappearing from view.

She ran, forcing her body to move, even though her legs felt like jelly beneath her.

Out of nowhere, a firm grip encircled her arm.

She flailed wildly, attempting to free herself.

"Let go," she yelled, but she couldn't make out her own voice.

Her captor held firm, then cupped her face under her chin, gently turning it.

It was Sheriff Perkins, his eyes filled with concern. Although she couldn't hear him, his lips moved, mouthing the words, "It's okay. You're safe."

42

In the moonlit parking lot, outside the wreckage of her motel room, Sam sat with her legs hanging off the back of an ambulance, teeth chattering. The thin blanket provided by EMS offered scant warmth against the chill. Or perhaps her shivering stemmed more from the aftermath of adrenaline rushes from narrowly escaping death twice that evening, rather than from the cold itself.

All around her, teams from various agencies scurried about, busily bagging and tagging, documenting the events that had unfolded. Sheriff Perkins had fatally shot Isaac, ending the threat he posed with his shotgun aimed at Sam. An investigation was imminent, yet it was clear the sheriff's actions were justified.

After finishing his discussion with a deputy, Sheriff Perkins approached Sam, his brows knitted in genuine concern. "You holding up okay, Doctor?"

She nodded, then she voiced the question she'd wanted to ask since the ordeal had ended.

"How did you get here so quickly?" Sam asked, maybe

a little too loudly. Her hearing had returned somewhat, but her ears still buzzed.

"Turns out our suspect at the farm? It was Isaac's uncle all along," he explained. "When we finally got him to surrender, he let us know that Isaac had snuck out right before the standoff began, saying he was going to kill that 'bitch doctor.'" Sheriff Perkins' eyes held a mixture of anger and relief as he looked at Sam. "Sorry, those were his words."

"It's okay," Sam said.

"Anyway, I rushed here as fast as I could. I'm glad I got here just in time."

"So, did Isaac kill Dr. Carlisle too?"

Sheriff Perkins nodded. "Isaac had gained access to Luann's electronic medical records and read Dr. Carlisle's note about giving her an abortion the year before—"

"Wait. Dr. Carlisle never gave Luann an abortion," Sam said. "She had a miscarriage." Then it dawned on her. "But Dr. Carlisle had written 'spontaneous abortion' in her chart, which is the medical term for miscarriage."

"I see," the sheriff said, his expression shifting as he grasped the significance. "Then it seems like Isaac's misguided interpretation of Luann's records led him to kill Dr. Carlisle."

"That must be why he came after me. When Luann had another miscarriage, he thought I'd given her an abortion, because I used the same terminology—spontaneous abortion—just to be consistent with Dr. Carlisle's notes."

Sam took a moment to compose herself, the weight of the realization settling in. "It's horrifying to think that words on a chart can spark such violence," she murmured, more to herself than to to the sheriff.

Sheriff Perkins nodded solemnly, his gaze lingering on

the ground before meeting Sam's eyes again. "Yes, it was a tragic misunderstanding that had deadly consequences. Isaac's actions were fueled by ignorance and hate."

In the silent space between them, a shared understanding passed—an acknowledgment of the heavy toll extracted by the night's events and the lives irreparably altered.

"Thank you, Sheriff," she said, her voice steady despite the chaos of the evening. "Your quick action tonight . . . You saved my life."

The sheriff offered a small, sad smile. "That's my duty, Doctor. To protect and to serve."

THE NEXT MORNING, Sam slept in, having spent the night at Bonnie's house. Bonnie had made breakfast for the household before her son had gone to school, but she'd kept some eggs and bacon warm for Sam to have when she woke up. At that point, Bonnie had already gone to the clinic to let the FBI in to gather evidence, then she worked with Kelly and Tanya to cancel all of the appointments that day as well as the following week. Bonnie had been planning on taking some time off anyway, since her brother's murder trial was close to jury deliberations. After breakfast, Sam packed up her things and got ready to leave.

"Despite all that happened," Bonnie said, "it really was good working with you."

"Thanks," Sam said. "I enjoyed working with you too." She paused, then asked, "What are you going to do?"

Bonnie's brow furrowed with concern as she considered her circumstances. "Obviously, I can't reopen the practice by myself, and I'm worried about finding another doctor to become my supervisor so I can continue as a nurse practitioner," she admitted, her voice tinged with frustration. She gave Sam a hopeful look. "Would you still consider staying?"

Sam closed her eyes for a moment before responding. "I don't know . . ."

"No, that's okay," Bonnie said, looking defeated. "I understand . . ."

"I'm sure you'll figure something out." Sam placed a reassuring hand on Bonnie's shoulder. "There has to be someone who can step in."

Bonnie nodded, but her eyes remained clouded with doubt. "If nothing else, I could try to get a job over in Timmons at the VA hospital as an RN. The commute is longer, and I wouldn't be practicing to my full abilities, but at least I'd still be helping patients."

They stood there for a moment, the weight of their uncertain futures pressing down on them, since, for the time being, Sam would still be working *locum* assignments.

Then Sam remembered Renee. She'd mentioned Renee to Olivia before, but Olivia hadn't been that interested in making a connection, and now Sam knew why. There was always time for a fresh start. "You know, I have a friend who's a family medicine doctor, and she'd love to have a small-town practice. Maybe I could talk to her."

Bonnie gave Sam a grateful smile. "I'd appreciate that."

After saying goodbye, Sam sent Renee a quick text to ask for another chat about the opportunity at the clinic in Dry Wells. She then drove to Timmons to meet James and his reporter friends at a cafe off the town square. They'd all ordered sandwiches for lunch—except for Sam, since she was full after breakfast at Bonnie's—and then they switched to bottomless cups of coffee as they awaited the verdict from the jury.

Sam absorbed the reporters' rapid-fire analysis, their theories ricocheting across the table like a high-stakes tennis match, leaving her caught in the crossfire of speculation. The morning had started with the prosecution's closing arguments, followed by those of the defense. Then, right before lunch, the judge gave instructions to the jury and sent them out to deliberate.

"I guess they all get box lunches today," Troy said. "Do you think the defense's argument that the sheriff focused on Dr. Morton too soon because they'd had a bad personal relationship holds any water?"

"Not at all," Elena responded. "He wasn't really involved with the main part of the investigation, anyway. That was conducted by the Rangers, and they don't have any personal interest in the case."

"I agree," James added. "I think the defense is just grasping at straws, trying to conflate things." He turned to Sam. "Did you know the sheriff was dating Dr. Morton's sister? After all, you worked with her."

Troy and Elena whipped their heads around to face her. "You worked with her?" they asked in unison.

Sam shrugged and said, "She's the nurse practitioner at the clinic where I was filling in. It's not a big deal." She kicked James under the table, who then gave her an apologetic look.

Troy's eyes widened. "Hey, wait, so I found out the FBI arrested the office manager from that clinic last night. Surely you know about that?"

Sam glanced at James, surprised that he'd actually kept quiet about what had happened the night before. He raised his eyebrows, smiling like the Cheshire cat.

"I do," Sam said slowly.

Troy put his elbows on the table and leaned in toward her. "Tell us about it," he said.

She paused for a moment, then fibbed, "I only know because they had to close the clinic today."

"So what's she like?" Elena asked.

Again, Sam bent the truth a little. "I don't really know. I only worked there for a couple of weeks."

Elena's eyes drilled into her as if she knew Sam was holding back, but Sam was saved by Troy's musings.

"I bet the FBI is there," Troy said, "just like they were at that lab here in Timmons a couple of weeks ago. And did you know that the lab director, who was also arrested last night, is the cousin of the office manager?"

"No," James said, giving Sam a look that suggested he knew she needed backup. "Is there a connection?" Although he was diverting attention away from her, his interest seemed genuine. Sam was intrigued as well.

"So get this," Troy began, "the office manager was selling prescription drugs—"

He stopped when he noticed Elena's questioning look, then added, "Not opioids; it's something that usually isn't in the spotlight. But it's been on the radar of these anti-doping agencies."

After taking a moment to collect his thoughts, he continued, "Anyway, she got her cousin to create fake lab reports to make the prescriptions look legit, so Medicare would cover the costs. The twist? The FBI's investigation initially targeted the lab director because a doctor here in Timmons filed a complaint. She'd discovered that her credentials were being used to order all these labs and prescriptions without her knowledge." He turned to Sam. "I'm not exactly sure what scam they were pulling, but since you're a doctor, do you understand it?"

"No," Sam said. "This is the first I've heard of it."

She flashed James a look, signaling they could discuss it more later. However, she suspected Olivia's cousin was falsifying thyroid function tests to make people appear to have hypothyroidism, thereby justifying the Synthroid prescriptions. That would explain the unusually high number of cases she'd observed in the EHR. Furthermore, if Olivia aimed for large quantities of pills, mail ordering the prescriptions for ninety-day supplies would be a strategy. As for the other doctor in Timmons, it seemed Olivia's cousin might have become greedy and decided to replicate what Olivia had done with Dr. Carlisle's credentials.

Now Elena chimed in with her own juicy tidbits. "Did you know the doctor from that clinic was murdered?" She turned her attention back to Sam, her expression skeptical, as if doubting Sam had shared everything. "You knew that, right?"

"I did," Sam said, maintaining a neutral expression. "That's why I was filling in; he died earlier this year."

Elena narrowed her eyes at Sam, then continued, "Yeah, so they figured out who killed him last night. It was the same guy who'd killed his wife and her mother a couple of nights ago. He somehow escaped during that standoff with the State Troopers, and he tried to kill a doctor. But *she* was saved by the sheriff." Now she stared intently at Sam. "You wouldn't happen to know anything about that, would you?"

All three reporters focused on Sam, with James giving her a slightly hurt look. She hadn't had the chance to tell him what had happened, so she tried to signal to him one more time that they would talk later.

He seemed to get the message and then deflected for her again. "Are you sure it was a doctor?"

Elena sat back in her chair and crossed her arms,

appearing somewhat contrite. "Well, not really. But that's just what I heard."

They sat around the cafe a little longer, with Troy and Elena backing off after realizing they weren't going to get any information out of Sam. Finally, the owner of the cafe began giving them annoyed looks, as there was a cluster of customers waiting for tables by the front door. They paid their bill and walked back to the courthouse.

Sam looked at her watch. "I think I'll drive back to Austin now. Try to get there before the Friday evening rush."

"Don't you want to stay for the verdict?" Elena asked.

"That's your arena, not mine," Sam replied. "Plus, there's no guarantee the jury will come to a decision today, right?"

"That's true," Elena conceded.

James offered to walk Sam to her car, prompting her to say farewell to the others. Once they were out of earshot, he said, "Okay, you need to tell me what happened last night."

As Sam recounted the events at her motel, James's concern deepened with every detail she shared. "So you almost died twice. Man, I thought what we went through at the salon was bad enough."

He gave her a long hug, then said, "I'm just glad you're okay."

They walked the rest of the way to Sam's car, which was parked on a side street off the square.

As she pulled out her keys, poised to bid James farewell, the atmosphere around them charged with energy. The chatter of people intensified as many began streaming down the street toward the courthouse.

James stopped a couple of men walking by, who looked to be reporters like him. "What's going on?"

One of them remarked, "Sounds like the jury's reached a decision," before they continued their way down the street.

James turned to Sam and asked, "Are you sure you want to drive back now?"

"Might as well see this through," she replied.

43

Inside the courthouse, the atmosphere in the busy hallway outside the courtroom was charged with tension as people milled about, waiting for the jury to return. Sam and James stood in an alcove, making plans to caravan back to Austin after the verdict was announced. While they chatted, Sam saw many familiar faces, including Sheriff Perkins, who was speaking to a bailiff across the corridor from them. When he spotted her, he gave her a brief nod.

Then, Bonnie appeared, with her mother, a storm cloud of indignation, trailing behind her. The matriarch, her face flushed and her eyes fiery, went straight over to the sheriff and stood toe-to-toe with him. Her voice was shrill and venomous as she unleashed a torrent of accusations and grievances, drawing the attention of everyone nearby.

"You should be ashamed of yourself!" Bonnie's mother hissed, jabbing a finger into the sheriff's chest. "My son didn't approve of you and Bonnie, so you set him up for this!"

Sheriff Perkins, clearly taken aback by the ferocity of

her words, tried to maintain his composure. "Ma'am, I understand you're upset, but I assure you, the investigation was handled properly—"

"Properly?" The old woman cut him off, her voice rising. "That doctor died, and it was probably just a bad accident. You never considered anything else, except that my son killed her. You're trying to get him out of the way, so you can have Bonnie. This town won't stand for your dirty tricks!"

A small crowd began to form around them, watching the heated exchange with bated breath. As the tension continued to escalate, the bailiff stepped forward, his hand resting on his baton at his hip.

"Ma'am," he interjected, his voice firm but measured, "I'm going to have to ask you to tone it down or leave the premises. We need to maintain order in this courthouse."

Mrs. Wright glared at the bailiff for a moment before reluctantly taking a step back. Her eyes returned to Sheriff Perkins, the burning anger still evident in her expression. For the moment, at least, she held her tongue, allowing the bustling hallway to return to its previous hum of activity.

"Come on, Bonnie," she said. "Let's get this over with. I hope our fellow citizens can redeem Aaron." She shuffled toward the courtroom door.

However, Bonnie stayed back. "I'm so sorry, Ken."

The sheriff put his hand on Bonnie's and squeezed. "It's okay. We knew she was like this." He looked around. "We just didn't know she'd make such a spectacle of her bigotry."

Bonnie continued to stand with him, until her mother called from the courtroom entrance. "Girl, get over here!"

"Go on," Sheriff Perkins said. "We'll figure all of this out later."

Moments after Bonnie disappeared into the courtroom

with her mother, the mood in the corridor grew tense again as word spread that the judge was reconvening the jury. People began pushing toward the entrance, vying to get the best seats.

Sam and James slid into a bench near the back just before the bailiff put out his arm, telling those still in the hallway the courtroom was full. With a clunk, he closed the door.

Peering over the heads of the people in front of her, Sam searched for Bonnie. As she looked, she spotted Troy and Elena near the front, not far from Bonnie. She was sitting in the same spot as before, behind the defense's table, next to her mother, the devoted daughter ensnared within a web of conflicting loyalties.

Sheriff Perkins had remained near the back of the room, standing next to the bailiff by the door.

The chatter of the courtroom came to a sudden halt as another bailiff took his place next to the judge's bench. His authoritative voice boomed throughout the space. "All rise! The Honorable Judge Patricia Mendoza presiding. Court is now in session!" The room's occupants, a motley collection of the citizens of Timmons County and media from around the state, stood in unison, bracing themselves for the solemn proceedings that were about to unfold.

Judge Mendoza, clad in her black robe, strode confidently into the courtroom from her chambers, her austere yet dignified expression betraying no emotion. With a practiced grace, she ascended the dais, settling into her high-backed leather chair. A moment of silence ensued as she surveyed the room with a discerning eye before giving a nod of approval to the bailiff, signaling that the court could be seated.

As the spectators reclaimed their seats, Bonnie's brother was brought into the courtroom. Despite having his wrists shackled, he appeared stoic in his well-cut suit, slicked-back hair, and clean-shaven face. He was accompanied by two stern-faced guards, who maintained a watchful eye on his every move.

Upon reaching the defendant's table, the guards unshackled his wrists, allowing him to take a seat next to his defense attorney. As he settled into his chair, the attorney leaned over, murmured into his ear, then patted him on the shoulder. The room was now charged with anticipation, as everyone present braced themselves for the jury's decision.

At last, the jury entered, ushered by another bailiff. Each member seemed to sense the gravity of their duty, holding the balance of justice in their hands. They filed into the jury box, taking their designated seats, their expressions a mix of determination and apprehension as they prepared to pass judgment on their fellow citizen. None seemed to want to make eye contact with the defendant.

Once the courtroom had settled and every eye was on the bench, the judge glanced around to confirm the presence of all necessary parties. With a nod, she addressed the jury foreperson. "Is the jury prepared to deliver its verdict?"

The foreperson, a middle-aged man dressed in a plaid shirt and slacks, stood with solemnity befitting the moment. "Yes, Your Honor," he affirmed.

As he handed a slip of paper to the bailiff, a hush fell over the room, the tension hanging heavily, like a curtain before the final act of a play. The judge received it, pausing briefly to read the contents before looking up, her expression indecipherable. "The jury will now announce the verdict as it stands recorded," she instructed, signaling the moment of truth had arrived.

With a solemn nod from the judge, the bailiff took the slip of paper and made his way back to the jury foreperson. The courtroom held its collective breath as he, with a steady hand, unfolded the paper. His voice, clear and resolute, broke the silence, "In the case of the State of Texas vs. Aaron Morton, on the charge of first-degree murder, we the jury find the defendant guilty as charged."

The courtroom erupted into a maelstrom of emotion. Relief and shock resonated, a tangible release from hours brimming with anxiety and expectation. The family of the deceased doctor clung to one another, their faces displaying a mosaic of grief and tentative peace, marking a complex journey toward closure. Meanwhile, through fleeting views between the onlookers, Sam observed Bonnie's mother, her face contorted with rage. When Bonnie attempted to offer comfort with an arm around her, Mrs. Wright rejected it with a sharp, dismissive shove.

The judge gently tapped her gavel to restore order. Once everyone quieted down, she outlined the next steps, detailing the scheduling of the sentencing hearing. Then, she declared the court to be adjourned.

The spectators began to rise from their seats, murmuring to one another and filtering out of the courthouse with a sense of finality.

As she stood, Sam strained to get a glimpse of Bonnie through the crowd. Bonnie's face was a complex tapestry of sadness and resignation, her eyes glistened with unshed tears, and her lips trembled slightly as she struggled to maintain composure.

After the courtroom had cleared a bit, Sam approached her to offer condolences, with James following behind. "I'm so sorry," she whispered.

Bonnie's smile, fragile and fleeting, betrayed the

turmoil swirling beneath her stoic facade. "Thank you. I knew it was coming, but it still hurts."

They shared a fleeting glance, silently acknowledging the storm they had just weathered, when Sam's focus shifted to Agent Harper making his way toward her. He had attended the trial, and his presence had not gone unnoticed, as Troy and Elena lingered nearby.

"Dr. Jenkins," he began, "I didn't properly thank you last night."

"I'm sorry, Agent Harper,' Sam replied, puzzled, "I'm not quite sure what you mean."

It was evident he knew exactly what he wanted to say, yet hesitated to express it directly.

James, exchanging a knowing look with Sam, hinted, "I believe he's thanking you for—"

"For stepping into the line of fire," Agent Harper interjected, locking eyes with her in a rare display of vulnerability. "For pushing me out of the way. Thank you."

"You're welcome," Sam responded.

The agent gave her an appraising look, reminiscent of their first meeting. "Miranda was right about you. You really should consider joining the FBI." Extending his hand, Sam shook it. "I hope we meet again soon, Dr. Jenkins."

Sam nodded, touched by his support. "Thank you, Agent Harper," she said, her voice steady. "I'll definitely think about it."

As he walked off, feelings of exhilaration and possibility bubbled up inside Sam. The thought of joining the FBI both excited and terrified her. Images of chasing criminals, solving intricate cases, and helping people in ways she never could as a doctor filled her mind. But it also meant leaving behind her life in Austin, her friends, and the familiarity of the practice of medicine.

She paused briefly, weighing her options. The cascade of events that had led her to this point was impossible to ignore. The factitious hyperthyroidism cases among the high school girls, the murder of Luann and her mother, the exposure of Olivia's illegal activities, and finally, the dangerous encounter with Isaac—all of these incidents had stretched her abilities and her understanding of the world around her.

James's perceptive gaze met hers, his voice soft yet resolute. "Sam, you've got this, no matter what you decide." His support shone like a lighthouse through her tumult of thoughts, anchoring her in the present.

As they headed to their respective cars, Sam couldn't shake the feeling that her life was on the brink of a major change. Whether it would lead her to the FBI Academy or another clinic, she knew that the experiences she had faced in Dry Wells had irrevocably shaped her future. With a blend of nervousness and anticipation, she climbed into her car and followed James back toward Austin, ready to face whatever lay ahead.

ABOUT THE AUTHOR

Stephanie Kreml writes mysteries and thrillers after working as an engineer, a physician, and a life science consultant. She lives with her family in Austin, Texas.

Sign up for her newsletter and receive a FREE copy of *Accidental Truth: A Dr. Samantha Jenkins Novella*.

Go to
www.stephaniekreml.com/signup

ALSO BY STEPHANIE KREML

Truth Unveiled

Neglected Truth

Truth Promised

Coming Soon

The Undercover Doctor

Made in the USA
Coppell, TX
05 July 2024